Jerusha
Journey of a Heart

A NOVEL BY KIM OLSEN

MILLENNIAL PRESS
SALT LAKE CITY, UTAH

Millennial Press, Inc.
P.O. Box 339
Riverton, Utah 84065

ISBN: #1-930980-92-2

Copyright ©2002 by Kim Olsen

*This book is dedicated to
the memory of Joseph Smith, Jr.,
the great prophet of the Restoration*

TABLE OF CONTENTS

ACKNOWLEDGMENTS

Thanks to Avis Pickens, possessor of a small box made from Kirtland Temple wood. This story came to be after I was shown the box.

Thanks to my mother, Charlene Manwaring who has always told me I could do anything I set my mind to.

Thanks to Georgia Carpenter who saw potential and gave me a chance. My life has not been the same!

Thanks also to Darla Isackson for her outstanding editing skills. You make me look good!

Thank you, my dear husband, Darwin Olsen. I have spent almost as much time in the past with Joseph Smith as I have with you. It means so much to me that you have given me the chance to study and write. I adore you.

Thanks to Susan Christiansen, a true friend who is not afraid to tell me what needs to be changed and how to do it.

Thanks to Lindsey James for her exceptional typing skills!

PROLOGUE

I grew up thinking my parents were religious fanatics. Actually, I thought my mother was the fanatic. Dad was one of those level-headed, sure and steady, never-do-anything-wrong Mormons and I adored him. His roots went clear back to Hyrum Smith, whose daughter, Lovina, married Lorin Walker. They were the progenitors of my Grandpa Walker. My geneology may be confusing but I know Hyrum Smith is my great-great-however-many greats grandfather.

My mom, on the other hand, thought the religion was wondrous. She was a convert, Dad's first on his mission to Chicago. Mom fell in love with the gospel and Dad all at the same time. They corresponded his entire mission. Two weeks after his release, he was back in Chicago asking Mom for her hand, which she willingly gave. They traveled back to Blackfoot, Idaho—the "Heart of Zion," as Mom calls it. I often wondered how Blackfoot could in any way resemble Zion.

Mom and Dad settled eight miles northeast of Blackfoot, in a small farming community called Wapello. Dad raised milk cows and together they raised five sons and one daughter—me.

An example will illustrate how fanatical my mother was. She insisted that, because the blood of Prophets flowed through our veins, we all must have names to remind us where we came from—as if she'd ever let us forget! My oldest brother was named Joseph Smith Walker. Of course there was also Brigham Young Walker, John Taylor Walker, Wilford Woodruff Walker and Lorenzo Snow Walker. I am not making this up; it's the gospel truth! My brothers seemed to take their names in stride, accepting them as part of their heritage, but I had never accepted my name.

Maybe my parents ran out of clever ideas, since I was the youngest of six children and the only girl. Did they take my name from the Bible or Book of Mormon? No! Right out of the pages of Church history—that's where they found my name. They actually had the nerve to have it printed on my birth certificate: Jerusha Mary Walker. Can you imagine how a teenager would hate the name JERUSHA? What kind of name is that for a cheerleader at Blackfoot High in the 20th century?

"It's a beautiful name for a special woman in our history," Mom would say when I got huffy about it. Mom looked disappointed when I opted to give myself a nickname at age 13—Jerree—with two 'r's and two 'e's. I thought the name was darling, and I insisted everyone call me "Jerree." Everyone did but Mom, which I think was a big part of my teenage resentment toward her.

Dad became the buffer between his girls. "Don't be so upset, Jerree. Your mother loves you so much," he said after one of our fights. "Right!" I would counter. "That's why she cursed me with such a horrible name."

Dad inevitably tried to calm me down. "It's not a horrible name. You are named for one of the great women of the Restoration. You are a part of her lineage. The gospel means so much to your mother and your heritage is important enough that she doesn't want you to forget where you came from. Someday you'll understand and be glad."

Being a teenager, I would counter with, "I doubt it! There are tons of great women of the Restoration. How come she didn't insist on Emma or Eliza or even Lucy. Why Jerusha?"

Then Dad would remind me, "She was the first wife of Hyrum Smith who started this family. She stood beside her husband through so many hard things. She was a great woman and she left a name you can be proud of."

"I could have been proud of Suzy too, you know." He would chuckle and kiss my forehead. I loved my dad, but his little pep talks did not stop the resentment I felt about my name.

The question remained throughout my growing up years. If Jerusha Barden Smith was such a great lady, why isn't there more written about her? Her life has not been chronicled like Hyrum's or Mary Fielding Smith's. All I have ever been able to find is little blips here and there. Her name only comes up as a sort of footnote in Church history. Actually, many times while growing up, mostly because of my name, I thought myself as only a footnote.

Another evidence of my Mom's fanaticism about the Gospel was her adoration for the Prophet Joseph Smith. Now I'm the first to admit that he was a great man—a Prophet of God—but according to my mom there had never been a greater prophet on the face of the earth except for Jesus. I lived my entire life thinking she over-exaggerated his greatness, until the day I was allowed to sit at the Prophet's feet and listen to him teach....

CHAPTER ONE

When my mom died in the fall of 1990, she left me three things she said would become priceless to me. The first was a small square box, six inches by six inches. She claimed it had been made from wood scraps left over from the building of the Kirtland Temple. It was old and had been given a place of honor in our home my entire life. I wondered what I'd do with it in my own home.

Mom took care of that question by giving me the dresser I had coveted forever. Daddy had presented her with the armoire as a wedding present. He told her that Brigham Young had made it from the same wood as the box. The box had always sat on the armoire at Mom's house, so I put it there in mine. I loved the dresser. It had three long drawers in the middle with three shorter ones on both sides. An oval mirror was connected to it and was obviously very old. I often wondered how it made it from Ohio to Idaho in such good condition. Dad said it was a special chest of drawers. How right he was.

The last gift was a dress that had been found in the bottom drawer. Family tradition stated that Mary Fielding Smith wore it. Personally, I thought it was in too good of condition to be over a hundred years old. I took the heirlooms home and was grateful for them. I had long since gotten over my animosity for Mom's craziness. Marriage and motherhood mellowed me, allowing me to enjoy my mother's stories and even perpetuate a few.

Six weeks after I buried my mother, my youngest son, Cory, went to Ricks College, fifty miles away. I was having a great time feeling sorry for myself. I was fifty years old, all of my kids were now

1

grown, my parents were dead, and I didn't even have a job to keep me busy. I sat on the foot of my bed staring at my armoire, wondering if the Prophet Joseph Smith had any words of wisdom for a middle-aged woman who had lost her mom and son within six weeks. Okay, so I was being much too dramatic. I hadn't really lost my son; he was in Rexburg but it seemed like I had lost him. It was only a matter of time before he went off on a mission and then got married, and I'd have no one left at home.

Hot tears stung my eyes as I wallowed in self-pity. I had borne and raised four children. Two were married, David and Sarah, and doing their best to make me a grandmother several times over before I turned fifty-one. My son Joseph—yes, I had a Joseph too—was a missionary in Germany, and Cory was off to conquer the world at college.

My husband, Tom James, was a successful salesman and traveled extensively. He just happened to be gone on a business trip, which left me alone for the week. My eyes drifted to the picture of us hanging on the wall. How I loved my husband. Tom James had swept me off my feet two weeks after I arrived at Ricks College. He was a returned missionary, ready to conquer the entire world. He literally plowed me over as I walked down the hall of the Hart Building.

"Whoa! I'm so sorry. Did I hurt you?" he asked, his brown eyes looking at me with genuine concern.

"No. I'm okay, but I think a couple of my books might need to be rebound," I said.

He gathered my scattered things and insisted on walking me to wherever I needed to go.

"Let me take you to dinner sometime to make up for bulldozing over you," he said before he left me. I agreed and soon we were seeing each other regularly. Before Christmas break, he was begging me to marry him.

"We can't lose with names like ours—Tom and Jerree. A match made in heaven."

We married right after school got out for the summer. I became a mother before I was twenty.

My parents loved Tom, especially since he chose to live in Black-foot, which kept me close. His parents were from Shelley, sixteen miles away. Mom thought he was wonderful because he had a testimony to rival her own, right down to his great love for Joseph Smith.

"He'll help you find the testimony you've kept hidden in your heart," Mom whispered the day we were sealed in the Idaho Falls temple.

For the past thirty-one years, I had lived the part of the perfect Molly Mormon housewife, putting my energies into my husband and family. Mom was extremely proud of me before she passed away. But I knew that deep inside, where my heart beat, I still didn't FEEL the fire, the passion for the gospel that my husband and mother felt.

Sighing, I knelt on the floor in front of my mother's armoire and pulled the bottom drawer open. Mary Fielding Smith's dress lay neatly folded on the bottom, a few other clothes surrounding it. With a longing I did not understand, I reached into the drawer and pulled it out, pressing it against my chest. It smelled old and musty. It was faded, though I could still make out the peach-colored flowers, on what looked like cream gingham. I wondered if the dress had once been white. It was typical of the dresses worn in the 1800s.

Standing, I held the dress to me, marveling at how perfectly it suited my complexion and complimented my auburn hair. Looking at myself in my full-length mirror, I wondered if it would fit me. Turning, I flung the dress on my bed and hurriedly took off my jeans and BYU sweatshirt. Amazingly the dress fit! The front was lined with a row of buttons from the waist to the neck, and it took me a while to get them all fastened. The sleeves were long and straight, just a little poofy at the shoulder. The bodice was form-fitting and the skirt flared out below the waist. The entire look was very flattering, almost as if it had been made for me. I thought it was a shame that women didn't wear this style anymore.

Excitement surged through me and I hurried to my closet. All right, you might as well know—I adore shoes. I have a rack made especially for shoes and four shelves as well, plumb full of them. My family calls me the Imelda Marcos of Blackfoot. Luckily for me, I happened to have a pair of granny boots. I pulled them on, rushed to the bathroom to put my waist-length, auburn hair in a bun, then hurried back to my mirror to see the full effect.

The transformation was incredible! I looked like a woman from the 1800s. I spied the box that sat on the dresser and reached for it. Opening the lid, I found an old envelope, yellowed with age, lying at the bottom of box. The name "JERUSHA" was written across it.

A chill ran through me as I picked it up and stared at it intently.

I know this sounds horrible, but since my mom died and I had received my inheritance, I had not opened the box. I had dusted it off, made room for it on the dresser, and left it there, unopened. I had been too grief-stricken to care about the contents of a dusty old box... until now.

With a pounding heart, I sat on my bed, holding the envelope in my shaking hands. It was definitely old. It was dusty and smelled ancient. It had not been sealed, but the back flap had been tucked in so that the letter inside would not fall out. Was this letter to my great –grandmother Jerusha Barden Smith from Hyrum? Family tradition says that Mary Fielding Smith brought all Jerusha's belongings when the Saints came west. She brought Jerusha's children too, those who were still too young to be on their own. Some of these treasures were given to Lovina's children when they finally came to the valley.

Was there a love letter from Hyrum inside? Did Jerusha have a chance to read it before she died? Did I dare open it and read what was written? My curiosity got the best of me; I carefully opened the back flap and removed the letter slowly, not wanting to tear it. Before I read the contents of the letter, I glanced at the signature at the bottom and was surprised to find Mary Fielding Smith's signature instead of Hyrum's! Why would Hyrum's second wife write a letter to his dead first wife? I couldn't bear the suspense and began to read.

Dearest Jerusha,

I wish I had more time to write, but Brigham says I must hurry if I'm going with his party, and I am going. Nauvoo will soon be deserted, as the faithful obey the brethren and leave. My heart aches to know that the City of Joseph, Nauvoo the Beautiful, will be left behind, holding the bodies of my beloved Hyrum and his brother in its depths. I have faith they will remain safe, though there are still threats to find their bodies and desecrate them.

I had hoped to see you again before my departure but I've been told you have gone and won't be coming back. Know that I have grown quite fond of you and treasure you as true friend. You have given all of us comfort in our sorrow. We can move forward, toward the unknown west, knowing it will someday be home for thousands of Latter-day Saints.

4

Your stories of the "Mountain Zion" have aided me in keeping Joseph and Hyrum's dream alive! This church will survive the deaths of its Prophet and his brother. Thank you for that. Though I don't claim to understand, I'm grateful for the miracle that brought you here to us. I pray your experiences in our time have strengthened your resolve to hold on until the Savior returns.

I will safely guard these treasures that will be yours until I can pass them on to those who will see to it that you receive them. Be strong, my friend.

With much love and affection,

Mary Fielding Smith

I could hardly breathe as I finished the letter. Could this letter have been written to me 144 years ago? How could Mary Fielding Smith have known me? How could I have gone back there? I'd heard about time travel, seen all the movies, read all the books—but they were all fiction...weren't they? I didn't have a time machine. I didn't have some fancy car and I didn't have one of those chambers that could help me make a quantum leap.

Puzzled, I went back to the armoire and peered into the box. It definitely was too small to transport me anywhere. On the bottom lay an old pair of glasses, with a note attached with a small piece of burlap twine. I picked up the glasses, slipped the note off the rim, and opened it. It said:

"Oft times we cannot see
The truth before our eyes
Until we earnestly seek it
And win the glorious prize."

I reread the poem several times, completely baffled by the words. I already knew truth... didn't I? What prize was I looking for? Everything was too weird. I put down the note and took the glasses and placed them on my nose. Looking into the mirror made by Brigham Young, I was impressed with my reflection. I looked like a schoolmarm right out of *Little House on the Prairie*.

Suddenly my reflection began to fade, almost melting away as streaks of rain poured inside the mirror! How could it be raining inside my mirror? Leaning closer, I touched the mirror and gasped when my hand came away drenched. Standing on my tiptoes, I got as close to the mirror as I could, water splashing in my face. Through the downpour, I began to see the outline of a city, although nothing I could recognize. Where was the reflection of my bedroom? I should be seeing my queen-sized waterbed with the floral print comforter Tom said he'd endure only because he loved me. Where were the pictures of my kids and grandkids and the vanity table laden with creams and perfume?

Then, without warning, a streak of lightning and a clap of thunder boomed through the mirror. Before I knew it, a gust of wind sucked me in and as I began falling through the cold, wet darkness, I wondered if this was how Alice felt when she went through the looking glass....

CHAPTER TWO

"She's not Jerusha, my brother's wife, but she looks enough like her to be her sister. I thought I knew all of them but maybe I was wrong."

Those words brought me out of a deep sleep. The voice was deep and melodic, and I felt peace I knew I should not feel.

"Tell me again how you found her," a woman said, laying a cool towel on my forehead.

I tried to open my eyes but my eyelids felt like cement blocks. My head was pounding and I wondered if I had come down with some virus and was hallucinating. That would explain the weird events I thought I was experiencing.

"She was lying plumb in the middle of the road. I'd come to see Newell and the horse almost trampled her."

"She's lucky you saw her then. Who do you think she is?"

"Haven't got a clue, but it looks like we're about to find out."

With every ounce of strength I possessed, I opened my eyes and turned my head toward the man's voice. Moaning, I lifted a shaky hand to my head. I definitely had one gigantic goose egg.

"Don't try to move. You've taken a nasty blow to the head," the woman said, patting my hand tenderly.

"Where am I?" I croaked, looking about me in wonder.

"Above the Gilbert and Whitney Store, in Kirtland," the man said, smiling kindly at me.

Squinting, I tried to focus on his face, my eyes rebelling against the effort. He seemed familiar to me somehow. I had seen those eyes somewhere before.

"Kirtland? Ohio? I'm in Ohio?" I squeaked.

"Yes. Don't tax yourself. Rest now. Lizzie, could you fetch some water for our friend?"

"Of course, Brother Joseph," the woman replied and quickly left the room. As I watched her leave I, noticed that she wore a simple, floor-length dress, much like the one I was wearing when I fell through the mirror. Slowly turning my head, mostly because it felt like a lead balloon, I stared up at the man who was sitting beside me in a rocking chair. He was the most handsome man I had ever seen—even better looking than Mel Gibson or Kevin Costner. His auburn hair was windswept and wet, waving attractively against his face. His almond-shaped eyes sparkled like sapphires as he looked at me with concern.

He had long eyelashes, which seemed totally unfair since mine were short and stubby, even with mascara. His nose seemed slightly larger than it should have been, but it surely didn't detract from his good looks. His lips were full and seemed constantly in a smile. Very little beard marred his complexion.

I gasped as I began to realize who he was! Now I knew I was in Neverland. I tried to sit up but was seized with overpowering dizziness. As I sank back into the pillow, I was suddenly keenly aware that I knew this man! I knew him! I had seen pictures of him every day of my life. My mother had collected them and placed them all over the house. Though he was better looking in real life, if indeed this was real life, there was no mistaking that face.

"Joseph?" I asked hoarsely.

"Yes," he replied, his high, wide brow crinkling handsomely.

"Joseph Smith?"

"Yes," he repeated. I felt a chill run though me. He seemed to feel it too for he leaned closer to me, looking into my eyes as if to read my thoughts. I almost thought he could.

"The Prophet Joseph Smith." This was not a question but an expression of awe. He sat back again, smiling, rubbing his broad, square chin, "Yes, I am often called the Prophet. Do I know you?" Chuckling, I shook my head, moaning when excruciating pain shot through it. Joseph tenderly touched my forehead. I looked at him intently. How could I be in an upper room over a store in Ohio with a man long since martyred? This had to be a dream; nothing like this happened in real life, only in books or movies. Still, I heard once that anything you hear, even fantasy, is based on some truth. I shut my eyes and breathed deeply.

Any minute now, all the Munchkins in Munchkin Land would come out and break into a song—"Ding dong the witch is dead"— and I'd click my heels three times and be home in my nice little room, in my nice little house in Podunk, Idaho. Opening my eyes, I again met the steady, curious, blue-eyed gaze of Joseph Smith, the Prophet, deep concern etched on his handsome features.

"I don't think I'm in Kansas anymore," I muttered. The Prophet looked totally confused.

"No. You're in Kirtland, Ohio." I smiled and sighed tiredly.

"What year is it?" I asked, deciding it was better to play along with my overactive imagination.

"1831, of course. March, 1831."

"Of course," I repeated and closed my eyes tightly. "I guess that means you don't have any Advil."

"Advil?" he asked.

"Never mind. I'm so tired."

"Then sleep and we'll figure all this out when you're feeling better."

"Yes," I said, knowing that when I was feeling better I'd be home and this little fantasy would be over. I allowed my exhaustion to carry me to that place where sleep awaits to make everything right.

They say I slept for three days, which did not surprise me. I had lost my mother, sent my baby off to college, fallen through my dresser's mirror into 1831, and been rescued by none other than the Prophet Joseph Smith. I deserved a little R and R.

Strange noises roused me from the three-day nap. Horses whinnying and wagons rolling by sounded as if I were right in the middle of a western movie. I heard a hammer pounding and people hurriedly walking by on plank-board sidewalks. I could smell horses, fire, and bacon. My stomach growled noisily, testifying to the fact that I was indeed still alive. I also had an urgent need to find the bathroom!

Slowly I sat up, looking about me. My head felt tons better and for that I was thankful. The room was decorated in 19th–century fashion, complete with rag rugs and a wash basin with a pitcher on the bureau. As an antique collector, I felt I had died and gone to heaven, which seemed very plausible to me, considering I had had a conversation with Joseph Smith. I had always thought I'd be greeted by my parents when I passed away, but maybe Mom told Joseph about me and he decided he'd better come and let me know he actually was what he said he was.

In the far corner of the room sat a rocking chair, where a small girl sat, her head bobbing sleepily. When she heard me move, her head snapped up and she smiled brightly at me. "Hi," I said.

"Hello. I was beginning to wonder if you would ever wake up," she said, quite matter-of-factly. "Brother Joseph said you would, but I wasn't sure. I'm Sarah Ann Whitley." She came to the side of the bed and looked at me with curiosity.

"Sarah Ann. That's a beautiful name. My daughter's name is Sarah."

"Really? Is she my age? Could I play with her?"

"She's 28. She's married," I said.

"Oh," she replied, disappointment playing across her pretty face. "What's your name?"

"Jer...Jerree...Jerree James." Sarah Ann gave me a funny look and moved even closer, examining me as if she had never seen a sick woman before.

"Mama says you're a stranger here, with strange underwear." Gasping, I looked down at my attire and realized I was now wearing a flannel nightgown instead of the dress I'd donned before all of this happened. Panicked, I unbuttoned the first few buttons and looked down the front of the gown. Sighing, I laid back. My garments were still on me, but not my bra.

I'm sure little Sarah Ann thought I was crazy. She couldn't have been more than seven, with cherubic features and blonde hair curled into long ringlets down her back. She wore a blue dress with a white pinafore. Black-button shoes covered her feet. My own Sarah had a porcelain doll that looked similar to Sarah Ann Whitney.

"You hungry, Miss Jerree James?" she asked, leaning against the bed, staring intently at me.

"Starved," I said.

"Mama says I need to tell her when you wake up. Brother Joseph wants to know too. He's down the hall with Brother Rigdon. I'll run and fetch them."

Before I could protest, she was gone, her tiny feet pitter-patting down the hall. It seemed forever before the door opened. Joseph Smith came in carrying a tray filled with delicious-smelling food.

"Ah, our guest finally awakes. You look better," he said, smiling kindly at me. I hadn't dreamed him! He was real—or as real as anyone could be in this strange situation. He came to the bed and held the tray out to me. His hair was combed and well-groomed today, though an unruly lock kept falling on his brow. The mother in me wanted to brush it aside.

He wore a smock-type shirt with an exaggerated collar and large cuffs at the wrists. A brown vest that matched his trousers was unbuttoned and I wondered who had made a vest large enough to fit his massive chest. He was a huge man, as well-built as any weight-lifter I'd ever seen. He stood at least 6'2" and was built somewhat like my own sons. This man was an uncle, several times removed, but the family resemblance was amazing.

"I bet you're starving," he said, bending to put the tray across my lap.

"I am but—" I stammered, unsure how to tell a prophet I needed to go to the bathroom, quick! "Do you have a bathroom?" He didn't have the foggiest idea what I was talking about. With a puzzled look on his face, he sat the tray on the table next to the bed.

"I need to…relieve myself," I explained, knowing my face was beet red. His eyes widened; he nodded and smiled.

"Of course. It's behind the house. Do you think you can stand?"

My legs felt like cooked spaghetti, but I managed to make it to the "privy," with Joseph's help.

He waited outside while I went in. I thought I would die of embarrassment. When I was safely tucked back into bed with a tray of food on my lap, the Prophet sat beside me, personally seeing to it that I enjoyed my first meal in 1831. The fried potatoes, bacon, and corn pancakes, that I later learned were called johnnycakes, tasted heavenly. The milk I drank was warm, fresh from the cow.

"Sarah Ann says you have a man's name," Joseph said, not seeming to be able to hold his curiosity at bay any longer. I looked at him and for the first time realized how very young he was. If it was indeed 1831, he couldn't be more than 25, just a few years younger than my son David. At 50 years old, I was old enough to be his mother!

"No. I mean, I guess it is. My name is Jerree Walker James."

Joseph nodded, his bushy eyebrows rising in surprise.

"I see you're married," he said, pointing to my wedding ring. I nodded, hungrily taking a bite of potatoes.

"Where is your family?" he asked. I knew he was testing me. "We ought to send a letter to them or maybe even a messenger."

I stopped chewing, looking directly into his blue eyes. I felt as if he could see right through me, into my very soul. He knew! He knew I wasn't really supposed to be here, of that I was sure.

"I doubt we could contact my husband. He's back East...on business."

"What type of business?" he asked, unconvinced. How did you fool a prophet?

"He's a salesman." Joseph nodded, refusing to break eye contact with me. Did he have any idea the effect he had with just his eyes?

"You're not from around here, are you Jerree James?"

"No," I whispered, not knowing what else to say.

"And yet you know me," he pressed, refusing to give me any kind of break. "You took one look at me and knew who I was— though I am sure I have never met you."

"I've seen several pictures of you. My mother had quite a few of them. She used to say you were the greatest prophet that ever walked the face of the earth...except for Jesus." Yes! I actually said that! My brain must have gotten scrambled in the fall I took. It didn't even dawn on me that I'd said anything strange until I looked at Joseph Smith's shocked face.

"Pictures...of me? I've never had a likeness drawn. How could you have seen a picture of me? Do I know your mother?"

"No. She's dead."

"What's happening, Jerree? Who are you really? Where do you come from and why do you look so much like my sister-in-law, Jerusha? I thought you were her until I saw your eyes. She has blue eyes but yours are green. I think it's time you told me the truth."

Though he was speaking softly, his deep voice echoed through the room and I knew he would not accept anything short of the truth. I hoped he was ready for it. Sighing, I laid against the pillows that had been propped up against the headboard. I rubbed my temples gingerly.

"It's all too strange for even me to believe. It's crazy...impossible. And yet...somehow it's really happening. I'll tell you the truth, but don't blame me if you can't believe it."

"I doubt you could surprise me with too much. I've seen a few impossible things in the past twelve years." His eyes twinkled with mischief. He had a point. He was, after all, Joseph Smith, Jr.

Nodding, I took a deep breath and began my story. "My name is really Jerusha Mary Walker. My father, David Smith Walker, is a direct descendent of your brother Hyrum and his wife Jerusha." Joseph's eyebrows shot up but he let me continue. "My husband, Thomas James, and I have four children and four grandchildren. I was born March 15, 1940, in a small town called Blackfoot, Idaho, a state in the Rocky Mountains. I guess you could say I am your niece, Brother Joseph. I don't know how it happened or why, but I seem to have stumbled onto a way to bridge the gap between my time and yours."

It was my turn to stare down my uncle, knowing that no matter how strange it seemed, I was telling the truth as I knew it. His eyes never left mine, though after a while I knew he was no longer seeing me. Chills danced up and down my spine as I witnessed the Spirit settle on this man I had been raised to believe was a prophet. Tears sprung to my eyes as I saw—no, felt—the prophetic mantle light the face of Joseph Smith Jr.

"What year were you living in?" he asked, his eyes focusing on me again.

"1990."

"Are you a member of the Church?"

"Yes. I was baptized at eight years of age by my father who was a bishop and a high priest." Joseph nodded, tears now springing to his eyes. He leaned over and touched my face, the gesture of a loving parent. Though I was twenty-five years older than he, for the moment he was the parent and I the child.

"You are the answer to my prayers, dear Jerusha. I was beginning to wonder if the Church would ever survive past this generation."

"But the Church is only a year old—to you."

"True, but I've been fighting to establish it for twelve years and sometimes I get so weary. But the Church has survived, clear to the turn of the 20th century. How many members are there? A hundred thousand?" I smiled at his childlike anticipation. He truly had no idea of the vast empire he was establishing.

"Well, if my memory is right, at the last General Conference in April, there were about six or seven million members, worldwide."

Joseph gasped, sitting back in his chair, breathing as if someone had sucker-punched him right in the stomach.

"Worldwide?" he whispered. I nodded, smiling.

"You said yourself this church is destined to fill the whole earth."

"I did?" he asked, his eyes round with wonder. I realized that in 1831 he might not have said that yet, but how would I know, since I never paid attention to any of the specifics my mom said about Joseph Smith? I sure wished I'd listened now.

"Mom said you did and no one knew more about you. She had a complete bookcase filled with books she had collected, written about you and your teachings."

"A bookcase?" he asked in wonder.

"Yes. Joseph, don't you know the destiny of the work you're doing?" I asked.

"Yes, I know…but I never, in my wildest dreams, imagined six or seven million members worldwide!"

"I do live 160 years after the organization of the Church. Things are bound to grow and change. There have been thirteen presidents of the Church since you."

Joseph nodded, trying to absorb all the information I was giving him.

"Has the millennium started yet?"

"No, but we pray it will soon. The world is a very wicked place in my time. Every day that goes by testifies of your prophetic calling. So many of the things you said would happen are happening before our eyes and the world as a whole is totally unaware."

"Then times aren't that different." Joseph stared at me, measuring me, I guess. Did he wonder if I was lying?

"We need to come up with an explanation for your presence. These people might accept angels and gold plates—but a person visiting from the future might be stretching their ability to believe."

"But you believe me, don't you?" I asked, knowing the answer but wanting to hear it from his own lips. He looked at me and smiled, reaching over and squeezing my hand with his massive one. He was a huge man, young and strong, and I could see how he could influence so many. He had a charismatic nature that drew his fellow men to him. Even if he hadn't been called of God he would have been a force to reckon with.

"Testing me, niece? Everyone feels they need to. While you were telling me your story, the future was made known to me and I know that what you say is true. It's amazing but true. Besides, you look so much like Jerusha that everyone will assume you are family. But since Jerusha doesn't know you, I will have to tell my family the truth. They will believe."

"I'm amazed at how much the family resemblance has been carried to my generation. I have a son, my Joseph, who could be your twin. I doubt anyone would think we were strangers... though no one from the family knows me...yet."

"So, we'll have to say that you've come here to be with the Saints while your husband is away on business. That much is true, isn't it? All of your children are grown so that's easy to explain. If you've seen pictures of me, why haven't you seen one of Jerusha?"

"I think she died before photography was really starting." Joseph's face went white and I realized I was saying things I shouldn't.

"I'm sorry. I forgot that you don't know everything I know about the future—which I admit isn't much. I really didn't listen to all the things my mom had to say about you." He smiled kindly and squeezed my hand again, his eyebrows raised in mirth, a gesture I would come to love about him.

"I think I know why you've been permitted to come here, Jerusha. Are all the people of your day as lax about the past?"

"No, many people study Church history avidly. But I guess there's plenty of us who haven't really paid much attention to the past."

"Which always leads to trouble. How can we ever improve ourselves if we don't know of the struggles our parents went through, or appreciate the sacrifices made in our behalf?"

"That's probably why the world is so horrible now. We've got it so easy nowadays that it's easy to forget there were those who gave their all to give us our comforts."

"But you'll return and remind them. Now you look exhausted and I want you to get some more rest."

"But..."

"No, don't argue." As he bent to take the tray from my lap, I impulsively touched his cheek. He looked enough like my Joseph that all my maternal instincts kicked in and I couldn't resist.

"All my life I was told you were real—the greatest prophet who ever lived—but until this moment I never truly believed."

Tears sprang to his eyes, fell to his cheeks and then to my hand.

He nodded, swallowed hard and straightened, taking the tray to the door before turning.

"Sleep now Jerusha..." His voice cracked and he hurried out. Tears filled my own eyes as I settled back on the pillow. Sighing, I allowed myself to drift off to sleep, knowing that soon I'd be well enough to begin my life in 1831.

CHAPTER THREE

It wasn't long before I felt like my old self. I ached to explore my new surroundings. Little Sarah Ann Whitney and her friend Mary Elizabeth Rollins insisted on keeping me company.

Their endless chatter was like an antibiotic and I learned so much about everyone in Kirtland that I could hardly wait to meet them all. The sixth day I got up and insisted I be given my dress. Elizabeth tried to argue with me but I wouldn't take no for an answer.

"I'm dying of boredom, Lizzy. I've never been to Kirtland. I can't wait to see all I've been hearing about." I knew I had won by the compassionate look on her face.

"All right. But I know Brother Joseph wants to talk to you." Joseph had stopped by to see me every day, though his duties with the Church kept him from staying very long. I wanted to spend hours with him, partaking of his spirit and listening to his experiences. It was beginning to dawn on me why these early saints readily gave up all they had to be in the Church and close to him.

"Good. When will he get here?"

"Oh, he's here. He and Brother Rigdon are already closed up in that office of theirs."

"What do they do in there all day?"

"Translate the Bible."

"Oh yeah! I heard they did that," I said, mainly to myself, but Elizabeth heard me and gave me a funny look. "I mean, I heard they were doing that. May I please have my dress?" She smiled, nodded, and headed for the door. "Thank you, Lizzy—for everything. How will I ever be able to repay you?"

"There's no need, Jerree. I've been glad to do it. Any member of Joseph's family is a member of my own."

When Elizabeth was gone, I sat on the bed contemplating all that had happened to me. By some miracle I had fallen from my time into the early 19th century, smack dab in the middle of the beginnings of Church history. I had been found by none other than the Prophet Joseph Smith and was being nursed by Newell K. Whitney's wife. If this was a dream, I hoped I wouldn't wake up for a while. I was beginning to really enjoy it.

At fifty, I was older than most of the people around me, though having lived in the 20th century all my life seemed to have kept me from aging as quickly as these women apparently did—probably due to all the preservatives that are found in the food in the 20th century. Elizabeth Ann and the girls had been awestruck by my well-manicured hands and the diamonds I wore on my ring finger. When I fell through the mirror I had also been wearing the diamond studs Tom had given me for our twenty-fifth wedding anniversary, a gold watch the kids had given me, and my gold CTR ring.

"You must be quite wealthy," Lizzy commented as she stared at my hands. I'd never thought much about my wealth, having always had everything I needed or wanted.

"I suppose I am," I agreed, surprised at the revelation. I had always taken my material possessions for granted.

"When I grow up, I want hands that look like yours," Sarah Ann said, comparing my hands to her mother's. I felt ashamed of them for the first time in my life. I had always spent hours keeping them beautiful. I had had many compliments because of them and they had always been a source of pride...until Lizzy Whitney sheepishly hid her work-worn hands under her apron.

"There's nothing wrong with hands that show the hours of work that must be done. I've led a very pampered life—up until now."

Lizzy gave me a grateful smile but I knew my words were lame. I had taken my whole life for granted, never once considering the sacrifices my ancestors made so I could have what I had. I was now getting a crash course in appreciation.

I missed small things such as hot showers, toilet paper, toothpaste, deodorant, and soap that smelled nice. I would have given all my diamonds to have those small conveniences we take for granted. I again realized that maybe this adventure happened to show me that I should never take anything for granted. Everything we have in my century was bought at an infinite cost.

"I would never have made it as a pioneer. I can't live without my dishwasher." These words, spoken in jest, now came back to haunt me. It looked as if I was about to find out if I could.

How long would I have to stay in 1831? Was there a way to get home? I was sure Tom was home from his trip by now and going crazy trying to find me. I needed to get back but I definitely hadn't had my fill of being in the presence of the Prophet.

Lizzy's knock brought me back to what was now my present. I called for her to come in. She brought my dress and my bra, which she had washed. She gave them to me, questions shining in her eyes. I giggled, lifting the bra up by the shoulder straps.

"It's like a corset but it's much more comfortable. Where I come from every woman wears one."

Lizzy's face reddened but she sat on the bed and leaned toward me conspiratorially.

"Do you think you could make me one?"

"I've never made one. They sell them in the stores but if I ever get home, I'd be happy to get one for you."

Lizzy was totally scandalized at the thought that such an intimate object of apparel was sold in stores where everyone could see it. How would it be to live in such innocence? Those of us in the 20th century had no such luxury.

"I better get downstairs. It's my day to oversee the counter," Lizzy informed me.

"Thanks again, Lizzy."

"Thank you," she said, standing in the doorway smiling.

"For what?"

"It's nice to have another woman to talk to. You remind me of my mother."

I smiled back at her, knowing that I probably was the same age as her mother. I nodded.

"Yes, and you have helped me not miss my daughter quite so much."

"Maybe you could send for her and she could come and visit,"

Lizzy replied innocently. A look of sadness must have flashed across my face because she came back into the room and sat on the bed beside me. "Are you all right, Jerree?"

"Yes, it's just that I doubt I could reach her at the moment. Don't worry about me. I'll be fine."

When Lizzy was gone, I dressed, did my hair, and left my room, happy to finally be out of there. I stood in the hall for several seconds, listening to determine exactly which room Joseph was in. I could hear his voice coming from the last room down the hall so I hurried to it and without even thinking knocked loudly. Joseph's voice stopped, a chair slid back and footsteps came toward the door. When it opened, I was shocked to come face to face with Sidney Rigdon instead of Joseph. He looked down at me a bit impatiently. I felt he was put out that I would dare disturb him.

"Can I help you, madam?" he asked. I was not impressed with his attitude.

Sidney Rigdon, THE Sidney Rigdom, was an older gentleman. His features were aristocratic; his dark hair was slated with gray. He wasn't as tall as Joseph, but well-built for his age.

"I have come to talk with Brother Joseph," I said, refusing to be intimidated by him. He shook his head and kept his hand on the door, barring me from peering into the room.

"He cannot be disturbed. We are in the middle of important business." Inside the room I heard a chuckle, footsteps, then the door was taken from Sidney, and Joseph stood there, an arm around Sidney's shoulder, smiling down at me.

"Sidney, this is the cousin I was talking about. She's come all the way to Kirtland to see her cousin Jerusha, who happens to be in New York. She was involved in an accident. I think we can take a break. It's just about lunchtime anyway and I need to check on Emma. Go home and see your wife. She'll probably appreciate some time with you. Sister Jerree, I'd like for you to meet Brother Sidney Rigdon, my right hand man. Brother Sidney, this is Sister Jerree James."

Instinctively, I stuck my hand out to shake his hand. For a moment he looked down at it as if he wasn't sure what he should do.

"I've heard so much about you, Brother Rigdon. This is truly an honor for me."

One bushy eyebrow arched and he genuinely smiled at me for

the first time. Joseph brushed past Sidney and looked back over his shoulder at his assistant.

"Give my love to Phoebe, Sidney. See you later."

Without waiting for a reply, Joseph led me down the hall and to the stairs. Sidney shut the door muttering something about the disrespectful way some people acted. Joseph chuckled as we descended the stairs. I gasped as we entered the store. It was amazing, straight out of the westerns I'd seen in my life. Lizzy was busy behind the counter, helping a customer. She nodded to us, turning her attention back to the woman, who seemed unable to make a decision.

The sights and smells captivated me. Brown sugar, molasses, cinnamon, straw for brooms, and some type of kerosene filled my nostrils. Wooden barrels encircled with iron straps lined one section of the room, the names of their contents stamped on each one.

A pot-bellied stove sat in another corner, a few chairs surrounding it, ready to heat the room when needed. Pans, baskets, tools, and lanterns hung from hooks in the ceiling. Shelves behind Lizzy were stocked with everything from dishes to hats. One corner of the counter was used as a post office; a cabinet with slots filled with envelopes was sitting on top. It was all so wonderful to behold. Joseph chuckled, escorting me out the door.

"Don't look so enthralled; people will think you're crazy. Do you think you're strong enough to walk a little? I left Isaac's wagon at the livery stable just down the way."

"Brother Joseph, I'm used to walking a mile a day. A little bonk on the head won't slow me down."

He looked at me and rolled his eyes.

"All right. Maybe it did a little, but I'm fine now. I'm certainly tired of lying around doing nothing, especially when there's a whole new world to explore."

"I thought you had been reading the Book of Mormon."

"I was...Did...it's just that there's so much to see. I need to get out." Joseph laughed and squeezed my arm.

"Yes you do, Jerusha from the 1900s. Step lively; we're almost there."

The Gilbert and Whitney Store stood on the corner of Chillocothe and Chardon Roads. Across the street on the southwest corner was an inn owned by a man named John Johnson. Joseph led me down Chardon Road toward the livery.

When the wagon and team were ready, Joseph helped me up, then easily jumped up to sit beside me. I felt like a young girl taking my first ride in a horse-drawn wagon. As we traveled, he pointed out homes and businesses along our way, trying to familiarize me with the area. He was a very humorous tour guide, telling short stories about those we passed. There was no gossip in the stories. Joseph Smith loved his fellow man and he showed it in the things he said and did. Soon we came to a fork in the road. Joseph steered the horses northeast on a road called the Painesville Road.

"It's only about eight miles or so from here. We live on the Morley farm. Isaac built us a small cabin behind his house. Emma is happy there. She says it's a nice place for our child to be born."

"She's expecting?" I asked, racking my brain to remember which of their children was born in 1831. To my dismay, I didn't know.

"Yes. She's due sometime in May. But then you must already know that," he said pointedly. My face reddened with embarrassment.

"Oh Joseph, I really don't. I'm sorry to say I only half listened to my Church history lessons." He looked a bit disappointed but smiled all the same.

"Don't fret. That's probably why you've been permitted to come here. It's just as well you don't know, for I've prayed about you and the Spirit says that having you here is a blessing. It will not frustrate the plan, but you must not tell those things you know about my life and I'm not to ask. I must confess I'm a little disappointed for I've got a million questions. But I suppose I'll have to be patient and just wait and see."

"Have you asked about how I'm to get back?" I questioned, finding I wasn't too thrilled about going back this second. He smiled and nodded.

"You must return exactly the same way you arrived. It's all rather simple." My heart skipped a beat. I felt I might lose the lunch Lizzy had made for me. Hot tears filled my eyes as I calculated how long I'd have to stay in the 19th century. I wanted to stay for a while but I wanted to have the say about how long.

I did know that the Kirtland Temple wasn't dedicated until 1836 and that Brigham Young had not even made it to Kirtland yet! Both the box and the dresser were built from wood left over from the construction of the temple, AND Brigham built the dresser! I could be in Kirtland for up to six years! I'd wanted to spend some time in Kirtland but not six years!

"What's wrong Jerree? You look like you've just seen a ghost.

"I'm stuck here! It's not simple at all! The heirlooms that helped me get here aren't even made yet. They won't be for at least four to six years! I can't stay here that long! Tom will go crazy! I'll miss the birth of Sarah's baby! My own Joseph will be home from his mission next year! Cory just left for college. He'll be sending in his mission papers in January. I can't stay here!"

To say I was hysterical is an understatement. Joseph reined the horses to a halt and took my arms in his huge hands, staring at me intently. Gasping for air, and sniffing loudly, I looked into his eyes. Suddenly I could no longer breathe as some force, some powerful energy, shot through him to me.

As we sat in Isaac Morley's wagon, on a rut-filled road in the Western Reserve of Ohio, I witnessed the prophetic mantle illuminate Joseph's face, causing it to shine. It seemed his very spirit was on fire and the glow could not be contained. His eyes were like the blue flame of a welder's torch.

"Be at peace, Jerusha. The Lord is aware of all that is happening. *He* is in control. Your family will be fine. You will be returned to them unharmed, as they will be. This I promise."

My mind screamed that he couldn't possibly know what he was talking about, but the Spirit was using my spinal cord as a xylophone.

The Prophet Joseph Smith had just given me a promise. I could not deny the power with which he was speaking. His promise made as much sense as anything else I was going through, so I nodded and tried to smile.

"Okay...thank you," I whispered, tears freely coursing down my face. He smiled, touching my right cheek.

"Don't fear, little niece. All will be well. You've been given a chance to see history for yourself. I hope you're a more attentive student than before."

I chuckled, took his hand in both of mine and pressed it to my lips.

"I plan to be, uncle. You can count on it."

J E R U S H A

CHAPTER FOUR

Isaac Morley owned a considerable amount of land, much of it covered with a variety of trees. His well-tended fields were being readied for planting. As we neared the Morley home, I spied several log cabins stretched out like a small subdivision. I must have looked surprised, because Joseph chuckled and began to explain.

"Every single person who lives on this land is a member of the Church. They were part of a group searching for the truth, trying to live as early Saints did with all things in common. Isaac had the most land and so he was chosen to "share" it with everyone. When we got here, Isaac Morley was being taken advantage of horribly. He's so patient, so loving. He can never say "no" to anyone. It didn't take long for me to see this set up was wrong, so I asked the Lord what should be done, and—"

"And you got the Law of Consecration which was nothing like they were living," I interjected, proud of myself for knowing something about what he was telling me. His blue eyes twinkled as he nodded and reined the horses to a stop in front of a small, well-kept cabin.

"Very good! That's right. It's only been a few weeks since the Lord gave me the Law, but already I can see it's going to be difficult to live."

"I'm sure. No one likes to have to give up their money. The Saints in my day promise to live the law in the temple—" Joseph's eyes were round with anticipation as I forgot who I was talking to and that temples were not even in existence yet. I smiled, brushing a stray hair from my eyes.

"I guess I'm saying too much, huh?"

"Yes, though I must confess I was hoping to get a little information. I'm sure I'll get it soon enough, though, from the Lord. C'mon, Emma's dying to meet you. I'm sure she heard us drive up." My heart began pounding in my chest. It hit me that I was about to meet Emma Smith—THE Emma Smith I had heard so much about, good and bad. I wondered how I would get along with her. Technically, she was my aunt, though I was just old enough to be her mother. Would she believe Joseph's far-fetched story or was I walking into trouble?

The cabin they lived in was small but immaculately cared for. As Joseph ushered me in, my eyes took a moment to adjust. Then I saw her! She sat in a rocker, her hands filled with needlework, peacefully stitching. She smiled up at me kindly. She was everything and nothing like I imagined. Though she was seated, I could tell she was tall, much taller than most women of her day. Her obvious pregnancy did not detract from her natural beauty. Her raven-colored hair was pulled back into a neat bun. Her olive complexion complimented the russet brown eyes that eagerly looked at me. All the austere pictures I had seen of her did her no justice. Emma Hale Smith was beautiful, the perfect mate for her handsome prophet husband whom she obviously adored. Emma had a sweetness about her that made me feel naturally drawn to her.

Without even an invitation, I went to her side, placing a kiss on her cheek. She smiled up at me and touched my face, looking intently into my eyes. She then looked me over from head to foot, shaking her head in awe.

"You're right, Joseph. She's identical to Jerusha, except for the eyes, green like emeralds. Slide a chair over here for her so she can talk comfortably to me."

Joseph promptly obeyed, ceremoniously helping me be seated, then plopped on the bed and began to pull off his boots, sighing contentedly. The cabin was only one room, sparsely furnished with a spindle bed in one corner, covered with an exquisite quilt done in a pattern I was totally unfamiliar with. A small table with a basin and pitcher sat beside the bed. A steamer trunk sat at the foot, filled with linens and the like, I was sure. On the opposite wall sat a wardrobe for their clothes.

A small dining table separated the sleeping area from the kitchen. They owned two kitchen chairs and a rocking chair. Emma cooked over a fire in a fireplace, equipped with a hook where a cast iron pot hung. Pots and pans hung from hooks in the ceiling. A Dutch oven sat on the hearth. A pie-safe held dishes and utensils and a steel wash basin sat on a butcher's block with legs. I could smell stew cooking.

"Joseph tells me your name is Jerusha and that you are a direct descendent of hers." She spoke as if my being here in their time was as natural as the sun rising. She seemed to accept it even better than I did. Of course she was the wife of the man who had seen God the Father, His Son Jesus Christ, translated an ancient record from gold plates given to him by an angel, and had continuing revelation. A time traveler must be small stuff compared to all that.

"Yes," I said, unsure of what to say. Emma laughed, and took my hand, squeezing it affectionately.

"There's no reason to be shy. I'm hoping we'll be good friends. Did Joseph tell you Isaac Morley has offered you a room at the big house? No? Well, he has and I hope you'll decide to stay. I'd feel better knowing a member of the family was near since I'm so close to my time."

"Where are the others?" I asked, feeling stupid for not knowing. Emma smiled, looking over at Joseph who winked from his resting place.

"In various places on the way to Kirtland. I've written to Hyrum and he'll be coming with Father soon. Mother is leading a group of Saints from New York with Newell Knight. Before spring is over our entire family will be reunited," Joseph explained.

"Oh," I said breathlessly, a little nervous to think of meeting the whole Smith family.

"Don't worry. They'll all love you. Now tell me all about yourself," Emma soothed, keeping my hand in hers. It was easy to talk to her. Soon I felt like an old and trusted friend.

One can only imagine my wonder at being in the Prophet's home. He was tenderly solicitous to Emma, insisting on dishing the stew into bowls and serving both of us with great flourish. He then sat in a chair next to Emma, took her hand, and folded it to him as he bowed his head to pray. If I live to be a thousand, I don't think I will ever know such joy again. I don't think anyone I ever knew actually "prayed." Not that prayer wasn't a part of our lives, because it was, but our prayers were a continuous repetition of words and phrases so that they hardly resembled what I was hearing now. The Prophet Joseph Smith talked to Heavenly Father his God as if they were intimate friends.

Taking a peek at him through my eyelashes, it struck me that Joseph had been tutored by angels, standing in the very presence of God and Jesus Christ. The Savior would in time call him servant, brother, friend. Tears streamed down my face; my entire frame was filled with a warmth unequalled to anything I had ever experienced. This was the burning Mom had told me would come if I was truly listening to the spirit. For the first time in fifty years I actually felt the seeds of testimony sprouting in my heart. When the prayer was over, Joseph smiled at the tears he saw on my face and began to eat heartily. Emma stretched out her hand, inviting me to place mine in hers, squeezing it affectionately.

"Don't worry, you'll get used to it. I swear I wept the entire first year of our marriage."

"That's true. I began to think she regretted marrying me," Joseph teased, tearing a chunk of bread from the loaf sitting in the middle of the table.

"I've never regretted it, Joseph. My soul still rejoices when I listen to you pray or speak."

"And I'm grateful for that," he replied, kissing her forehead. Emma blushed prettily, aware that I had been watching with great interest.

"You have to forgive Joseph. He hardly ever sticks to convention."

"Which is exactly why you chose me over all those stuffed shirts your father introduced you to."

Emma laughed and nodded. "You are right there."

I sighed as I listened to Joseph and Emma banter with each other. Tom and I had that easy friendship too. I missed him and wondered how he was doing.

"You miss your husband, don't you?" Emma asked compassionately. She seemed as good at knowing the thoughts of others as her husband was.

"I do. I hope he's not crazy looking for me. We've been together for thirty-one years. He's gone on many business trips and we've been separated longer than this, but he's probably frantic by now, especially if he can't reach me by phone."

"Phone?" Emma asked curiously. I nodded and was about to explain when I caught Joseph's eye. He shook his head, reminding me of his counsel not to reveal to them things I knew about the future. Sighing, I smiled and took another bite of stew.

"This is wonderful stew, Emma." Emma looked at Joseph, silently communicating with him. Finally she smiled, placing a hand on his arm.

"I see I won't have the pleasure of knowing about the wonders of the next century. So be it. Let's finish eating and go over to meet the Morley's. I hope you'll consent to stay at the big house so that we can be close and get to know each other."

"I'm not sure..."

"Don't worry. Isaac and Lucy Morley are wonderful people and they are eager to meet our 'cousin.' You'll love them."

The Morleys were everything Emma said and more. They were also the first people I'd met that were close to my age! Even Sidney Rigdon was twelve years my junior. Isaac Morley was a forty-six-year-old farmer and cooper who was deeply devoted to Joseph and the church he had established. Lucy Morley was a small woman, with a sweet, round, cherubic face. She literally fawned over Emma, insisting she sit in the most comfortable chair in the parlor.

"Lucy, I'm fine, I'm fine! Jerree, come rescue me. Isaac, Lucy, this is Jerusha Smith's cousin, Jerree James. Jerree, these are the Morley's, the kindest, best people in the world."

"Brother, Sister Morley, it's an honor," I said, extending my hand to Isaac. He took it in his huge, work-worn one and smiled kindly.

"Joseph says you came to visit your cousin but she hasn't arrived yet. Have you been baptized yet, Sister James?"

"Oh yes! Years ago...um, years ago I had searched for the truth...and, well, I finally found it...just recently." I looked at Joseph, who was enjoying my attempt to smooth over my slip of the tongue. His blue eyes sparkled as he nodded his approval. Isaac insisted that I stay with them, saying the big house could accommodate me better than Emma's small cabin. Before I knew it, Lucy and Isaac were showing me my room.

"I hope this will do, at least until your family arrives," Lucy said, searching my face for a reaction. Joseph, who was standing next to me, felt me stiffen as I thought of my family, knowing they would not be joining me here—at least not the family I knew. Joseph took control of the situation, explaining that I would be here indefinitely—that my children were all grown and my husband was traveling, so I did not know when he might arrive.

The room was decorated in the furnishings of the time. I thought it was beautiful. I told Lucy as much, which pleased her greatly.

"Shall I go and fetch your trunk?" Isaac offered. Joseph shot me a warning look and again took over the explanations.

"Sadly her trunk was lost in the horrible storm we had the night I found her. We'll have to help Sister Jerree renew her wardrobe. Now Isaac, I've been meaning to talk to you about purchasing some more land for those who are coming from the East." Joseph put a hand on Isaac's shoulder and led him out of the bedroom. He did not want to be pressed for more details to explain my existence in 1831. I smiled and turned my attention to Lucy Morley who was showing me around the house.

CHAPTER FIVE

I remember my mother had once wished I had had a chance to listen to the Prophet Joseph Smith speak. I would have been convinced of his divine calling, she said. As if she had ever heard him! She had been born a hundred years too late but I think all of her study sort of jumbled her brain. She talked as if she really knew him and had sat at his feet while he preached.

Now as I sat on a makeshift bench in the middle of Joseph and Emma's cabin, listening to a prophet...THE PROPHET...I yearned for my mother to be with me. I could picture her on the other side, plotting with Joseph himself to push me through the Mirror of Time just for this moment. Fifty or sixty people were crammed into the small house to receive instruction from the prophet. Joseph had insisted on introducing me to those he knew, then took great delight as he watched me try not to faint at some of the names.

Sidney and Phoebe Rigdon were there with their children Nancy and John. Newel and Elizabeth Anne Whitney were there with Sarah Anne. Mary Elizabeth Rollins had come with her uncle A. Sidney Gilbert who also brought Orson Hyde, a clerk at the store and a nonmember—for the moment. Edward Partridge, the first bishop of the Church, came. I was struck with how handsome he was. Only Joseph outshone him in looks. Of course the Morleys came, as did another couple that made me stop and do a double take.

"John! Julia! I'm so happy you could come, considering Julia's obvious condition," Joseph said, glancing lovingly at the woman's very pregnant belly. Julia giggled like a young girl, though she was older than Joseph.

"You must come and meet one of our long-lost family members. Jerree James, this is our good friend Julia Murdock and her husband John."

My face must have gone completely white at the mention of their names, for Joseph looked at me with concern. His eyes questioned me but I avoided eye contact, as I tried to meet these two people with some sense of decorum. I knew if I looked into Joseph's eyes he would see that I knew something about these two that was important. I knew that Julia would give birth to twins at the same time as Emma. Emma's babies would die, as would Julia. Motherless babies and a baby-less mother.

This woman who held my hand so kindly would soon die. Emma, who wanted a child so badly would soon lose the ones she carried. For the first time I wished I didn't know the little I did know about these people's future.

"Are you all right, Jerree?" Joseph asked, taking my arm, almost forcing me to look at him. Unwillingly I looked up into his eyes, begging him not to ask me. He seemed to sense he shouldn't, escorting me to a place where I could sit, explaining to Julia that I had had a bad fall and was still quite weak. Julia sat close, hoping to help me if need be. Emma joined her. They visited happily, comparing the size of their bellies and the hardships of being so big. Sarah Anne and Mary Elizabeth sat on the other side of me, chatting happily. It seemed the only one who was upset was me. Joseph looked at me with concern. How could I act as though nothing was wrong when I knew that the babies Emma was carrying and julia would soon die.

"Brothers and sisters...friends. It's so good to see you all here. It makes my heart glad to know you would travel out here so that my dear Emma might be able to join a body of the Saints in worship. I thank you for that. I've asked Bishop Partridge to open this meeting with a prayer. Bishop." Joseph waited for Edward Partridge to come forward, shook his hand, sat down, and waited for him to pray.

A sweet, peaceful calm spread through the cabin, so tangible that I was sure everyone could feel it. I had the feeling that someone was among us, someone angelic; I opened my eyes, hoping. I must have not been ready for such a vision because I saw only people bowing in prayer, no angels. Joseph met my gaze, smiled, nodded, and closed his eyes again. I guess I wasn't mistaken after all.

When the prayer was finished, Joseph stood and looked at his congregation, smiling lovingly at them. A lump formed in my throat, realizing that I was actually sitting in the presence of the Prophet Joseph Smith, about to hear for the first time his testimony from his own lips. My mother would have loved to have been there. I hoped that somehow, in the grand spectrum of things, she was, and that she was filled with as much joy as I felt. Looking at Joseph, I could feel the love he had for his fellow men.

"I know there are some here tonight who aren't members of our church and are here seeking answers to questions about us. First, let me say that we do believe in the Savior, Jesus Christ. Rumors are spreading that we are not Christians, but nothing could be further from the truth. I would dare to venture that we worship Christ with more integrity and faith than the rest of the world."

A few murmurs were heard but it didn't seem to affect Joseph's concentration. Mary Elizabeth leaned over and whispered in my ear.

"Watch him. Any minute now he'll begin to glow." I looked at her curiously. She nodded, smiling. Turning back I watched intently. Joseph Smith was a handsome, charismatic man, with a deep melodious voice. He had the natural ability to reach out and grab his audience, drawing them right into his vision. As I listened to him, I could hardly breathe, I was so caught up in his words. Then, to my amazement, my whole frame was on fire, the Spirit flowing from the Prophet to fill the room. Suddenly I noticed that he was enveloped in light, his face so transparent I was sure I could see his cheekbones.

Such joy filled my heart that I began to weep, unable to hold back the tears. Mother had been right. I would never feel the same again, after hearing Joseph's story from his own lips. No wonder these early Saints were willing to give their lives, and all they had, for him and his cause. Who could deny the truth as told by Joseph Smith Jr.?

I don't remember all the words he spoke that day, but I will never forget the way they made me feel. Joseph Smith was REALLY a prophet! He REALLY had seen God and the Savior. An angel had come to him, entrusting him with a sacred record. It was true! All of it was true! My heart was filled with unspeakable joy.

All too soon he was finished. He then invited those who had

questions to feel free to ask. He seemed invincible. There was no question he didn't have an answer for, either by his own knowledge or through the Spirit.

"Is it true that you have been given the priesthood as Christ had it?"

"Yes."

"How?"

"It was conferred upon my head, and Oliver Cowdery's, by John the Baptist, and Peter, James, and John, the three leading apostles of the Savior."

"Then, if you do have it, can you perform miracles with it?" I turned to see who was asking these questions. A sour-faced, self-righteous looking man stood in the back, mockingly asking these questions. Joseph seemed unruffled by his blatant attempt to stump a prophet.

"No. I can perform no miracle—of myself. But God can perform the miracle, using me, through the priesthood power. He bestowed it upon me—and those who are worthy can also receive and hold the priesthood."

The man seemed somewhat satisfied with Joseph's answer, though I could tell he was trying to find fault with it. Joseph answered many other questions, always genteel and loving in his response. At times he had the entire room filled with laughter with his quick wit. I felt as if I were hearing the gospel message for the first time. It was glorious to my heart. I couldn't seem to get enough.

"If he has the Priesthood of God, then he should be able to heal the afflicted. Here is Mrs. Johnson. She is crippled with rheumatism and has been for six years. Has God given any power to men on earth to cure her?"

The man, whom I later learned was a local preacher named Ezra Booth, hadn't said it very loudly, just a mumble really, but I knew Joseph heard the remark. He refused to give Mr. Ezra Booth the satisfaction of knowing he had heard and continued to answer other questions, though his eyes often traveled to Mrs. Johnson, who sat shyly by her husband. Suddenly Joseph stopped speaking, his eyes boring into Elsa Johnson's. Once again he became defused in light, walking slowly to the afflicted woman. No one even dared to breathe as he bent and took her crippled hand in his, smiling tenderly down at her.

"Woman, in the name of the Lord Jesus Christ, I command thee to be whole." No one moved. Joseph's voice echoed through the small room. He squeezed her hand, smiled, and walked out, his head held high. I wanted to run after him, to touch his face, hoping to feel the power that was glowing there.

"Praise the Lord!" Elsa Johnson whispered. "Thank God! I can move it! John, I can move it and it doesn't hurt!" Tears streamed down her face as she painlessly moved her arm up and down. No one else said a word, knowing they had just witnessed a miracle. Ezra Booth stood in the back, speechless, his face red with shock.

I looked at Emma who smiled and nodded, her eyes filled with tears. I laughed, tears flowing down my face. I had seen priesthood blessings heal sick children and comfort the dying. I knew priesthood power "worked" but seeing it work through Joseph Smith was an experience I would never forget.

＊　　　＊　　　＊

March ended and April brought the prospect of the Smith family being reunited. Joseph had written to Hyrum urging him to hurry to Kirtland. I was overjoyed to know that I would finally get to meet my "grandfather," three generations removed.

Life at the Morley settlement was peaceful. I soon fit in as if I'd done 19th-century work all my life. I learned to cook over a fire in the fireplace. I learned to extract yeast from the hops plant, which I never knew it came from. I learned to make potash soap and yearned for "Coast" or "Zest." I became proficient in identifying useful herbs and what they were used for. I learned how to sit on the three-legged milking stool to milk cows. My dad would have been so proud. I even learned to make butter! It took longer than running down to Albertsons to pick up a couple of pounds, but it tasted so much better.

My well-manicured hands soon became a distant memory. I wished I had some hand lotion and a nail file. Emma told me lard worked as a softening agent for hands. It smelled horrible but it worked. With so much to do every day, I hardly had time to worry about my family, though I did wonder how they were doing.

Emma was finding it harder to move about. I spent most of my time with her. She taught me the fine points of sewing by hand. I soon had two new dresses and some much-needed underwear. I was afraid my garments wouldn't last the entire time I was in Kirtland, though they seemed to be holding up quite well. I hoped the Lord would understand why I didn't wear them the days they were being laundered.

I wished often that I didn't have the knowledge that the babies Emma carried would not survive. She was looking forward to their birth and was fearful of losing them as she had little Alvin, her first child. She seemed to feel she was somehow unworthy to be Joseph's wife because she had not borne Joseph living posterity. I tried to comfort her, reassuring her she was just the right wife for Joseph.

"Sometimes, though, I understand how Sarah felt when she had Abraham take Hagar—or Rachel giving her servant to Jacob. A prophet deserves posterity."

"And Joseph will have that—through you." Emma seemed to brighten, knowing that I knew things about her future she did not. She laid the shirt she had been working on in her lap and clasped my hand in hers.

"Oh Jerree, I do give him children then, right? I'm so glad you came here. I've needed comfort and hope—and the Lord gave me you."

"I'm honored to be here with you. I've needed comfort too. I never realized how much I would miss my mother until she was gone. She loved studying about Joseph and constantly told me how wonderful you both were. I'm glad I've had the opportunity to find out for myself." She smiled, patted my hand and resumed her sewing.

"I'm just a woman, Jerree. Joseph is just a man. So many people think we should be perfect because of our calling, but nothing could be further from the truth. God has given Joseph many gifts—such as healing the sick and translating—but he's still human. He can't spell worth beans and it's all I can do to listen to him read one paragraph. I'm too strict, stodgy, and impatient. I voice my opinion far too often. Sidney barely tolerates me."

"Well, I doubt he'll be too happy with me before it's through. Women have much more say in the world I live in. Some women are even presidents of companies in the 1900s."

"It sounds like heaven. Have things changed that much in over a hundred years?"

"Oh yes! Nothing seems the same—except for the gospel and even that seems to have been refined. Being a Mormon in 1900s is certainly different than in 1831."

"Is it true that the country extends from sea to sea and that the Rocky Mountains are filled with Saints?"

"Yes. We call the Rockies the Heart of Zion—though Zion is not really there, it's—" Emma was listening with rapt attention and I realized that in 1831, Zion had not yet been identified. I smiled and stood, going to the fire to place another log in it.

"I doubt Heavenly Father would appreciate me revealing things that Joseph is supposed to. Why don't you rest for awhile? Joseph will be home soon and dinner isn't done yet."

"Yes. I am tired. I'm so glad I have you to keep me company." I helped her stand and walk to her bed where she laid, trying to find a comfortable position to rest in.

"Me too," I said, bending to drape a quilt over her. When she was comfortable, she smiled up at me, reminding me of my daughter. I couldn't help leaning over and kissing her forehead.

"Sleep well," I whispered. She nestled closer to her pillow and sighed contentedly.

"It's nice to be mothered," she mumbled as she drifted off to sleep.

Tears stung my eyes as I thought of the fact that she had left her parents, in Pennsylvania, on bad terms. I knew she would never see them again. She was only twenty-six, turning twenty-seven in July. I was old enough to be her mother. I needed someone to nurture as much as she needed a mother. I felt honored to be a surrogate mother for her.

J E R U S H A

CHAPTER SIX

It was the third week of April and spring was finally getting serious. I was glad of it. As the days grew warmer, I began to yearn for short-sleeve blouses, knee-length pants and sandals. Having to keep the body totally covered was becoming a drag. I felt truly sorry for 19th century women. At least at night I could retire and lay in the privacy of my own room. I was gratefully resting one evening when a knock was heard on my door.

"Yes?" I asked, scrambling for my nightgown.

"Sister Jerree, Brother Joseph is downstairs. He asks to see you," Lucy Morley said through the door.

"All right. I'll be down in a moment." I wondered if Emma had gone into labor and my heart was beating clear into my throat. I wished I could remember the actual date of the birth of Emma's twins. Then again, knowing would have made things even worse. When I was presentable, I hurried downstairs to where Joseph was sitting in the parlor talking quietly to Isaac and Lucy.

"Ah Jerree! Sorry to disturb you but I thought you should know that Hyrum and Jerusha are finally here. They are extremely anxious to see you," Joseph said, crossing the room to take my hands in his. They trembled slightly and he squeezed them reassuringly.

"Are you up to it tonight?" Filled with excitement, his blue eyes searched mine. I wished I had put my hair up instead of letting it fall down my back in a fiery tangle of curls. "They are at the house visiting Emma and when I told them you were here they couldn't contain their excitement."

I nodded, unable to speak. He laughed and wrapped his arm around my shoulders, pulling me tight against his side. I had looked forward to this moment all month, but now that it was here I was scared to death. How did you prepare to meet your progenitors?

"Come on. I've got a lantern on the back porch and if you'll trust me, I'll lead you home."

He said good-bye to the Morleys and led me though the house to the porch. All I could do was think of his last words… "If you'll trust me, I'll lead you home." What a profound statement for a prophet to make. All we need to do is trust any prophet of God and he'll lead us home. No truer words were ever spoken.

When we were safely out of the Morleys' hearing, Joseph chuckled at my sudden attack of timidity.

"Don't be nervous. Hyrum is as gentle as a kitten. He's quite excited to meet a direct descendant. Jerusha is very skeptical. She thinks I'm playing one of my jokes on her. Father seems to have no opinion."

"Father?" I asked, stopping in mid-stride. Joseph let go of my hand and lifted the lantern so he could see my face.

"Yes, my father—Joseph Smith Sr. Hyrum brought him with them. He's been on a mission with my brother Don Carlos. He's the one, now, whose imagination has run away with him. He thinks I should send him back with you to learn all he can to help us here. Don't worry, Jerree. They are all your family too."

"With one major difference. I'm not even supposed to be born for over a hundred years."

"Only a minor detail. Family is family. Now come on; it's not polite to keep folks waiting."

With a pounding heart and clammy hands, I followed the prophet across the field to his cabin where happy laughter could be heard. Joseph paused at the door to smile kindly, then flung it open with a dramatic air, ushering me in. At once all eyes were on me. Gasps of surprise were heard all around. Joseph blew out the lantern, left it on the porch, and shut the door behind us.

"Everyone, let me introduce Jerusha Mary Walker James, a direct descendent of Hyrum and Jerusha Smith."

"H…H…Hello," I muttered as these strangers, who were my family, stared at me in speechless wonder. Finally, three-year old

Lovina, who would one day be my grandmother, toddled over and looked curiously at me.

"Mama, she wooks just wike you." Her innocent honesty seemed to activate everyone and Jerusha Barden Smith came to stand directly in front of me. She was indeed a mirror image of me, down to our height. Of course our eyes were different colors and I was definitely older, but we resembled each other enough to have been twins. It hit me that I had always thought of this woman as insignificant—a footnote. Yet now she was standing in front of me, wonder in her eyes, as real as I was and so much more than a mere footnote.

"It's true! I thought you were pulling one over on us, Joseph, but it's true. Your name is Jerusha?"

"Yes, after you. My mother said you were...are...one of the great women of the Restoration. Everyone calls me Jerree."

Tears fell down Jerusha's face as she touched mine. Lovina danced around us, begging to be held. Hyrum scooped her up and stood beside his wife, staring intently at me.

"And here I thought you were one of a kind, dear. Hello Jerree James. Welcome to the family." Hyrum Smith was a big man, though not quite as tall as Joseph. The Smith family resemblance was marked, though Hyrum's nose was not as big nor his lips quite as full as Joseph's. His hair was darker than Joseph's and he wore sideburns that were very bushy, which I found amusing. He was devastatingly handsome. I thought there couldn't have been a more handsome man than Joseph, but Hyrum equaled his brother in that respect. Though I tried hard not to, I kept comparing him to his younger brother. He held up quite well under the comparison. They complemented each other. Hyrum was more quiet and reserved, while Joseph loved to laugh and tease.

It was apparent that Joseph took the lead, despite the fact that Hyrum was six years older. Yet there seemed to be no jealousy or malice in his attitude toward Joseph. He seemed content to follow Joseph and adored him as much as everyone else did.

"Hyrum," I whispered, realizing my hand was being grasped by one of the greatest men in the early Church. He smiled, kissing my cheek as any loving father would.

"Amazing! She really looks like Jerusha! Are you really from the 1900s? Are there really seven million Saints? Am I really your

41

uncle?" Don Carlos asked, gushing with teenage enthusiasm. I laughed and nodded vigorously. An elderly man placed a hand on his shoulder and stared at me with wise, blue eyes. He was tall, though not as tall as his sons. He was an older version of Joseph.

"I must admit, I thought nothing in this world could ever shock me again, especially coming from Joseph, but this does. It is good to know that this family and the Church will continue into the next century. Welcome, child."

Father Smith enfolded me into his arms where I was overwhelmed with a sense of love and acceptance that brought tears to my eyes. These people were my family. I belonged to them. They had lived and worked so that I could have all that I had. I felt reborn, recharged, and knew that my association with the Smith family would change my life forever.

CHAPTER SEVEN

April 30, 1831 is forever imprinted in my memory. There's nothing like living through history to help one remember it. Emma began to complain about a nagging backache two days before but brushed it off because her due date was still at least three weeks away. Try as I might I couldn't remember the date of birth of her twins. I'll never forget again. Joseph was worried on the morning of the 30th, declaring he would stay home instead of going into Kirtland to work with Sidney.

"Don't fuss Joseph. I'll be fine. It'll be weeks yet. My back hurts because I'm so big. It's more work to have you home." Joseph snorted, looking at me for support.

"Jerree, tell her I should stay," he commanded, his eyes pleading. I smiled, shaking my head.

"You can't bully me, Joseph Smith. Emma's right. You'll just stomp around the house and get bored and be too hard to get along with. If I need to, I'll send someone to get you."

"You're no help. All right. I'll leave, but I'll be home for lunch."

"I'm sure you will," Emma said, patting his cheek as he bent to kiss her.

"I love you, Emma," he whispered, then went to the door, looking back worriedly. She smiled, waving him on.

"I'm glad he's so concerned. Some men aren't," I said. Emma nodded, pain etching lines in her face.

"Are you all right?" I asked, touching her belly. It seemed too hard. "Are you having contractions?" She nodded.

"I'm frightened, Jerree. This is how it started before. It's too early. I can't be ready yet."

"You should lie down. I'll go get Lucy. She'll know what to do."

When I had her lying down, I rushed to Morley's filled with dread. Emma was going to have premature twins that did not live. I knew this. Not far away, Julia Murdock was struggling to bring twins into the world and she wouldn't live. I wished I could take them through the mirror into my own time where they might have been saved with proper medical care. When Lucy and I returned, Emma was sobbing. Rushing to her I noticed a dark patch under her. Gasping, I stroked her forehead, trying to calm her.

"My water broke! It's not time! I can't have this baby now!" she said between gasping breaths.

"Looks like the little tyke is in a rush to greet this cruel world. Jerree, go fetch Cordelia and have Isaac go for Brother Joseph. Try to relax, Sister Emma. It' going to be all right."

When I returned from doing as Lucy said, I got a crash course in mid-wifery. Having a baby in 1831 was definitely different than having one where I came from. There would be no hospital, no doctors, no life saving equipment—just boiled water, sheets torn into rags, twine, scissors and faith. Pain had to be endured for there was not Demerol nor epidurals. No one wore masks or sterile gowns but I did insist that everyone must wash their hands.

Emma was a true lady, refusing to disgrace herself by screaming. Tears and sweat rolled down her face. She insisted I sit by her, holding her hand. The hardest thing I ever did was to comfort and encourage Emma Smith as she labored to bring babies into the world I knew would not live.

An hour or so later, Joseph burst into the room, unmindful of the protestations of the women attending Emma. I tried to avoid his eyes, knowing if I looked at him he would know. Joseph Smith refused to allow me to ignore him. When his eye met mine, I was sure he knew my very thoughts. Tears filled my eyes as he knelt beside his wife, whispering words of love to her.

As the hours wore on, I knew I was going to go insane. Emma would be devastated and there was nothing I could do nor say to change that. I wished I had never come here. I hated this situation. There was nothing to do but wait. Finally, Emma delivered a small baby boy. His cries were weak but any crying was a good sign to his mother who sobbed joyously.

"He's beautiful, Joseph. Look he has your nose."

"Poor boy, but he has his mother's hair, so there's hope for him yet."

They fawned over the babe for several minutes before Emma was seized by horrible pain.

Lucy checked Emma and looked at Joseph in shock.

"Twins! She's having twins!" Joseph took the baby from Emma and stood back as she again labored to bring another baby into the world. Soon she brought forth a daughter, laughing and crying at her good fortune.

"Two to make up for Alvin," she said, placing kisses on her daughter's forehead. I helped clean things up and left the Smiths to enjoy their babies.

The next three hours were the closest to hell I hope to ever go through. Even a casual student of Church history like me knew exactly what was going to happen to the twins Emma bore. I walked slowly to the Morley house, went to my room, laid on my bed and sobbed. I was still lying there when Joseph arrived, knocking quietly on my door. When I opened the door he looked down at me with red, swollen eyes. He took my hand. I followed him down to the parlor where we sat together on the davenport. He stared intently at my face, still grasping my hand as if it alone kept him from drowning in the sea of sorrow so evident in his eyes.

"How's…"

"Just as you would expect her to be. You knew, didn't you? Twins…that die." His voice was toneless, his eyes dry and unyielding.

"Yes, but I couldn't tell Emma that her babies would die." He nodded his head and squeezed my hand.

"Of course you couldn't. I'm the one who told you to keep your knowledge to yourself and the Lord is the one who told me. I guess even a prophet isn't privy to all things. Tell me this, Jerusha, will my Emma ever bear a living child? I love her so much. She thinks she needs to give me a child to be justified as my wife. I don't care about that. I only want Emma, alive and happy."

"Yes, Joseph. She will have living children; that I know. And soon you will see God's plan for Emma…and it will bless your lives. Have faith. God is mindful of you." It seemed perfectly natural for me to say this, though later I wondered if Joseph thought I was a little out of line. He, after all, was the prophet, not me. But at this moment, he was a grieving man who had lost two children. Since his mother had not yet arrived in Kirtland, I felt I should try to fill her shoes and offer the comfort I felt she would have offered.

"Thank you for reminding me of that. I'm grateful to you, Jerree. I don't think Emma could weather this storm without having you here. It will help her heal, knowing that you know she will have living children. Thank you." He took me in his arms and held me to him. We wept together, in the Morley's parlor. I prayed that comfort would come to these two people I had learned to love…and I prayed for the Murdocks.

Facing Emma was one of the most difficult things I've done in my life. Joseph escorted me in, where she lay weeping quietly. Jerusha sat next to her, clasping one of her hands. Emma looked up when she heard us come in. My heart wrenched with the pain I saw there.

"Emma," I said, my voice trembling, partly from grief, partly from fear. Would she hate me for not warning her?

She reached up to me with her free hand and waited for me to take it. With a sob, I knelt by her bed, bowing my head, crying harder than I had since my mother died.

"I'm so sorry, Emma." She squeezed my hand and touched my face.

"Just tell me again how I'll give Joseph living children."

"Oh you will—that I promise. Strong, healthy children that will live to a ripe old age."

Sighing, she smiled and looked up at her grieving husband. He nodded, placing a hand on my shoulder.

"Jerree, will you help…prepare the babies for…" His voice cracked.

"Yes, I'd be honored."

Emma nodded, exhaled shakily and fell into a fitful sleep, tears still glistening on her cheeks.

"Jerusha, please stay with her. Come, Jerree." I stood and put my hand over his, which still rested on my shoulder.

Isaac and Lucy Morley helped us bury the babies—such sweet, perfect babies, that, had they been born in the 1990s, would probably have lived. Thaddeus and Louisa Smith were buried in the Morley cemetery, quietly, with only their father and three strangers to witness. Joseph stood silent and grieving long after the Morleys left, staring at the freshly-dug graves. Though he stood a good foot taller than me, my maternal instincts would not allow me to leave him alone. Slipping an arm around his waist, I stood near him, my head on his arm.

"Have you lost a child, Jerree?" he finally asked, slipping an arm around me also.

"Not like this. I've had a few miscarriages, but never a child that lived and then died. Tom and I wanted a big family. We felt blessed we were able to finally have four," I replied dully. How could I comfort him? What words of wisdom do you give to a man who knows God better than anyone you ever knew?

"Why Joseph? Why did this happen? No one wants a baby more than Emma. No one deserves it more and yet..." Joseph turned and looked down at me sadly, shaking his head.

"Dear Jerree. You know God's plan even better than I do, at this moment. I'm not sure why Father has taken these children but whatever the reason..." His voice trailed off as he shook his head and turned, hurrying off. I looked again at the small graves, then walked back, praying that Emma would be able to weather this newest storm.

JERUSHA

CHAPTER EIGHT

The Smith's grief was felt by all the Morley settlement. No one knew how to comfort them. Joseph hardly left Emma's side, both of them clasping hands and weeping often. I spent as much time as I could with them, making sure they ate and took care of themselves. I had forgotten about the Murdocks until three days later when Newel Whitney rode out with the news of Julia's death. Joseph was sitting on the porch of their small cabin, peeling potatoes, while I was inside preparing lunch. Emma was asleep. She had barely moved from the bed in three days. We were both worried about her. Newel reigned his horse to a stop and climbed down, tying the reigns to the hitching post.

"Brother Newel. What brings you way out here?" Joseph asked, smiling tiredly.

"We heard about the twins, Joseph. Everyone sends their love and condolences," Newel said tenderly, leaning against the rail of the porch. Joseph nodded, unable to find a reply.

"I've just left the Murdocks," Newel said.

Gasping, I hurried to the door, wiping my hands on my apron. Newel looked at me with a puzzled expression.

"How's Julia? I know she was close to delivering too," Joseph asked. I came out onto the porch and put my hand on his shoulder. He looked up at me and seemed to sense something in my eyes. I only looked back at Newel.

"Julia died, Joseph, six hours after giving birth...to twins." Newel's voice was almost a whisper as he locked eyes with Joseph. A shiver ran up my spine. My eyes filled with tears. I had known this would happen but hearing the words spoken, about someone I knew, filled me with such grief that I could not contain it. Joseph stood, placing the bowl of potatoes on the porch.

"How's John?" I heard Joseph ask.

"He's overwhelmed. There are seven children now with no mother to care for them. Two of them need a mother's milk. John's asking for you." Joseph looked down into my eyes. I nodded, and he seemed to understand that this was something he should do. I could see the thoughts racing through his mind. Twins without a mother and a mother without her twins. Emma was still complaining that her milk would not dry up.

"Go, Joseph. I'm here and I won't be leaving. You need to go." He nodded and hurried to ask Isaac for the use of his wagon and a team of horses. I turned to Newel and asked him if he'd like a glass of water, which he readily accepted.

The Murdocks lived approximately twenty miles northeast of Kirtland. Isaac's land was eight miles out, so I knew Joseph would be gone the rest of the day. Would he bring the babies home tonight? Would John Murdock's family be all right? I wondered what I should do. I couldn't go to Morley's and tell them to cart down all the baby stuff they had just put away. How could I explain my knowledge of what was going to happen? I was so happy for Emma. She wanted a baby so badly. It took all my efforts not to act too happy or excited because I knew she would have two babies very soon. Guilt would seize me then. Everyone was still mourning and now another family would be also. How could I be so heartless? Seven children had just lost their mother and a man his wife. Still Emma desperately needed these babies to help her heal and she would soon hold them in her arms, so my excitement would overwhelm the grief. I thought I might just go insane before Joseph returned.

The hours seemed endless. How I yearned for TV or radio, something to help drown out the silence and grief that pervaded the Smith cabin. Emma woke several times during the day, barely speaking at all. I helped her to the outhouse, gave her lunch and sat with her, reading the Book of Mormon. Tears streamed down her face and I knew they were not for the destruction of the Nephites. How I wished I could reveal what I knew was soon to happen. I longed to see the light back in Emma's brown eyes and a smile on her beautiful face. But I had promised I wouldn't reveal what I knew about their lives, so I waited in anxious silence. It was 10 p.m. when I heard a wagon rolling in. Another sound aroused Emma, who sat up, looking at me questioningly.

"Do you hear that? Tell me I'm not going insane. Is that a baby crying?" she asked, swinging her legs over the side of the bed, hope shining in her eyes. I nodded and lit the lantern.

"It's definitely a baby crying—wailing like a banshee as a matter of fact. Don't get up. I'll go see what's happening."

Hurrying out the door, holding the lantern high, I peered into the darkness, smiling as the wagon came into the circle of light. Newel was driving. Elizabeth Anne and Joseph were in the back, each holding a squalling baby. Having waited all day for this moment, I laughed heartily, knowing at least two of the people in the wagon thought I was insane.

"Hurry, Jerree, I think this baby senses I'm a novice. Good, hand the lantern to Newel. There, now take little Julia and let's see if Emma can accommodate her. She refuses to take a bottle we made for her," Joseph said, bending to hand the baby to me. He then jumped down and turned to Lizzy.

"Here, Lizzy, hand the boy to me. Let's go meet Aunt Emma," he said when baby Joseph M. was in his arms. Emma stood in the doorway, her eyes as big as saucers. Joseph's face was beaming as he walked to her, a baby in his arms. I followed, Julia already quieted, nestled against my woman's body.

"Joseph, where did you get them? Why..."

"Come into the house and sit, Emma. Here, take this baby. He's starving."

"But whose?"

"John and Julia Murdock had twins the same day we did. Six hours later, Julia died. John has been beside himself, and when he heard about us...he hoped we would... could...take care of them. Do you think we could, Emma?" Emma was already unwrapping the baby, cooing softly to him. She looked up at Joseph with tear-filled eyes and nodded.

"Poor John. Poor babies. Of course we'll take care of them. It's a good thing my milk never dried up. Here you go, sweet baby..." She unbuttoned her nightgown and offered the hungry babe a breast, unconcerned with the audience she had. Newel smiled, and touched my arm.

"I think we should leave. Isaac offered Lizzy and me a room for the night. Jerree, let us escort you home." I nodded. As I handed baby Julia to Joseph, I reached up to touch his cheek.

"Enjoy this blessing, Joseph. God did have Emma in mind all along."

"I see that," was all he could say. As I reached the door, I turned and took a final look at the Prophet Joseph Smith and his new family. Little Joseph M. was already nursing greedily while Joseph sat, rocking Julia and humming.

"Come, Sister Jerree," Newel coaxed. Sighing, I closed the door and followed the Whitneys to the Morley's house.

Joseph dearly loved Emma. That was evident in all he did for her. The pain of losing three children was almost too much for her. He stayed close to her, providing for her every need. When Julia Murdock died, leaving newborn twins, Joseph brought them to her, then stayed close by to help. He refused to leave her side, sharing her bittersweet joy of having babies to care for.

A few days after the Murdock twins were delivered into their care, John Murdock came to the Smith's, looking weary and grief-stricken. Joseph held him as he wept for the loss of his beloved wife. Seeing how well the twins were doing in the Smith's care, he pled with them to adopt them, to raise them as their own.

"But John..." Joseph protested.

"Don't, Joseph. I can't care for them the way they need. It would be an honor to place them in your care. I can hardly do justice to the older ones. Julia would want this also. She loved Emma. She would have wanted her to be happy. I see that the babies make her so. I feel strongly that this is the right choice."

John Murdock was a big man, with dark hair, a square jaw-line, and full lips. He looked to be in his late thirties, too young to be a widower with seven children to care for. That he loved Joseph was evident. Joseph nodded, again embracing him, letting his own tears fall unashamedly.

"We'll raise them the best we can, John. Feel free to come over whenever you wish to visit them."

"Thank you, Joseph. Thank you for everything."

Thus Joseph and Julia Murdock became the adoptive children of Joseph and Emma Smith. I don't think anything aided Emma's recovery better than those two sweet babies. Though they were a handful, she thoroughly enjoyed them, which enabled Joseph to get back to the business of running the Church.

Sometime during all this, Lucy Mack Smith arrived with about eighty Saints, including Newel Knight. Joseph's mother was a small woman, even shorter than my five feet. Though small, there was nothing frail about the mother of the Prophet. I soon learned that she was a living well of love and understanding from which the entire family could partake. She accepted me, and the story of my arrival, as if that sort of thing happened all the time. I guess with Joseph Smith as a son, it did.

J E R U S H A

CHAPTER NINE

"The revelation is clear, brethren. If you have land, it needs to be shared with those coming from the east. If the land needs to be purchased, then we'll have to find the money to buy it. Edward has chosen John Corrill and Isaac Morley to counsel him. I think they can handle it. There are more pressing matters—such as how to feed all those who are arriving," Joseph said, as he sat in counsel with Sidney Rigdon, Edward Partridge, Lyman Wight, Isaac Morley, Hyrum and Father Smith.

It's amazing how fast your mind can adjust to the changes you're forced to make. I had been in Kirtland only two months, and already it seemed commonplace to meet people with great historical names. I was also getting pretty good at cooking over an open fire, though Joseph and Emma empathized with my struggles more than once.

"In my own time I'm an excellent cook," I retorted.

"Hopefully they have found easier methods than what we have now, or I fear for the rising generations," Joseph teased.

"It's easier, and faster, and better," I snapped, tossing the burnt johnny cakes I'd just destroyed out the door where even the dog refused to eat them. Joseph laughed loudly, causing Emma to chide him for fear he'd wake the babies.

I hated laundry day and learned to do it only out of necessity. I longed for my matching Kenmore set and Tide with bleach. The soap used in the 1800s was abrasive and smelly. I wondered how anything could get clean from a mixture of potash, animal fat, and lye. My poor hands were doomed.

But in spite of discomforts, I felt privileged to be witnessing a young Prophet establish an organization that would stand until the Savior returned. Many of the men around him were older than he was. Sidney Ridgon was 38, as was Edward Partridge. Isaac Morley was 46, Hyrum was 31, and Father Smith was 60. Joseph was only 26. Yet no one questioned his leadership. They all came to him for counsel and advice.

"Not everyone is willing to just give their land away," Sidney said, startling me out of my reverie. He turned to me and gave me a stern look. I had been doing dishes but had stopped to listen to them and to reflect. I smiled sweetly and returned to my duties. Joseph still insisted on staying close to Emma, so this meeting had been held in the Smith's small cabin.

"It's true, Joseph. I've been around to as many people as I can and tried to explain the Law of Consecration and Stewardship but it hasn't been accepted," Bishop Partridge said.

"I know, Edward. The Law is perfect but we as humans are not. It's hard to give away something we've worked so hard for. Maybe that's why the Lord has blessed us with poverty."

The men chuckled, nodding their heads. Many of them were financially strapped, and sometimes it felt good just to joke about it.

"Have patience, brethren. It takes time to make saints out of ordinary people."

"Patience doesn't feed and house the hungry, Joseph."

"True, Brother Sidney, but we are commanded to have it nonetheless. I think if we all work together we can find a solution to our problems. The Lord has commanded us to convene a special conference that will begin June 3rd. Many of these problems will be addressed. Now, brethren, let's close this meeting and go outside. It's terribly hot and I need to stretch my legs. Father, could you please pray for us?"

"Of course. Thank you," Father Smith said, standing and folding his arms. As he prayed, it struck me that this man had been the example to a son who was now called to be a prophet. Father Smith was everything the father of a prophet should be. I thanked the heavens that I could get to know him—and that I descended from him.

Sidney Rigdon wanted to complain more after the prayer but Joseph would not hear of it, winking at me as he ushered the men out of the cabin. I smiled and wiped my hands, tip-toeing to the blanket that divided the sleeping area from the kitchen. Peering behind it, I saw Emma sleeping soundly with baby Joseph M. and Julia beside her. Sighing, I walked out onto the porch, breathing in the fresh May air. Joseph was leading the small group up to the big house, laughing and enjoying the companionship of his friends.

In one week I would be able to attend my first conference where Joseph Smith would preside. How I wished Tom could be here to enjoy it with me. Was he frantically searching for me? Was I presumed dead? Had my picture been plastered across bulletin boards throughout the country? I could see my family being interviewed by Robert Stack on "Unsolved Mysteries." What was happening to my family? I hoped my own Joseph would stay on his mission and not come home because they could not find me. As I watched Joseph escort the men to their horses, a sweet sense of calm came over me. Everything would be alright with my dear family. A prophet had promised:

"Be at peace, Jerusha. The Lord is aware of all that is happening and is in control. Your family will be fine. I promise it."

Having been raised in the Church, General Conference was a way of life. Twice a year my parents gathered their children, insisting we sit through every session. I was spared one session due to the fact that I was a girl, but I thought it was still four sessions too many. Every Saturday morning session, without fail, my mother rose early, made cinnamon rolls and hot chocolate, and blissfully parked in her favorite Lazy-Boy to hear all the words of the brethren.

"We are so fortunate to live in a time when we can listen to the words of the Prophet in our own home," Mother would say. Now her words flooded my memory as I sat in the Sunday session of the special conference of June 1831. I had sorely missed going to the Friday session because it was a Priesthood session. For the first time in my life, I seriously wished that I was a man. It didn't help when I began to hear reports about the meeting.

June 2nd, the day before the conference, Joseph had prophesied that the Man of Sin would be revealed. Because I was *such* a student of Church history, I had no idea what that meant. I wonder if Joseph ever was discouraged by my lack of knowledge. I assured him that there were people in my time that knew much more than I did. I was

57

really a poor representative of my generation.

Joseph spoke powerfully to the brethren and many said he was surely speaking by the power of the Holy Ghost. The Spirit was strong. Lyman Wight was blessed with the spirit of prophecy. He said the coming of Christ would be like the brilliant sun rising in the east. The world would be illumined by the Savior's presence and that brightness would consume the wicked of the earth.

He prophesied that some of the brethren would suffer martyrdom for the gospel of Jesus Christ, sealing their testimonies with their blood. He professed to see the Son sitting upon the right hand of the Father. I was envious, having always wished for such a witness.

Not to be outdone, Satan exercised his power by seizing John Murdock and Harvey Whitlock, hindering their speech and restraining the movement of their limbs. Joseph masterfully rebuked him, in the name of Jesus Christ, and the men were set free. John told me later, on one of his visits to the twins, that feeling the dark power of Satan was worse than the grief he felt at Julia's death. He hoped never to feel it again.

The first high priests of this dispensation were ordained during that June conference. There were nineteen. Isaac Morley and John Corrill were sustained and set apart as counselors to Bishop Partridge. What seemed natural to me was wonderful and strange to these Saints in Kirtland. Again I was struck with the fact that this was an infant church I had fallen into. What to me seemed a matter of course was exciting and new to everyone else. It did my heart good to see the Church through their eyes.

Sunday June 5th was glorious, with bright sunlight and blue cloudless skies. Summer had definitely come. With its heat came humidity, the like I had never experienced. I longed for a T-shirt and some knee-length shorts. The fashions of this century were certainly not conducive to comfort. Because so many people had shown up for the meeting—a whopping 300—it was decided that Sunday services should be held in the grove on the Morley Settlement.

I found myself seated on the ground on a beautiful quilt amongst the entire Smith clan. Four-year-old Lovina had taken to me, saying that she loved me because I reminded her of her mother. She planted herself solidly in my lap, playing with my hands. My rings fascinated her. On my right hand, I had a 14-karat gold CTR ring that I had worn for years. It had been a Christmas present from Tom. She traced the letters in the shield over and over with her tiny fingers.

"What do the letters mean?" Jerusha asked, sitting close by, holding two year-old Mary.

"CTR means 'Choose the right.' A CTR ring is quite a popular item of jewelry where I come from."

"The people in your time must be very wealthy," she said, refusing to allow Mary to run about the trees. Mary began to fuss and I wished for a Tupperware bowl full of Cheerios.

"Yes, I guess we are. There are many poor people, and I never considered myself wealthy, but I guess I am. I've taken so much for granted." Jerusha nodded and focused her attention on Mary, magically presenting her with a cookie from a small handbag that hung from her wrist. Ah! A 19th–century diaper bag!

Before long, Sidney Rigdon stood. The grove that had buzzed with visiting people became instantly quiet. Sidney looked over the crowd and smiled. For some reason, Brother Sidney rubbed me the wrong way. I knew he was a very intelligent man and a forceful speaker, but knowing of the choices he would make later in his life bothered me.

Some people in the congregation had been his followers when he was a Campbellite minister. They thought he was nigh unto perfection. I wanted to heartily disagree with them. I might have been the poorest student of Church history ever born, but I did know that Brother Sidney Rigdon would not stay faithful and I had a pretty good idea pride had a major role in that.

"Brothers and sisters, it does my heart good to see so many of you gathered here on this glorious Sabbath morning! This Church is but a year old and look at its growth! The field is definitely white and ready to harvest. To open this meeting we'll sing the "Alleluia Chorus" by St. Francis of Assisi, after which Brother Martin Harris will offer the invocation."

I was grateful I knew this hymn. In some meetings these early Saints sang songs I'd never heard. Sometimes they sang words I knew to a different tune, which fouled me up royally. But this song, "All Creatures of our God and King," was sung exactly as I knew it. Though there was no organ, I don't think I've ever heard it performed more beautifully than on that Sunday in a grove of trees in 19th century Ohio.

After Martin's prayer, several men were called upon to bear their testimonies. I found Newel Knight's very interesting, for he related his experience with evil and the miracle that was wrought in his behalf. This was a story I had not heard before.

"Last April, shortly after the Church was organized, Brother Joseph visited Colesville, where my family lived. We had known Joseph since 1826. He had even worked for us a few times. Through him we learned of the gold plates and his visitation from the Father and the Son. Joseph was only twenty, but I was deeply impressed with the truthfulness of his statements concerning the plates of the Book of Mormon which had been shown to him by an angel of the Lord."

"While Joseph was in Colesville, he held meetings where he preached powerfully about the restored gospel. In one such meeting, he asked me to pray. As I attempted to do so I was attacked by an evil spirit that lifted me from the floorand tossed me about most fearfully. Frightened, I begged Joseph to cast the devil from me. Joseph grabbed my hand and said, "If you know that I can, it shall be done.""

"I knew he could and with a booming voice he rebuked the evil one, commanding him in the name of Jesus Christ to depart." Newel's voice cracked. For a moment he could not speak. Only then did I realize how intently I had been listening to him, totally caught up in his story. He smiled and brushed a hand over his eyes, trying to regain his composure.

"I'm sorry. Sometimes I can't contain the joy I feel at remembering this event in my life. As soon as Joseph touched me, I saw the devil leave me and my body was returned to normal. The Spirit of the Lord then fell upon me. The visions of heaven were opened to me. Needless to say, I was baptized, eager to join the kingdom Joseph was establishing. My family and I have already been reviled and persecuted, counting ourselves lucky to say as Paul, "Be not thou therefore ashamed of the testimony of our Lord, nor of me his prisoner, but be thou partaker of the afflictions of the Gospel according to the power of God.""

Jerusha took my hand, bringing me back to the present. I then realized that I was weeping, something I very seldom did in church meetings. I had always considered "weepers" weak, and prided myself with fortitude to stay dry-eyed. Yet, here I sat, in a grove of trees crying like a baby, listening to what I learned later was the story of one of the first miracles performed in this dispensation.

Jerusha seemed to understand, in spite of my embarrassment. She squeezed my hand. Jerusha Barden Smith was a small woman, quiet, soft-spoken. She was the perfect companion for Hyrum Smith who was sober and thoughtful. Jerusha quietly experienced the new gospel through her husband. That's where I differed from her. I was too much like my mother, I guess. I wanted to experience everything for myself. I wanted to feel the sensations I had when I heard Newel Knight's testimony, or listened to Father Smith pray, or witnessed the prophetic mantle fall on Joseph as he declared, "Woman, in the name of the Lord Jesus Christ, I command thee to be whole."

Suddenly, I realized that I was sounding like my mother. It was wonderful! I really did want these experiences and reveled in them. How I wished she were here now. Here I was, tasting the Spirit and liking it—loving it in fact—and I knew she would be proud.

J E R U S H A

CHAPTER TEN

Later that evening, the Smith family dispersed throughout the Morley settlement, resting after a day of worship. I was at Joseph and Emma's cabin helping with the twins. Joseph was in counsel with Bishop Partridge and his newly sustained counselors. The Saints' poverty was a distressing problem. Though the Lord had revealed His plan to alleviate poverty, many people complainied.

I looked at Emma, who shrugged and smiled. She seemed used to such meetings and was content to have them in her house. At least Joseph was close to her then. I wondered how often they got any time alone.

A knock interrupted the meeting. Joseph rose, obviously happy for the diversion. Newel Knight stood on the porch, his handsome face etched with worry.

"Newel? What's wrong?" Joseph asked, drawing him into the cabin. Everyone focused their attention on Brother Knight.

"I just received word from Thompson. Leman Copley has ordered us off his land. He brought a sheriff with him. He's giving us a week. The Saints are frightened and confused. They've asked me to consult you."

Joseph's expression changed from cordial to pained sadness. He placed an arm around Newel's shoulders and led him to a chair.

"Leman made a covenant! How can he do that?" John Corrill asked, his face flushing with anger.

"The State of Ohio recognizes no such covenant," Isaac replied softly. Joseph nodded silently.

"What do we do, Joseph?" Edward asked, feeling the weight of his calling even more heavily. As bishop, he would have to help these now–homeless people find homes.

"I must ask the Lord," Joseph mused, walking to the door. "Will you brethren stay until I return with an answer from the Lord?" They all readily agreed. Who wouldn't? I planned to stay. I had been raised to believe in prophets and prophecy, but never in my life had I witnessed first–hand a prophet asking and receiving an answer directly from heaven.

"How long will he be gone?" I asked, earning impatient looks from a couple of men. Emma understood and smiled.

"It depends. Could be a few minutes or it could be hours. I'll wager you brethren could use something to eat. Jerree, will you help me prepare a little something for these good men?"

"Of course," I said. Emma put Julia in her cradle and joined me in the kitchen. Joseph was gone exactly long enough for us to fix dinner, feed the men and clean up. I was just wiping my hands on my apron before picking up Joseph M. when he came in, his countenance tranquil and shining. Emma immediately went to the steamer trunk at the foot of their bed to retrieve paper, an inkwell, and a quill pen.

"Would you like me to write for you, Joseph?" Emma asked. She seldom got the chance to do that for him now, with the babies here and Sidney, of course. He smiled and nodded. When Emma was seated and Joseph was sure everyone was listening, he began.

"Behold, thus saith the Lord, even Alpha and Omega, the beginning and the end, even he who was crucified for the sins of the world—" Joseph Smith's deep voice, which was rich and resonate, when under the Spirit's influence, vibrated with intensity that pierced my soul with exquisite joy. He spoke slowly and distinctly, stopping at intervals to give Emma time to write what he said. He never had her read back what he had just said; he seemed to have the revelation seared in his memory, like the Ten Commandments on the stone tablets.

He just stood, waiting patiently, until she said "Go on," then resumed the revelation exactly where he left off. Watching him dictate the revelation, I too was drawn into the spirit of it and could not contain the rapture I felt. Once again, tears began to flow. I couldn't believe what a baby I was becoming.

"Behold, verily, verily, I say unto you, my servant, Newel Knight, you shall stand fast in the office whereunto I have appointed you.

"And if your brethren desire to escape their enemies, let them repent of all their sins, and become truly humble before me and contrite.

"And as the covenant, which they made unto me, has been broken, even so it has become void and of none effect.

"And wo to him by whom this offense cometh, for it had been better for him that he had been drowned in the depth of the sea."

There was a collective gasp, as all of us stared at the prophet. Joseph did not seem to notice and continued, Emma having to write faster to keep up with him.

"But blessed are they who have kept the covenant and observed the commandment, for they shall obtain mercy.

"Wherefore, go to now and flee the land, lest your enemies come upon you; and take your journey and appoint whom you will to be your leader, and to pay moneys for you.

"And thus you shall take your journey into the regions westward unto the land Missouri, unto the borders of the Lamanites.

"And after you have done journeying, behold I say unto you, seek ye a living like unto men, until I prepare a place for you.

"And again, be patient in tribulation until I come: And behold, I come quickly, and my reward is with me, and they who have sought me early shall find rest to their souls. Even so. Amen."

For several moments everything was silent, Joseph looking at each of us with great love. He sighed and placed a huge hand against Emma's face. She pressed her cheek into his palm, her tears wetting his fingers. What a wonderful experience! I can't describe the feelings I felt but suffice it to say, I will never be able to read the Doctrine and Covenants without hearing the clear, melodious voice of Joseph Smith. Some of his critics said that he received revelations too conveniently for them to be from God. Those critics never sat in a room while he dictated a revelation or they would not have been able to say those things. Joseph Smith was truly the Lord's mouthpiece, and I am so thankful to have received that knowledge.

Emma volunteered to walk me home, mostly to let the men discuss the revelation. Joseph promised to listen for the babies and lit the lantern for us. He walked us to the door, handing me the lantern. His face still radiated with the Spirit's glow. I couldn't resist reaching up and touching him, wanting to feel even a small portion of the power that flowed through him. He covered my hand with his.

"Thank you," I whispered. He chuckled and squeezed my hand.

"Don't thank me. The Lord gets the credit for your little adventure. Now get out of here; these brethren would like to get home sometime tonight."

The men inside collectively agreed. We all laughed, Joseph kissed Emma's cheek and we walked into the night, leaving the prophet to counsel with his brethren.

The Colesville branch, as it was called, packed up and started on the 880–mile journey to Missouri less than a week after Joseph's revelation to Newel Knight. I was amazed at how readily these people obeyed the word of the Lord. They had already traveled from New York to Kirtland, Ohio, a trek of over 300 miles and had tried to establish a community outside Kirtland called Thompson. Now they had to pull up stakes and begin again.

Could I have put my faith in the promise of one man, albeit he was a prophet? Could I give up everything and WALK an additional 880 miles to a strange place, all for the sake of the gospel? I hoped so, but could not be sure. The greatest trial I'd ever faced was the loss of my mother and I knew she was in a far better place. I knew then that my generation of saints had no idea about the depth of these people's faith nor their fortitude. I trembled at the thought.

Along with sending sixty plus families off to Missouri, twenty-six men were called on missions, traveling two by two. I learned that until this time, many men traveled alone. They were to go throughout the region to meet in Missouri for a conference. Everyone was to go straight there except Hyrum Smith and John Murdock, who were to go to Detroit first. Joseph Wakefield and Solomon Humphrey were sent "into the eastern lands."

All the other brethren were to stay to watch over the branches in Kirtland. I learned there were three branches in the Kirtland area—one in Kirtland, presided over by John Whitmer, one in Warrensville, and one in Mentor. John Murdock and Sidney Rigdon presided over them respectively. With so much happening, I never learned who presided in their absence.

Joseph would be going to the conference. He seemed filled with mixed emotions. On one hand, he was going to a place where Zion would be named. The entire body of Saints was anxious to know the location of the land of their inheritance. Leaving Emma so soon after the birth and death of their twins was a sore trial for him.

I promised to help in any way I could. Though Emma was feeling stronger every day, I knew caring for the Murdock twins alone would be too big a strain. All of Joseph's family assured him she would never be alone. Satisfied, Joseph prepared to depart, his companions being Sidney, Edward Partridge, Martin Harris and Sidney Gilbert, who was taking his family to Missouri to settle. They left on June 19, 1831 in a wagon filled with as many goods as they could carry. Though I knew they would miss each other, Joseph and Emma parted tenderly, excited to learn the Lord's will. Joseph embraced each member of the family that had come to see him off, including me.

"Good-bye, Jerree. Thank you for being here to care for my family," he said as he kissed my cheek. I smiled and gave his back a pat.

"Don't thank me. It's the Lord that brought me here. Remember?" He laughed and turned to his wife. Embracing her once more, he then jumped into the wagon and rode off amidst tearful farewells. We all stood waving until the wagon was out of sight.

"Come on now, let's get out of this sun and have a cool drink of water," Mother Smith said, wiping her eyes and putting an arm around Emma's waist.

"Good idea, Mother Smith," Jerusha said, letting baby Mary down to toddle after her older sister.

Having their men go to promulgate the gospel was becoming a natural thing to these women. My husband took many business trips and I missed him, but we had access to all the modern devices that allowed us to communicate daily. Being in 1831, without telephone lines and cell phone towers, made me see what a sacrifice the early Saints made to spread the gospel. Again I prayed I could have as much strength as these great women.

The summer of 1831 passed uneventfully for those of us left behind in Kirtland. All the action was 800 miles away and we'd be told all about it when Joseph returned. I did know that Joseph would be told that Zion was in Jackson County, Missouri with Independence being the center place. That was the extent of my knowledge about Joseph's first visit to Missouri. So I waited as anxiously as the rest of the Saints to hear all the news.

As the summer progressed, it got hotter and more humid. I would have traded my diamond ring for a T-shirt, a pair of shorts, and some sandals. I knew I would die of heat stroke in the 19th century. There was no way to get cool. Even going barefoot was out of the question with all the foliage and underbrush. Snakes and rodents were too plentiful.

I yearned for a tall glass of ice water. That one simple pleasure seemed like the greatest luxury—one I had taken for granted all my life. Ice was not a commodity in the middle of summer in 1831. I had to be happy with cool water from the well.

In Joseph's absence, Emma began to compile hymns for the hymnbook she had been asked to make in 1830. She seemed happy to have this task, for it helped fill the lonely hours without her husband. The twins kept us both busy.

Joseph Smith was such a charismatic man, so full of life and energy that when he was gone nothing seemed right. He breathed life into everything around him. His exuberance was contagious, so that even without his prophetic gifts, being in his presence was always a joy. He was sorely missed, and we all anxiously waited and wished for his return.

CHAPTER ELEVEN

August 27, 1831
Kirtland, Ohio
Morley Settlement

> "I am a child of God
> And he has sent me here.
> Has given me an earthly home
> With parents kind and dear.
>
> Lead me, guide me
> Walk beside me
> Help me find the way.
> Teach me all that I must do
> To live with Him someday."

Quietly I sang that beloved song as I rocked Joseph M. to sleep. The heat was stifling. He had been cranky most of the afternoon. Now that the sun was setting and a breeze was beginning to blow, little Joseph M. could finally relax enough to fall asleep.

Emma had taken Julia over to the Morley's, hoping that separating the babies would help them settle down.

Heaving a tiny baby sigh, four-month-old Joseph Murdock Smith drifted to sleep, clothed only in diaper and a loose cotton gown. I dared not stop rocking him, just in case he'd wake up.

"I am a child of God
And so my needs are great
Help me to understand His word
Before it grows too late.
Lead me, guide me
Walk beside me
Help me find the way.
Teach me all that I must do
To live with him someday."

"You have a beautiful voice," Joseph said. He was standing in the doorway, smiling. Even with dust caked on his clothes and hair, Joseph Smith was a magnificent–looking man. I gasped, startling the baby, who began to whimper. Joseph chuckled, crossed the room, and took his adopted son from me.

"Shhhh, sweet boy. Papa's here now. Go back to sleep." He quieted the baby, then looked at me curiously.

"I've never heard that song. It's quite beautiful…and true."

"Yes, I know. It's one of the many we teach our children to help them learn the gospel. All of my children could sing it before they could talk."

Joseph nodded and sat down, patting the baby's back.

"I'm glad. I approve whole-heartedly. Will you teach me the words?" I looked at him in surprise. He laughed.

"Are you sure it's not against the rules?" I teased.

"I think we can bend the rules on this one. Where's Emma?"

"At the big house. The children have been fussy all day. She'll be so happy you're home. We all will. You must be starving. Let me get…"

"Don't. I ate at Sidney's. Phoebe insisted. I think I'll go fetch my wife, though. I've missed her sorely," he said as he put the baby to bed.

"I'm sure you have. Here, let me heat some water so you can wash up. I'll go get Emma." I turned to pick up the water bucket and felt his hand on my shoulder. Looking at him, I saw concern and compassion in his eyes.

"How are you, Jerusha? You must miss your family something fierce." Tears sprang to my eyes at the gentleness in his voice. The use of my given name added to the ache for my mother and Tom.

They were the only ones brave enough to call me Jerusha...except for the Prophet Joseph.

"Oh, Joseph, I do miss them. I wonder every day what they are doing and if they are frantically worrying about me."

"Be comforted. I don't know how all of this came about or why, but the Spirit whispers that all is well and God's purposes are being fulfilled in your being here. Learn what you need to learn and this experience will not have been in vain. Run and tell my wife her husband is home while I wash up. Tomorrow I will recount all my experiences in Zion."

I nodded and rushed to the door, turning back as I stepped onto the porch.

"I'm so glad you're home, Joseph. Emma will be too."

"No more than I am," he replied, sitting on his bed and pulling off his boots off. I hurried to Morley's, the last rays of the setting sun lighting my way.

✻   ✻   ✻

I had been in Kirtland five months and had not yet had the privilege of meeting Oliver Cowdery. He had been in Missouri to help organize the area. When my opportunity finally came, I had long since gotten over the wonder of meeting the "Who's Who" of the Restoration.

On August 28, a special meeting was held to report all that was accomplished in Zion. Many tears were shed to finally have a place the Lord decreed would be for the Saints. News of the death of Polly Knight was received reverently. Polly Knight was Newel's mother. She had not been well when they began their journey to Missouri. Many times her family begged her to stop until she was well enough to travel but she was determined to reach the promised land. She was so sick at one point that Newel bought lumber for her casket. She refused to die before setting foot in the land of Zion. She died a few days after their arrival.

"There's a woman with faith. I can say with assurance that she sleeps in Jesus till the resurrection," Joseph said, tears lingering in his eyes.

There was a collective gasp when it was reported that cornerstones had been laid for a temple to be built in Zion. Sidney

Rigdon dedicated the land where the city of Zion would stand, and the Saints were already beginning to build a city.

"The inhabitants of Zion must cleanse themselves of all unrighteousness, for Zion means the pure in heart, and the place of Zion is where the pure in heart dwell together in righteousness. We must all strive to do these things," Joseph counseled.

After the meeting, Joseph made a special point of bringing Oliver Cowdery to meet me. He was a handsome man, standing only 5'7", with refined features and a slight build. I'd always pictured him as tall as Joseph but even Emma was taller than Oliver by two inches. He was younger than Joseph and I was again struck by how young the men were who were leading the Church.

"Oliver, this is Sister Jerree James, Jerusha's cousin. Jerree, this is Oliver Cowdery, my right hand-man. This church would not run without him." Oliver laughed and nudged Joseph's side.

"I wouldn't let Sidney hear you say that; he thinks the Church can't run without him. Hello, Sister James, so nice to meet you. Joseph has said so many good things about you. How long do you plan to visit?"

"Indefinitely," Joseph chimed in, seeing my hesitation. "Her husband travels extensively and all of her children are grown so she's come to dwell with the Saints. She's a valuable member of our family and such a wonderful help to Emma." I felt my face go red under his tender gaze.

"I'm grateful to be here, Joseph. It's wonderful to finally meet you, Brother Cowdery." I held my hand to him. He took it, smiling brightly at me.

"It's an honor to meet you, Sister Jerree, and now I must go and visit with the Whitmers. Elizabeth Anne is looking a bit perturbed that I'm mingling again. I'll see you later." He pointed to Joseph and hurried off to join a very pretty, very impatient girl. Joseph chuckled and shook his head.

"I hope he marries her soon. It's hard to get him to concentrate on anything."

"Who is she?"

"Elizabeth Anne Whitmer, David's sister."

"Oh," I said. I hadn't realized Oliver married into the Whitmer family. Joseph saw my surprise and laughed.

"Dear Jerree. I hope you are recording all you are learning. You've been a very poor student of your own history. I admonish you to go home—to your own time—and educate those like you who feel that ignoring their past won't hurt them. How can the future ever be better without knowing the past? Come, I see Emma."

He squeezed my arm and led me to his wife, his gentle rebuke still ringing in my ears. I vowed then to do just as he advised. My generation would know about the Saints who built the kingdom, I would see to that.

Because Joseph had been gone more than two months, many problems needed attention. He began spending more time in Kirtland than with Emma. Knowing he was needed there did not lessen her loneliness. I don't think anyone could fully understand her pain without witnessing it. Emma Hale Smith was then twenty-seven years old. She was a strikingly beautiful woman, with raven-colored hair and russet brown eyes. She stood 5'9", was slender and well-built. She was a perfect match for her giant of a husband. That she adored him was obvious in everything she did for him.

She had been raised in comparative wealth, but had forsaken all, including association with her family, to marry Joseph Smith. She truly believed he was a prophet and was determined to be a proper helpmate for him. Her greatest sorrow was being unable to bear a living child for him. The Murdock twins had helped ease that pain, but she longed to give Joseph his own child.

I was grateful for the time I spent helping Emma with the daily tasks a woman had to perform in the 1800s. At times the tasks were tedious and time-consuming, and I would have rather not spent so much time working. But I learned to love and appreciate Emma Smith so much more by working beside her every day. I knew that for the rest of my life I would refuse to hear or read anything derogatory about Emma Hale Smith, for now I knew her. I spent hours talking to her about her feelings, about the gospel, and about Joseph.

It broke her heart to see the world vilify her husband. A man by the name of Ezra Booth wrote several articles against Joseph and had them published in *The Ohio Star*, the local paper. He had been converted the day Joseph healed Elsa Johnson but had lost faith when he learned that these types of miracles were not the norm. God expects His children to live by faith, not by grand displays of power. Joseph seemed to take the bad press in stride. He smiled at Emma as she fumed about Ezra Booth.

"Moroni said my name would be had for good and ill. Ezra's claims are false and petty. Those who want to believe him will. There's nothing we can do to stop them. But the honest in heart will see the lies for what they are," Joseph said, taking a bite of his breakfast.

Emma threw the newspaper on the table, huffing to the fireplace to check the water she was trying to boil. Joseph chuckled and looked over at me. I was mixing cornmeal mush to make into johnny cakes.

"I'll bet there's still many things said about me in Jerree's day. Aren't there, Jerree?"

"Yes, good and bad," I replied, wondering if I should say any more. Joseph nodded and turned to Emma.

"See dear, nothing to be done."

Joseph brushed off the verbal attacks, but I knew they worried him, too. Enemies of the church were threatening violence and he was not naïve. He had been attacked before, and it bothered him that his family might be in danger. Along with his worries about his family, the Church seemed to have a lot of internal struggles in his absence. Ezra Booth was not the only apostate. This broke Joseph's heart. Asking for the Lord's help in this matter he received his answer.

"Hearken, O ye people, and open your hearts and give ear from afar; and listen, you that call yourselves the people of the Lord, and hear the word of the Lord and his will concerning you.

"Yea, verily, I say, hear the word of him whose anger is kindled against the wicked and rebellious;

"Who willeth to take even them whom he will and pleasure; and destroyeth when he pleases, and is able to cast the soul down to hell.

"Behold, I the Lord, utter my voice, and it shall be obeyed.

"Wherefore, verily I say, let the wicked take heed, and let the rebellious fear and tremble; and let the unbelieving hold their lips, for the day of wrath shall come upon them as a whirlwind, and all flesh shall know that I am God.

"And he that seeketh signs shall see signs, but not unto Salvation.

"Verily, I say unto you, there are those among you who seek signs, and there have been such even from the beginning;

74

"But behold, faith cometh not by signs, but signs follow those that believe.

"Yea, signs come by faith, not by the will of men, nor as they please, but by the will of God.

"Yea, signs come by faith, unto mighty works, for without faith no man pleaseth God; and with whom is angry he is not well pleased; wherefore, unto such he showeth no signs, only in wrath unto their condemnation.

"Wherefore, I the Lord, am not pleased with those among you who have sought after signs and wonders for faith, and not for the good of men unto my glory.

"Nevertheless, I give commandments, and many have turned away from you, and others remain with you that hereafter shall be revealed."

Many more things were told to the Prophet and he recorded them all, though some people were offended, murmuring against him. The Lord commanded that Joseph and Sidney find other housing. That posed a problem, for Joseph had no money to buy a home or even rent one. The Lord took care of the problem for them.

CHAPTER TWELVE

"We will be honored to have you stay at our house," John Johnson said, squeezing the healed hand of his wife Elsa. She fairly beamed at Joseph, the look in her eyes nearing adoration. Joseph was very sweet to her. He smiled and bent closer to hear her soft voice.

"Oh yes! We owe you so much!" she breathed. Joseph shook his head, smiling at the loving couple.

"I did nothing. The Lord healed you, Sister Elsa. We do appreciate your offer, though. Emma and I have discussed leaving the Morley settlement since the Lord told us to find somewhere else to live. Sister Jerree has been an invaluable help with the babies. She's a part of our family. Would there be room for her?"

I was surprised by this request. I lived at the Morley's and had not thought of the possibilities of a move. Joseph smiled and winked as if to say I needed to continue my education.

"Of course, Brother Joseph. We'll be honored to have you and any of your family in our home," Elsa said. Joseph took her hand and smiled.

"The honor is ours. Thank you both."

* * *

Hiram, Ohio, was thirty miles south of Kirtland. The Johnson farm was large and productive, with acres of wheat and corn ready to be harvested. Apple orchards, a vegetable garden, and dairy cows testified of the industry of these people.

The house was a large two-story frame house with many beautifully–furnished rooms. Joseph and Emma were given two rooms on the ground floor. Their room was on the north side of the kitchen and mine, which I shared with the twins, was on the south. A room upstairs was made available for Joseph, in which to conduct business. The Johnson home soon became the church headquarters. The Rigdons moved across the street to be more accessible to Joseph.

Life became busier, if that was possible. People came all the time to find out what the Lord wanted them to do. This puzzled me. Why did everyone think they needed to ask Joseph? Didn't they know they could ask for themselves? I learned that it was the tradition of the day to have a spokesman who went to the Lord in prayer for each family. Often the father was the only one who verbally prayed. Individual prayer was a new concept to these people.

Joseph and Sidney began again to work on their revision of the Bible. Many Saints prepared to go to Missouri. When Joseph was asked why he was staying in Kirtland when Zion was in Missouri, he just smiled and said that Kirtland was to be a stronghold for the Church for the space of five years. After that it was up to the Lord where he would go.

Newel Whitney was told to retain his property but send as much money to Zion as he could. Sidney Gilbert sold his share of their business to Newel and took his family to Missouri. Isaac Morley was to sell his holdings so that he could use his talents in Zion.

He had a hard time for a while but eventually sold out to Hercules and Richie Carrell for $1,050.00. I was shocked! Isaac owned more property than most anyone else, and it seemed as if he deserved more than a thousand dollars for it all. I don't know how much real estate was worth back then, but I felt he had been ripped off. Everyone else was very pleased. I guess I had a lot to learn.

Three large farms were purchased, the Peter French farm being the largest. A council of high priests was convened to decide what to do with the lands. Newel Whitney was called to be the bishop of Kirtland. He was to head up the disposition of the lands. It was revealed that a temple should be built on the French land. Lots were to be divided for those seeking an inheritance in Kirtland. It was an exciting time, and Joseph seemed to have one foot on this side of the veil and the other foot on the other side. Everyone wanted to know what the Lord wanted them to do. Some people were happy about the revelations and some were not. Joseph sighed and shook his head.

"If they don't like what the Lord has to say they shouldn't ask. He won't sugar coat anything and neither will I."

"And that could get you into serious trouble," Emma said.

"You are right, my dear. But I would be in worse trouble with the Lord if I tried to make His revelations nice and pretty for the weak- minded."

"True. I suppose you had better keep the Lord happy first."

"That, my dear, is sound advice," he said, kissing her forehead.

The first baptism I witnessed in the 19th century was that of Orson Hyde, on the first Sunday in October. Summer was definitely gone and autumn was trying to hang on but Old Man Winter was winning the battle. Everyone bundled up, stood on the banks of the Chagrin River, and watched as Sidney Rigdon and Orson Hyde took off their shoes, socks, coats, and vests and strode into the icy water. I shivered just thinking how cold it must be.

"Brother Orson Hyde, having been commissioned of Jesus Christ, I baptize you in the name of the Father and of the Son and of the Holy Ghost. Amen."

Sidney's voice boomed with authority, in spite of how cold he was. He smiled genuinely as he brought Orson up from the water and embraced him affectionately. Orson had been a Campbellite minister just as Sidney had been and had even tried to deny the truth when he first heard it from Oliver Cowdery and Parley P. Pratt. He felt 'reproved by the Spirit' and made further inquiries. Now, almost a full year later, he was being baptized.

Joseph was waiting at the water's edge with a blanket, which he wrapped around Orson, then urged him to kneel. There on the banks of the river, Joseph confirmed him a member of the Church and ordained him to the Priesthood.

I stood beside Miranda Johnson, daughter of John and Elsa, who could hardly contain her joy at witnessing Orson's baptism. You would have to be awfully dense not to see that Miranda was crazy about Brother Hyde. By the way he went to her and squeezed her hands, still dripping, his eyes brimming with tears, it wasn't hard to see that he felt the same way about her. I stole a look at Elsa. She seemed very pleased with her daughter's choice.

The chilly weather of that October morning intensified the warmth of the Spirit. The river's flow, the puffs of steam from the people's mouths, Joseph Smith the Prophet standing at the water's edge, brought so many things into focus for me. I couldn't help but compare this service to the ones we had in Idaho. A warm building, warm water, electricity, were all things I had taken for granted throughout my life. These people didn't need those conveniences to feel the Spirit's fire.

Never again would I complain that the Relief Society room was too cold because of a stuck air conditioner control. No excuse sounded reasonable for not driving the four blocks to church, even in ten inches of snow. I could attend Home, Family, and Individual Enrichment meeting or inservice or any of the other meetings I thought weren't important in the wake of watching Isaac Morley sell all he had, or Sidney Gilbert move his family to an unsettled part of the country, or Orson Hyde buried in freezing water to enter the Kingdom. I had been such a complacent member of the Church all my life, taking for granted even the smallest blessings. Sighing, I vowed to be an active participant in the gospel, in both centuries.

The winter of 1831/1832 passed in a flurry of conferences and revelations. Joseph worked with Newel Whitney in his new calling as bishop to establish the Law of Consecration and Stewardship. Many people willingly gave, expressing a great desire to give their all for the Lord.

"I have nothing to consecrate to the Lord of the things of the earth, yet I feel to consecrate myself and my family. I am thankful that God has given me a place among the Saints, and feel willing to labor for their good," Joseph said, in response to the new law.

On November first, a conference was held to decide on the publication of a book of the revelations given thus far. The Lord approved and gave His own preface to the book. It is now known as Section One in the Doctrine and Covenants. Sixty-five revelations were to be printed under the title "Book of Commandments." Ten thousand copies were to be printed.

During the conference, William McLellin loudly questioned the grammar and language of some of the revelations. He was a school teacher and fancied himself considerably more educated than Joseph. He tried to write a better revelation but failed miserably.

Joseph chuckled when he told us about it saying, "William has more learning than sense."

Oliver Cowdery and John Whitmer were charged with carrying the revelations to Independence where W.W. Phelps would print them. A printing press was purchased in Cincinnati and shipped to Missouri.

In December, Joseph and Sidney were called on a mission to neighboring regions to call upon the inhabitants of the earth and bear record, and prepare the world for the commandments and revelations which were to come.

Ezra Booth had been writing slanderous articles and publishing them in *The Ohio Star*. People were becoming increasingly leery of the Church and for this reason, Joseph and Sidney left Kirtland to preach. I was surprised that they would leave so close to Christmas until I learned that Christmas was not celebrated as I knew it. That was a hard blow, since I loved all the Christmas festivities. I lived through it, but December was not the same without *White Christmas, Rudolph the Red-Nosed Reindeer,* or *Frosty the Snowman.*

Elsa Johnson was surprised by my lack of knowledge about cooking in the early 19th century. Emma just laughed and wrapped an arm around me.

"Jerree's family was very wealthy and she's never really had to do much kitchen work. I think she's learned quite a bit since she's been here. Come, let's show her how to use your oven."

Elsa's kitchen was equipped with a brick "bustle" oven, which was built right onto the fireplace wall. I thought it was really quite ingenious. Hot coals were shoveled into the oven and fanned into a flame. When the fire was roaring, the door was shoved forward, forcing the smoke and fumes up the flue. Since there weren't any temperature gauges to test the temperature of the oven, you put your hand in the oven and counted slowly. If you hand was uncomfortable at twelve seconds the oven was hot, at eighteen seconds it was "quick," moderate at twenty-four seconds, and warm in the thirties. The coals were removed, loaves of bread were placed inside, and the door pushed in as far as possible. It sure beat cooking johnny cakes on hearth stones, covered with ashes. I heartily learned to use this oven, soon becoming quite proficient at it.

I enjoyed living at the Johnson home. Elsa was a kind woman with simple faith and we became quick friends. Miranda was sweet.

She was very much in love with Orson Hyde, who was becoming a frequent caller. I had a hard time reconciling myself to the fact that this sixteen-year-old girl should be courted by the twenty-something, future apostle. I may have been living in 1831 but I still had a 1990s mentality. Girls started to DATE at sixteen, not get married. Elsa seemed happy about the match, so I didn't voice my 20th–century opinion.

John and Elsa readily accepted the Law of Consecration and were willing to comply completely. Several of their sons complained, saying they would lose their inheritances if John consecrated it all. John tried to convince them that they would be more blessed under the law but that did not pacify them. Ezra Booth's persistent complaints kept them in a constant uproar. Some of his charges were that Joseph was wanting in sobriety, prudence and stability. Joseph possessed a spirit of lightness and levity, with habitual proneness to jesting and joking. Ezra also accused him of having revelations too conveniently to originate from God.

Joseph took this all in stride, but I could see that it hurt him deeply every time an article came out in the paper. There were nine articles in all. Another man, named Simonds Ryder, apostatized because Joseph Smith, the Prophet, once spelled his name wrong. He claimed that if a prophet could spell his name wrong, he must not have the Spirit; therefore he was a false prophet.

"What a crock!" I blurted out, winning for myself some very shocked looks. These people were not used to a woman saying that type of thing. I smiled sheepishly and pointed to the paper.

"This Simonds Ryder claims he found papers that outline a secret plot to take people's property and give it to Joseph. Anyone with a brain will know that's a lie," I said, defending my slang words. Joseph nodded, smiling sadly, squeezing my arm, and taking the paper from me.

"But some people won't see it as a lie. Let's just put this away for a while. I'm tired of hearing what apostates have to say." He rolled the paper, tucked it under his arm, and left the kitchen with a somber look on his face. I looked at Emma, who stared after her husband with fear in her eyes. He might be tired of hearing what his enemies had to say, but were they tired of saying things? Emma turned to look at me, silently asking me to assure her that he would be all right. I knew that was one thing I could not do.

CHAPTER THIRTEEN

Christmas, for my family, was a tradition-filled holiday that was the highlight of the year. I planned for months in advance, driving Tom crazy with my extravagance.

"I think you can tone it down a bit this year, Jerree. The local economy will not fail if you don't spend a zillion dollars on Christmas," Tom would complain as he watched me try to hide the mountains of gifts I purchased. Smiling, I would give him a quick kiss and go about my life, planning the best Christmas ever.

That Christmas, the first spent with the Saints in Kirtland, was bittersweet for me. Would my family be upholding the traditions started years ago by my grandparents? Would they be mourning for a mother that just fell off the face of the earth? And yet...to be in the home of the Prophet and see him interact with his family, day to day, was a joy indescribable.

He was so tender with Emma. He catered to her every need, as often as he could, often caring for the babies when she was too exhausted to do anything more. One night I heard him pacing the floor, softly singing. His "office" was right above the room I shared with the twins. Julia had been extremely fussy. Both babies were teething, loudly pronouncing their discomfort. I took Joseph M. and got him to sleep but Julia would not be comforted. How I missed children's Tylenol.

Quietly, so as not to disturb Joseph M. or Emma in the next room, I donned my robe and climbed the stairs, tiptoeing to the office door, which was ajar. Julia was nestled against Joseph's chest, her head lying on his shoulder. He walked back and forth, swaying slightly, singing:

"Lead me, guide me
Walk beside me
Help me find the way.
Teach me all that I must do
To live with Him someday."

Tears stung my eyes as I listened to him sing the song I had taught him. He said it was a beautiful melody with truth ringing from every note. It seemed fitting to have the Prophet singing it to his infant daughter.

"Did I wake you?" Joseph asked, seeing me in the hall. I shook my head and went into the office, sighing tiredly.

"No. I couldn't sleep."

"Emma has often said my singing keeps her up, too. Sit and talk to me for awhile. I think the little one is finally giving up the fight. Joseph M. must be asleep?"

"He is," I replied and sat in one of the chairs by Joseph's desk. He looked tired—his shirt was untucked from his trousers. His suspenders hung down in comical loops that hit his knees as he walked. His usually immaculate hair was tousled; some strands even hung down his high forehead into his eyes. He looked like a very young man, which he was. I again felt the pangs of longing for my own sons.

"If my singing isn't keeping you awake, what is?" he asked, sitting down carefully, trying not to jar Julia.

"I miss my family," I breathed forlornly. His expression was compassionate and loving.

"Ah! Of course you do. It must be hard not knowing when you'll see them again."

"Yes. Especially this time of the year."

"Oh? What's special about this time of the year...besides my birthday, of course," he teased trying to coax me out of my depression.

"Christmas is a big thing in my day. It is a worldwide celebration, with parties and gifts and family. All my family would be gathered at my house—except for my Joseph who's off on his mission—and we'd laugh and cry and eat and love each other. It's a wonderful time of the year."

"But why is Christ's birth celebrated in December? He was born on April 6th. That was revealed to me awhile ago and the Saints know that. Don't the Saints in your day know that?"

"They do and we recognize that day as Christ's birth but the rest of the world has not taken your word on it so they still celebrate Christmas on December 25th. We join in the celebration hoping our love of the Savior helps promote the peace and goodwill that is the theme of the Christmas season. It's the spirit of the occasion we celebrate. Oh, Joseph! You should see it! For one day our tired world pauses and remembers the greatest man ever born! Men at war have been known to put aside their weapons to worship the Prince of Peace on that day. People give to total strangers; children marvel at the magic of the spirit of giving personified in a man called Santa. The Christmas story is retold, acted out in many languages, and for a few hours, millions of people think of Jesus together. Even the Jews respect the day. I miss that."

"It sounds wonderful," he mused. I nodded and sat quietly, as he rocked Julia, seeming to be lost in his thoughts. When he looked at me again, his handsome face was puzzled.

"I know I told you not to disclose anything important…things you know…about this time…but I need to ask you one question."

"All right," I said tentatively, unsure how I should respond.

"Was the law of celestial marriage and the plurality of wives lived?"

I don't think I could have been more shocked. I knew he taught plural marriage, but I didn't know it was this soon. I was sure polygamy didn't even start until the 1840s. I was so confused.

"Yes. We are all taught that polygamy is a celestial law. However, the Church has not practiced it since 1890 when…when Wil…one of the prophets was told to rescind the commandment. Celestial marriage, as we know it, has to do with being sealed in the temple by someone with the proper authority. All worthy members can be married in this way—but only to one wife. I have teased Tom though, telling him which single women I'd let him marry should the Saints ever be commanded to live polygamy again."

Joseph smiled at the attempt to lighten the mood. He waxed silent again, until I couldn't stand it anymore.

"Are you going to begin…"

"No!" He spit out, frightening the baby, who began to cry. For a few moments he was busy trying to calm her. Then he looked at me again. "It's not time yet—and I'm glad. I was not happy when the law was revealed to me. I wish it hadn't been. Nothing the Lord has ever asked me to do is harder than this. I love Emma. I want only Emma, but in the process of translating the Bible, the question of polygamy came up so I asked about it. Sidney was disgusted with the answer and relieved we're not commanded to live it yet. But we will be—I don't know when—you probably know but I'm not in a hurry to know. I would like nothing better than to ignore the whole thing, but I have been shown some of the women that are to be given to me as plural wives. I actually met one in my travels recently. Oh, Jerree, how can I ever do this? I know Emma will oppose it. She already thinks she's unworthy to be my wife because our babies keep dying. I don't think she will ever be able to consent to this."

All I could do was nod sympathetically. I did know how Emma would react and the grief it would cause. I hadn't known of Joseph's knowledge of who would be his other wives. I didn't know translating the Bible had raised the question, nor did I know how to comfort him.

"Don't tell me anymore. What will be, will be and I'll have to face it, no matter what. It's just nice to be able to talk to someone about it who doesn't think I'm wicked or crazy. Please don't tell—"

"Do you really think you have to tell me that, Joseph? You are the man chosen to reveal those types of things, not me. I only know this by virtue of the fact that I was born to a mother named Dorothy Tatum Walker, who spouted Church history like a fountain. I'm here to learn, not give away trade secrets."

Standing, I went to him and took the sleeping baby, cuddling her close to me and kissing her chubby cheek. Joseph rose and touched my face, his eyes shining with happy tears.

"Has anyone ever told you how remarkable you are, Jerree James?" he asked.

"A couple of times—but it means so much more when a prophet says it. Thank you," I replied and stood on my tiptoes to place a kiss on his cheek. He folded me close, holding me as a father would his daughter. We both heard the gasp at the same time and turned toward the door to face Eli Johnson's horrified expression. Eli was one of John Johnson's sons who was not happy with the revelation on consecration. He was Ezra's Booth's friend also. His eyes narrowed and a look of wicked pleasure crossed his face.

Our actions had been innocent, those of two people belonging to the same family giving each other comfort. Joseph Smith was my uncle! Of course, no one knew that except the immediate family. Eli Johnson would not look on our embrace as an innocent act but something torrid and evil. I was, after all, in my nightclothes, Joseph had his shirt untucked, with his suspenders hanging down. The disgusted look in Eli's eyes made it clear what he thought was going on. It didn't matter that I was holding a sleeping baby in my arms. I felt like throwing up. Angrily, Eli stomped off, raw hatred burning in his eyes. I looked at Joseph, who only shook his head sadly.

"Go down to bed, Jerree. The wicked will always turn purity and innocence into something ugly. Don't fret."

I nodded and hurried from the room, my heart pounding wildly. I knew Eli Johnson would not let what he saw lie. It didn't matter that I was the same age as his mother or that both Joseph and I were married. Eli thought Joseph and I were…I couldn't even bring myself to think of it. Fear gripped my entire being. I knew the time would come when I would be accused of doing something unthinkable with my great-uncle the Prophet Joseph Smith.

✻   ✻   ✻

February 16, 1832

In an upper room, in the southeast corner of the Johnson house, one of the greatest revelations ever given to man was received by the Prophet Joseph Smith. He called it a transcript from the record of the eternal world. Twelve men had gathered for a meeting. The Johnson home had become the headquarters of the Church by virtue of the fact that Joseph lived there, and I found myself helping Elsa and Emma care for the needs of all the visitors.

On this day I was asked to look in on the men to see if they were in need of anything. Because of my ignorance of Church history, the 16th of February, 1832 had no special meaning to me. As I pushed the door open and slid inside, I had no idea what I was about to witness.

Joseph stood beside the table he used as a desk, one hand at his side, the other out-stretched to the ceiling. He was peering intently up at something, his eyes darting back and forth as if viewing a fast paced video. He was surrounded by a glow of light that ebbed and flowed about him, causing his hair to appear deeper auburn, his skin like fine porcelain. Sidney Rigdon seemed to be able to see whatever Joseph saw, for he nodded, his face rapturous and tear-stained.

Ten men sat, awestruck, watching the other two, listening intently to what they were saying. Philo Dibble noticed me and quietly beckoned me to be seated.

"What do I see?" Joseph asked in a booming voice. My heart jumped into my throat as I was enveloped in a blanket of intense spiritual power.

"I see the resurrection of the dead—all they who hear the voice of the Son of Man. They shall come forth, all those who did good in the resurrection of the just and those who did evil, in the resurrection of the unjust."

"I see the same," Sidney said, his voice trembling with emotion.

"What do I see?" Joseph asked again. His handsome face breaking into a smile, the light growing more intense around him.

"It is the Son, in wondrous glory sitting on the right hand of the Father. He has received a fullness from the Father and all the holy angels and the sanctified are before His throne, worshipping God and the Lamb, forever."

Sidney was sobbing now, clutching at his chest as if his heart could not hold all the joy he was experiencing.

"I see the same!" he gasped. "I see my Redeemer and my God! He lives! He lives!" A collective gasp was heard throughout the room. Tears flowed down my face. I suppressed the urge to reach out and touch Joseph, wanting to feel the energy of the spirit that surrounded him.

"What do I see? What do I see now?" the anguish in his voice matched that on his face. A chill raced through my body. "No! I see an angel, once bright and beautiful, rebel against the Only Begotten Son, who was loved by the Father. Now he is cast out and thrust down from the presence of God. He is called Perdition and the heavens weep for him." Joseph's voice cracked, his hand wiping tears from his eyes so that he could continue to peer into heaven. It struck me that Joseph Smith actually had compassion for Lucifer, weeping with the heavens over the loss of one of the great ones. "He is Lucifer, a son of the morning. He is fallen, he is fallen, even a Son of the Morning," he whispered, his voice choked by sobs that wrenched my heart.

"I see the same," Sidney replied in a strangled whisper. I was thankful that I could not see what they saw. It was so traumatic that two grown men stood sobbing as they looked.

On and on it went, Joseph reciting what he was seeing and Sidney affirming it. No one else in the room could see the vision, but we all witnessed the light and felt the power of the Spirit. Someone to my left was writing as fast as he could, trying to keep up with Joseph's words.

The fate of the ungodly was given in graphic detail. From Joseph's description, I could imagine all too well and shuddered at the thought. Just when I thought I might faint from fear, the vision changed and the fate of the just was revealed. I hoped I would be counted worthy to be in this group. Such promises, such blessings, such happiness! The look on Joseph's face was so sublime that if I live a million years more, it will never be erased from my memory.

"I want that," I thought. "I want the reward of the just."

Joseph described celestial, terrestrial, and telestial glory. This was not new doctrine to me, but I could tell it was to the rest of the people in the room. They had been taught there was only one heaven and hell, nothing more. Hope filled the face of each man as Joseph talked.

"Great and marvelous are the works of the Lord, and the mysteries of His kingdom which he showed unto us, which surpass all understanding in glory and in might and in dominion," Joseph said, sighing and looking about him for the first time in over an hour. He raised his eyebrows when he saw me, but smiled and sat down, breathing deeply. Sidney all but collapsed into his chair, trembling visibly, so pale I thought he might faint.

"Sister Jerree, Brother Sidney needs a drink of water. Could you fetch some for us?" Joseph asked, turning to Sidney, patting his back.

"I feel so weak, Joseph. Why aren't you?" Sidney asked, wiping his face with a shaky hand. Joseph chuckled.

"Oh Sidney, you're just not as used to this as I am."

I left the room amidst the soft laughter of the men before they bombarded Joseph with questions. I hurried to the well and drew a pitcher full of fresh water, almost spilling half of it trying to get back to the room before I missed too much. Naturally everyone was excited, wanting Joseph to expound on the revelation.

"Brethren, I understand your zeal and all the questions will be answered in due time. For now, let's adjourn to rest for the remainder of the day. Sidney looks as though he's been through a war. Thank you, Jerree. I need to read through what's been written and make sure everything the Lord wants revealed is recorded. Brother Newel, could you please pray for us?"

They waited for me to leave before praying. Slowly I walked down to the kitchen, my spirit still soaring from what I had been privileged to witness. How many times had I read that section in the Doctrine and Covenants? It would become known as Section 76. How many lessons had I sat through as the concepts of that revelation were discussed?

Nothing Joseph had said was new to me. I had been taught these principles my entire life, but never once had I felt the impact of what it meant to be sealed by the Holy Spirit of Promise and to be numbered among the Church of the Firstborn. Not until that moment, when I stood only a few feet from the Prophet as he witnessed the vision, had I actually ached for the blessings promised to the faithful. The feeling was so intense, I was loath to lose it. Setting the water pitcher down, I went into the room I shared with the twins and quietly shut the door. Joseph M. and Julia were napping and I did not want to disturb them. Sighing, I laid on the bed, curling into a ball and let my emotions flow with my tears.

"Thank you," I whispered. "Thank you." I could find no other words to express my feelings. A sense of overwhelming peace filled me as I fell asleep, basking in the love of my Savior, knowing He was mindful of me...in 1832.

I was putting the last of the dinner dishes away that night when Joseph came into the kitchen. He looked tired, to say the least. Smiling, he took the Dutch oven and placed it by the hearth, trying to be of service.

"Thank you," I said.

"You've been rather quiet tonight. Are you all right?"

"Oh yes! It's just that I never really looked at that revelation in such a way before. I've known about those truths all my life but never given them much thought... until today. Does that make me a horrible person?"

Joseph chuckled, shaking his head. The dishes were done, and he invited me to sit beside him at the table. I gladly obeyed, placing my hand in his outstretched one. The house was quiet. Everyone had retired early. I loved the times like these that I spent with Joseph. Knowing I would learn something incredible, I'd really listen. It was amazing that I knew anything considering the fact that I had given the gospel little thought most of my life.

"You're a normal person. Most people don't think about something they've had all their lives. It's sad though; I'm sure many of the people of your day are as you are... were. This gospel is so vital to their well-being and they take it for granted. Tell me your thoughts about what you heard today."

"Oh, Joseph. It was marvelous! I have grown to love being in your presence when you are filled with the Spirit. It's amazing! And the things you said...and how you said them! I pray I can live worthy to be with the just in eternity. I've never had the desire before... never really thought about it. Even when my mother died, I was too numb to think about the fact that we can really truly be together again. Now it's the most important thing I want—to be with my family forever in the Church of the Firstborn."

"Good girl. I know you will receive your heart's desire."

"Do you, Joseph? Do you really know what is going to happen to me? Will I get home? Will my family be all right? Is this really part of some grander scheme?"

He smiled and squeezed my hand. His blue eyes captured mine as he kept his fingers tight around my hand. I could feel power flowing from him into me and I began to tremble.

"Dear Jerree. After all you've seen today, all you've seen this past year, can you doubt? I don't claim to know everything, nor the reasons why Father does some things, but I do know that your being here is no accident. You are here to learn, to grow, to experience these things so that you can help those of your time struggling with the truth. After today, can you ever doubt that God lives, or that he loves His children?"

"No. One look into your eyes, one sermon from your lips, would have been enough to convince me. I know now why all these people are willing to give up all they have to be a part of this great work."

"Don't think that you will be excluded from that blessing. I've peered into your time and I can tell you that the saints of your era will be called upon to give up their all for the kingdom, too. And it will be a greater trial for them than it is for us because there is so much wealth and decadence. A great weeding out process will take place and only the truly faithful will stand and be counted. This experience will help you set an example. The wonders I just revealed will be worth whatever sacrifice has to be made. If the Lord would permit me, I could reveal a hundred times more than what I did today... but the world and the Saints aren't ready to handle it yet."

"A hundred times more! What you told us already is enough to keep a whole generation going! When will the rest be revealed?"

"As soon as the Saints are ready for it."

I sighed, feeling suddenly depressed. In the 1990s, no more of that revelation had been given to us. Would we ever be ready for it? Joseph smiled, seeming to know my thoughts.

"When you go back—when your time here is through—teach your people the things you've learned. Prepare them for the things to come...because they will come and those who are prepared won't fear."

"Will it be horrible, Joseph?"

"Yes...and wonderful...and exciting...and frightening. The Lord speaks truly when he tells us of the calamities that await the wicked. We should all try to be numbered among the righteous. Only then will we not fear."

"You make it sound so easy."

"Nothing worth having is ever easy...it's just what needs to be done. Don't fret any more tonight, Jerree. We've all had a busy day. Go to bed. You look tired. I'm headed there myself. I haven't had much time with my wife lately, and I think she could use a back rub. Good night."

He stood up, squeezed my hand, and went off to bed. Sighing, I followed suit, extremely exhausted but content in the knowledge that I was loved and known in such a vast universe.

CHAPTER FOURTEEN

I am a woman of the 90s, born and raised in a time where any crime imaginable could be viewed for $2.99 at the local video store. The nightly news flashes horror stories into living rooms worldwide, and hate crimes are a way of life. I thought I was pretty hardened, that nothing could shock me anymore. Never have I been more wrong. I have since learned that whenever a person faces evil head on, the shock is overwhelming.

It was March and I had now been in Kirtland for a year. I'd witnessed firsthand what my mother had only dreamed of. I didn't know how, but Joseph had promised all would be well with my family. Being a member of the Smith family had become so routine that I had allowed myself to be lulled into a sense of security that bordered apathy. The events of March 24, 1832 came as a bolt out of the blue.

Eli Johnson was a wicked man. I'm sorry if that sounds harsh, but I don't know how else to describe him. He took great pleasure in spreading the rumor that Joseph was being unfaithful to poor Sister Emma, who was once again in the family way. A select few knew about the revelation on polygamy, and it had leaked out that Joseph was happily complying. Rumors flew fast and thick.

Apostates caught hold of the newest ones, blasting Joseph long and loud. Threats were made and Hiram, Ohio, soon ceased to be a safe haven for any of us. Elsa and John were ashamed at the behavior of a couple of their sons, knowing that the things they said were bold-faced lies.

It was amazing how the story of Eli discovering Joseph and I together in his office took on a life of its own, becoming obscene. I thought only the people in my age were so crude, but I have since learned that evil men are crude in any age.

I hated being around Eli. He stared at me longingly, his eyes raking over my body in a way that disgusted me. I was old enough to be his mother! I could imagine the filthy thoughts behind those mocking eyes. I made it a point never to be alone with him. Because she was ill, Emma was spared most of the horrible gossip. Amidst the rumors and threats, Julia and Joseph M. came down with the measles and were also very sick. Being in the first trimester of pregnancy, it was not good for Emma to be around the babies. I was glad I was there to help. We all took turns walking the floors day and night with the miserable eleven-month-old twins.

On the night of the 24th, Emma was quite weak. We insisted she go to bed early to rest. Joseph took Joseph M. and made a bed in the hallway so Emma would not be disturbed. I had Julia. The entire household retired as soon as the sun set, needing the rest after a full day of sick children. Exhausted, both Julia and I fell asleep, snuggled together on my bed. It felt good to have a child close to me, and I drifted easily into oblivion.

Horrendous screams jolted me awake sometime in the night. Outside my door, Joseph was yelling at the top of his lungs while Emma screamed in fear. Little Joseph M. joined his parents, his small voice adding to the cacophony assaulting my ears. Upstairs I could hear the Johnsons pounding on their door, screaming to be let out. I later learned that someone had barricaded their door to keep them from helping Joseph.

"Hold him! Don't let him touch the ground or he'll run over the whole of us!" someone yelled.

I pulled my door open in time to see Joseph being carried out of the front door by several men, fighting with all his might to be free. One of his legs broke free and he kicked a man square in the face, knocking him backwards to the ground. Screaming, I ran after the men, grabbing one by the arm.

"Let him go!" I screamed. Growling, the man swung his arm, backhanding me across the face. I dropped to my knees, feeling blood flowing from my nose.

"Jerree!" Joseph screamed and fought harder to get free. The men grabbed him and swore they'd kill him if he resisted anymore. Behind me, Emma had scooped up the babies and rushed to my side.

"We've got to hide the babies!" she screamed, her eyes filled with hysteria. Before I could protest, she was running toward the back door, afraid some of the mob was still in the house. Wiping my face with my sleeve, I stood, following her, knowing I couldn't leave her alone. In the darkness, I could see her running toward the barn. Before I could start after her, I was caught from behind and roughly turned around. Eli Johnson wrapped me in a vise grip I could not break.

"Lookee here! I got me a right proper little piece of work now. Gimmee some of what you save for the Prophet," he sneered, trying to kiss me, bending his head toward me. His breath reeked of whiskey; his eyes blazed like a rabid animal. I turned my head and felt his lips on my neck. The scream I wanted to let loose was trapped inside my throat, I was so paralyzed with fear.

"Let go of me!" I screeched, struggling to free myself. He chuckled wickedly and groped at the front of my nightgown, whispering obscenities in my ear. I fought with all I had. I wrenched one hand free and scratched his face, feeling his flesh gather under my fingernails. He screamed and hit me hard on the side of the head, sending me reeling. He dropped to his knees, straddling me, laughing. I heard the fabric of my gown tear, felt a burst of energy and in a grotesque sense of slow motion, I watched Eli's startled face as I flung him from me. I saw him land with a thump some twenty feet away. He lay there, stunned, unable to move, staring at me in wonder. Emma was screaming at me from the barn. I stumbled to my feet and blindly headed toward her.

When I was safely in the barn, I blocked the door and went to Emma, huddling with her to keep all of us warm. Outside, screams and howls rent the night air. Light from several torches danced through the cracks in the barn walls. I imagined demons from hell couldn't have sounded any worse than those men did.

"Joseph! Oh dear God, Joseph!" Emma cried, burying her face in my shoulder. I silently prayed for him, too. I don't know how long we were in the barn. It seemed like forever. I was afraid Eli would crash through the doors at any minute but he must have decided to go help his cohorts. Neither of us had shoes on. We had been in bed before all this began. The babies were in warm nightgowns but both were feverish and winter was still gripping Ohio at the moment.

"Oh Jerree! Your nightgown! Did he—?" Emma asked, motioning to the rip in my gown. I pulled it closed with my left hand, shivering violently, Julia snuggling against me.

"No. Somehow...something stopped him—almost as if he had been shocked. He was thrown to the ground..." It was then that it hit me. He had ripped my gown and reached inside where my garments covered me. I had tried to take the best care of them that I could, knowing they were my only pair. I thought they were holding up quite well. My temple garments had saved me from unspeakable acts of violence. I had been wearing them and Eli had not been allowed to defile my body. Some unseen force, like a force field in Star Trek, had protected me from his vile plans. Gasping loudly, I began to tremble harder, sobbing uncontrollably.

"Thank God!" I said, rocking back and forth. "Thank God!"

The silence that followed was as ominous as the noise the mob had made. Quietly but swiftly, we ran back to the house, our feet frozen and cracking, leaving a trail of blood behind us. We hurriedly wrapped the babies to warm them. I ran upstairs and let the Johnsons out of their room. They gasped when they saw me. I had forgotten how horrid I must have looked.

My nose was swollen and caked with blood. My blood-splattered gown was ripped and I was half-frozen. Elsa gathered me in her arms, weeping, begging me for forgiveness. John hurried downstairs and threw more wood on the fire, telling Emma to bring the twins as close as she could. She tried to calm them.

"Joseph...they took Joseph," she said. John nodded, went to a corner and picked up a club.

"I'll go find him," he said, hurrying toward the door.

"No! They'll kill you," Elsa screamed.

"They took the Prophet, Elsa. Our sons—they took him and I have to find him." Elsa nodded, covering her face with her hands. He disappeared into the night, leaving the three of us alone with two sick babies.

Things get jumbled in my memory after that. Sometime later, we heard footsteps on the porch. The door was flung open and Joseph stood there, his body covered with something dark and sticky.

Emma gasped, stood, began to walk toward him, then fainted, crumpling to the floor. Elsa ran to her, gently trying to revive her.

"Joseph!" I cried and ran to him.

"No! Don't come too close, Jerree. They've taken my clothes and I'm naked." He moaned; his body was wracked with violent spasms.

"I'm old enough to be your mother, Joseph. Let me help you," I pleaded, staring into his eyes. He sighed.

"Get me a blanket, please, Jerree." Nodding, I ran to my room, pulling the quilt off the bed and hurried back, wrapping it around him. Only then would he enter, going straight to the fire. Elsa had revived Emma enough to escort her into her room, but the babies still sat by the fire, screaming at the sight of their father.

"Take them out of here," he pleaded. I gathered them up, taking them to my room where Elsa stayed with them. When I returned, I went to Joseph, unsure what to do. He was covered with tar and feathers from head to toe. His face was bruised and bleeding. He looked like a gross caricature of Big Bird.

"We have to get the tar off. They've put acid in it and it's burning," he croaked.

"I...I...don't know—" before I could finish the door burst open and several people hurried in, David Whitmer and John Johnson among them.

"He's tarred up!" David yelled and began barking orders. "Stand as close to the fire as you can, Joseph. Go get some lard. You get some spoons. Start pulling that tar off!"

"I'm so sorry, Joseph," I cried, tears streaming down my swollen face. He turned and seemed to really notice my disheveled appearance. He reached out and touched my face, his eyes full of compassion.

"What happened to you, Jerree?"

"Eli...tried to..." I couldn't verbalize the horrible things Eli had tried to do to me but Joseph saw my torn gown. He knew what had gone on. A look of great sadness settled on his battered features, and he wrapped the blanket tighter around him.

Someone returned with the lard and spoons, and we began to scrape the tar from the Prophet Joseph. He got as close to the fire as he dared, staring into the flames, his entire body trembling as people began to scrape the sticky goop from him. I learned that lard kept the tar soft enough to get it off the body, but more than one patch of skin was removed with it. Joseph refused to cry out in pain. He gritted his teeth and squeezed his eyes shut.

The news of the violence spread like a prairie fire and before long the Johnson house was full of concerned saints. Phoebe Rigdon came, hysterical because Sidney had been carried away from their house by the mob and could not be found. Several men volunteered to search for him. He was eventually found, wandering around, half out of his mind, his head gashed and bleeding. He had been dragged several hundred feet by his heels, his head taking a severe beating.

Emma came out of the room, almost fainting again when she learned what had happened. Someone went to her and coaxed her back into the bedroom with the twins. Joseph couldn't bear to have her see him like this. Sometime during the night, the rest of the Smith family arrived. Lucy sobbed at the sight of her son. I had been numbly standing beside Joseph, spooning tar from his arm. Jerusha came to me and stared in horror at my appearance.

"Jerusha, take her away," Joseph said. "She needs attention, too." I pulled my arm from her grasp, refusing to leave Joseph's side.

"No! I'm staying here and helping Joseph! This is all my fault! I'm not leaving!" Jerusha looked at Joseph questioningly. He shook his head and turned to touch my face, bringing my attention to him. His sapphire eyes were shining in the firelight, compassion etched on every feature of his face.

"It's all right. There are enough people here to help me. See, Mother is here. Let Jerusha help you." I shook my head, covering his hand with mine, pressing my bruised cheek into his palm.

"But this is my fault," I whispered. He chuckled and patted my cheek. Joseph Smith Jr. was such a paradox to me. He was twenty-six years old, a young man, close to the same age as my son, yet I felt like the child. He was comforting me although I was twenty-five years his senior. He clasped my hand in his and squeezed gently.

"Jerusha," he said firmly but quietly. I knew by his tone that he was talking to me, not his sister-in-law. I stared into his eyes as he moved closer to me.

"Is this incident recorded in your history books?" I thought desperately, knowing that if it was, my mother would have talked about it. I vaguely remembered a story of Joseph being tarred and feathered in his own backyard. I nodded, in awe of his ability to calm me. Not many people knew my given name so most would not know he was talking to me. He had spoken so softly that those standing around would think he was instructing Jerusha, but I knew he was addressing me and that was all that mattered.

"Then it would have happened whether or not you were here. I feel horrible because you were caught in the cross fire of it all. Please go with Jerusha and get the attention you need."

Jerusha put an arm around me and led me to my room. Tenderly she cleaned me up and helped me change my clothes. If she was curious about my garments she said nothing, though her eyebrows arched when I muttered that they had saved me. Speaking softly, the way a mother does to a distraught child, she ministered to my needs, tucked me into bed, and sat beside me until I was asleep. Jerusha Barden Smith was twenty-four years old. I was fifty-one. For this night she was indeed my grandmother, something I needed more than I knew.

It took the rest of the night to scrape the tar from Joseph's body. By morning he was able to be dressed, though it was painful indeed. He had red patches here and there where skin had been scraped off with the tar. His face, torso, and back had great gashes where someone had scratched him. His face was swollen and bruised, his lips cut in several places. The mob had tried to force a vial of poison in his mouth. One of his front teeth was broken and his lips were cut from the glass vial shattering.

Though it was Sunday, no one expected him to participate in the worship services. Actually no one felt much like worshipping at all, but Joseph insisted that the Sabbath would be observed as usual. Only Emma stayed in, the twins running high fevers from their exposure to the night air. My face looked like I'd been the loser of a boxing match with both eyes black and my nose swollen twice its size. I was told to stay in and rest, but I determined that if Joseph could get dressed to attend church, so could I.

A large crowd was already gathered in the Johnson's yard waiting to see if Joseph would appear. As I took my place beside Hyrum and Jerusha, I noticed Eli Johnson standing near a tree, surrounded by several other men from the mob that I had seen last night. His face was scratched on one side, evidence that he had actually assaulted me. I felt vindicated. Simonds Ryder, Ezra Booth, Edward Johnson and John Johnson Jr. all stood with him. A large man with a swollen face joined them shortly after. He was the man that had been kicked in the face by Joseph. He looked as bad as I did. I later learned his name was Warren Waste, which I thought was an appropriate name, considering he was certainly a waste of human flesh in my book.

I couldn't believe they had the nerve to show up looking so smug. They were so sure they'd stopped Joseph Smith and wanted to witness it for themselves. A cold rage settled over me. I wanted so much to take a machine gun and blow the smug looks right off their faces.

There was a collective gasp when Joseph appeared on the steps of the back porch. Most people hadn't seen him yet and couldn't believe anyone could be so wicked. The mobbers were shocked that he could even stand, let alone speak. Everyone had heard that Sidney was still incoherent, rambling madly and quite ill. Instantly the entire yard was silent. Even the slight breeze that had been felt was stilled, as if the elements waited to hear the words of the Lord's prophet.

I hoped he'd spout hellfire and damnation, commanding all of the mobbers to the lower regions of hell itself. He was justified. They certainly deserved it. I waited anxiously, feeling vindicated in my anger.

"Brothers and Sisters, how good of you to come and inquire about my condition and that of my family. It cheers my heart to know so many people care about us. By the providence of the Almighty my life has been spared and I have a great desire to sing everlasting praises for that marvelous gift."

Taking a deep breath, he looked out at the crowd, his eyes filled with such love I thought my heart might burst. It was hard for him to stand, for I saw him shaking, but he spoke no word in anger. He did not spout recriminations to those he must have seen from the mob. He condemned no one. He talked of forgiveness, brotherly love, and the privilege of being abused for Christ's sake.

As he spoke, I felt utterly ashamed. All I wanted was revenge. He urged the Saints to find mercy in their hearts, to forgive all or any who had despitefully used them. My tears started then and, together with the Prophet's words, washed away the anger raging in my heart.

I can't write everything he said because his exact words are lost from my memory. The feelings they evoked are not. In the world where I grew up and had raised my children, revenge was a way of life. Therapists actually touted revenge as a way of healing. Standing in the Johnson's yard, listening to the Prophet Joseph Smith forgiving those who had nearly killed him, I knew what was expected of me.

What a weak soul I had. How much I needed to know, to learn from my Uncle Joseph. Would I be able to forgive? Could I show loving-kindness to those who had hurt me? I wanted to blow Eli's face off, not forgive him. The struggle in my heart was so strong, the pain of it was unbearable. I didn't realize I had stopped breathing until Hyrum placed an arm around me, looking at me in concern. Leaning on him, feeling too weak to support myself, I tried to smile. How thankful I was for such a family at a time like this. Being close to Hyrum, knowing he was my progenitor, that he loved me, helped me make it through that morning.

The next few days did little to ease the burden of my soul. Little Joseph M. got worse instead of better. The cold night air had done its damage to the sweet baby. I remember my mother talking about one of the twins dying in infancy but what had that mattered to me— until I sat by Emma's side as she rocked the baby, already weakened by the measles, fighting for his life. We cared for him for five days, but in the end he could not fight the infection. On March 29, quite early in the morning, Joseph Murdock Smith's labored breathing slowed until it finally stopped and he was taken home to that God who had given him life. He was one day short of being eleven months old.

Emma was cast into a deep depression, her own condition weak due to anxiety and pregnancy. She was inconsolable. She refused to give up little Julia, keeping her by her at all times. She insisted Joseph M. be buried in a decent cemetery, not in some forgotten grave like her three other children. A plot was purchased in the cemetery in Kirtland, and Joseph Murdock Smith was laid to rest across the street from where the temple would one day stand.

Joseph also wept bitterly at the loss of this child. He declared Joseph Murdock Smith a martyr for Christ's sake as surely as any other who died for the gospel's sake. He would be crowned with glory in the Father's kingdom. Watching these people I loved mourn for their baby made the anger in my heart grow until I questioned the wisdom of forgiving such vile men. John Murdock came and wept with the Smiths, telling them how sorry he was for their loss. Joseph stood in his embrace, sobbing, telling him how sorry he was, that he should have taken better care of the boy. John chastised Joseph, reminding him that the Lord was in charge, not him. He knew that little Joseph was now with his mother Julia and that they were happy to be together. He thanked Joseph and Emma for taking such good care of his children and for loving them so much. I could not believe these people held no grudge against those who had caused this!

Sidney Rigdon spent several days totally crazy ranting, and raving about killing Joseph and his own wife, Phoebe. Joseph gave both of them a blessing, and Sidney began to recover. The hateful threats did not stop and within a week Sidney moved his family to Chardon, five miles south east of Kirtland. He was taking no chances. He wanted to be closer to civilization.

Joseph was preparing to go to Missouri and was not sure what to do with us. Emma was still mourning the baby's death and I definitely wasn't myself. Looking back, I now know that I was ill, but at the time all I could think about was the hatred I felt for those who had done this to us, especially Eli Johnson.

The day before Joseph left I was in the kitchen finishing the dishes after lunch. I felt horrible. Every muscle in my body ached. I was sure it had to do with the fact that I was still holding a grudge against Eli. Joseph had forgiven everyone and he was fine. Even Sidney seemed to be on the mend but I could not shake how awful I felt. I was sure I was the worse sinner ever born. Being in such deep thought and being immersed in my agony, I did not hear him come in until the sound of his voice startled me. I dropped the plate I was drying. It shattered into a million pieces. Eli Johnson chuckled, moving across the room to help me pick up the mess. He was too cocky, too sure of himself, and it angered me all over again.

"I don't need your help!" I snapped, feeling my blood boil. This man had attacked me! He had helped hurt Joseph. I couldn't believe he still had free reign of the house. His parents knew what he had done. The scratch marks on his face were proof enough.

"Oh, should I go get the Prophet to come help you?" he sneered, looking down at me contemptuously. His attitude angered me further. I stood, letting the broken pieces of china fall from my apron.

"You are a perverted jerk! Joseph Smith is three times the man you'll ever be!" I said, anger and fever raging through me, making me too bold and uncaring. His face turned three shades of red, making the marks on his cheek stand out more. He stepped toward me. "I'm old enough to be Joseph's mother. I am a married woman with four grown children of my own! Joseph Smith is a righteous man, which is more that I can say for you!"

He chuckled, stepping even closer. He had the art of intimidation down pat. I stood my ground, unwilling to allow him to intimidate me again.

"That's the story you tell everyone, but sweetheart, you don't look any where near fifty and I ain't never seen the man or the children you claim to have. All I want to know is why go for a married man when you could easily have a single one?"

His words startled me. How many other people thought I was lying because my family wasn't with me? No one would believe they existed in another time. I had always been proud of the fact that I looked fifteen years younger than I was, thanks to good genes and preservatives, but at that moment, standing less that a foot from Eli Johnson, I hated it. When he touched me, something inside me snapped. I lunged at him, screaming and scratching. I learned later, to my utter horror, that I used words and phrases 19th–century folks had never heard, much less from a woman.

Strong arms encircled me from behind and I was sure I was being attacked again. Eli fled the room but I continued to thrash about, screaming 90s obscenities.

"Jerree, it's all right. I won't hurt you. Please stop," Joseph whispered in my ear. His grip was like a vise and I had a firsthand demonstration of his great strength. Gasping, I went limp against him and began to sob. He turned me around and pressed me gently to his chest. Emma rushed in, followed by Elsa and Miranda.

"I'm sorry, Joseph. I'm so sorry. I've tried to be forgiving like you but I can't. All I feel is hate and anger! I hate that man! He's horrible! I'm just too weak to find forgiveness for him. I can't do it! I can't do it! I'm so sorry!" I buried my face in his chest and sobbed bitterly.

"Shh. It's all right, Jerree. Come, let's get you to bed. She'd burning up—she's got a high fever. Don't fret anymore, Jerree. It's going to be fine." The Prophet Joseph Smith picked me up and carried me to my room. The world went dark then. I don't remember anything else until I woke several weeks later.

JERUSHA

Chapter Fifteen

The summer of 1832 passed quickly, at least for me. The exposure to the cold that March night aided in giving me pneumonia. I was quite ill for several weeks. Of course there was no pharmacy to run to for an antibiotic, so the process of healing was a slow one. The Saints of the 19th century were ingenious though, using herbs to aid in my recovery. I remember waking up with a foul-smelling poultice on my chest and feet. I might have vomited if I hadn't been so weak. I smelt a mixture of vinegar, mustard, and cayenne. It was horrible. Jerusha sat beside me, smiling, feeling my forehead for a fever. She didn't seem to mind the smell.

"Good afternoon, Jerree. How are you feeling?"

"What is that smell?" I croaked, my throat feeling like sandpaper. She chuckled and reached for a cup on the table next to her. She helped me sit up so I could take a swallow of the tepid liquid.

"We put a mustard poultice on you to help draw out the infection. There are also rags soaked in vinegar and cayenne wrapped around you. The infection is gone now, so I think it worked. I expect you'll start mending real soon."

"Where am I?" I asked, noticing I was not in my own room. Nothing around me seemed familiar, except for Jerusha.

"At my house. Joseph's off in Missouri and Emma is stayin' either with the Cahoons or the Williams, I'm not sure. He was afraid to leave you all out in Hiram and, well, we felt you should stay with us, seein' as we're family."

Jerusha Barden Smith was nineteen when she married twenty-six-year-old Hyrum, in November of 1826. Now at twenty-six, she had four-year-old Lovina, who was destined to be one of my progenitors and three-year-old Mary, who was as beautiful as her mother. Jerusha was in the first trimester of pregnancy again. Tears stung my eyes as I realized she had been the one taking care of me.

"Thank you, Jerusha. I'm so sorry to be a burden—especially right now."

"You're nothing of the kind. I'm happy to do it for you. Watching you sleep has been like stepping out of my body and seeing myself, as I'll be when I'm your age. At least I hope I look as good as you when I'm fifty-one. It's still hard to believe that you are descended from Lovina and that after more than a hundred years there'd be someone who looks so much like me. But here you are. I feel honored to be of service to you. Now rest, you need to regain your strength."

Sighing, I happily obliged, drifting off to sleep, not even minding the foul-smelling poultice.

The balance between life and death is so precarious that there are times when we mortals realize how insignificant we truly are. I learned this when my mother died. I had always had a small amount of pride which dictated that I had some control over the events in my life. Then right out of the blue, Mom had a heart attack and was gone. I was numb for days and then I wept for many more days. I would have spent more time mourning if I hadn't been transported from my time to this time in the world's history.

April 1832 was a time of bittersweet rejoicing for the Smiths. Sophronia Smith Stoddard was delivered of a baby girl they named Maria, on April 12, and within hours, Catherine Smith Wilkins was also delivered of a girl named Elizabeth. The babies were precious, and we all took turns lavishing attention on the newest additions to the family.

One month to the day of Joseph Murdock Smith's death, more tragedy was felt in the family. Little Mary Smith, three years old, died in Hyrum's arms. One day she was a healthy, happy toddler; the next she drifted to sleep, never to wake again, against her father's chest.

All the Smiths (except Joseph, who was out of town nursing Newel K. Whitney, because he broke his leg on the return trip from Missouri) rallied around Hyrum and Jerusha. Emma was especially compassionate, knowing firsthand the heartache of losing a child. Jerusha often said that having me there at that time was a great comfort to her. I was happy to be of service to these people who were my ancestors. They had given me far more than I could ever give them.

Living with them, day after day, experiencing their joys and their sorrows, gave me a greater appreciation for the lives they led. Somehow, my mother had felt this same appreciation simply by studying their lives. I guess I needed firsthand experience and though I was separated from my family, I was grateful for it.

Joseph returned in June, promptly coming to Hyrum's house to comfort his brother and mourn with them. Joseph Smith was such a strong man, yet I have never known a more tender one. He embraced both of the grieving parents, crying, promising them that their Mary was not lost to them. The gospel's light would shine even beyond the grave. They would yet have claim to their daughter and would raise her in a future day. They took great comfort in this promise from the prophet. Always one to think of others, he came to me and smiled lovingly at me.

"I'm glad to see you on the mend, Jerree. You were quite sick when I left."

"Jerusha took good care of me. I'm so glad you are back, Joseph. We need your strength."

"Oh, I'm replaceable. No one knows that better than you, Jerree."

"Maybe as a president but never as a person. There's only one you, Joseph."

"I'd say the same about you, but if I turn my head I see your twin," he teased.

The business of the church soon consumed his time, making family life sporadic for him. He immediately began to work on the Bible again. I felt for Emma who wanted only to spend some time with her husband. He did the best he could, but the Lord's work was the most important thing he did. He would not let that go. He would say, "I have learned when the Lord says to do something, DO IT!" He lived by this motto—thus his wife spent many lonely hours waiting for him. Her love of the Lord and his prophet was her only comfort at times.

One of the things he accomplished while he was in Zion was to establish a newspaper, *The Evening and the Morning Star.* The church had no good press from worldly papers and it felt good to have righteous views in print. The first issue was received in July and was quite a treat for those of us in Kirtland. I actually thought they were pretty bold to print the articles they did. In the 1990s, writing must be politically correct. William W. Phelps did not seem to worry about sugar-coating anything.

"With the help of God, the first issue of The *Evening and Morning Star* comes to the world for the objects specified in its prospectus which was published last winter. That we should now recapitulate some if its leading objects, and briefly add a few remarks, will naturally be expected; and we cheerfully do so, that this generation may know—

"That the *Star* comes in these last days as the friend of man, to persuade him to turn to God and live, before the great and terrible day of the Lord sweeps the earth of its wickedness;

"That it comes not only as a messenger of truth, to bring the revelations and commandments of God which have been, but to publish those that God gives now, as in the days of old, for He is the same yesterday, today, and forever.

"That it comes according to the will of God from those who are not ashamed to take upon them the name of Christ and walk lowly in the valley of humiliation, and let the solemnities of eternity rest upon them: Knowing that the great day of the Lord will soon usher in the Sabbath of creation, for the rest of the Saints, that the Savior may reign His thousand years of peace upon the earth while Satan is bound...

"That it comes when war, and the plague, or pestilence as it is called, are sweeping their thousands and tens of thousands to the grave, to show that the day of tribulation spoken of by our Savior is nigh at hand, even at the doors;

"That it comes to show that no man can be too good to be saved but that many may be too bad."

Joseph thought my reaction to the paper was quite funny.

"Don't tell me that newspapers are obsolete in your day," he chided, his sapphire eyes dancing merrily. I shook my head, sighing, and put the newspaper on the table.

"No! There are newspapers—but the writers of our day aren't quite as bold. William has no fear, does he?"

"No. I must admit he can be over-zealous but it is our duty to warn the world. Don't the prophets do that in your time?"

I thought about his question, trying to remember the things the prophets had said in my day. They did warn the world and were just as bold; still it seemed different, somehow.

"Yes, they have been bold in my day too, just in a different way. I remember how a lot of my friends were irate when President Benson said women should stay home instead of getting a job. A couple of them almost quit going to church over that." I had no idea I was revealing more than I should until I saw the shocked looks on everyone's face. I shot Joseph a look of apology. He just smiled at me and shook his head.

"Do you mean the women of your day actually go to work outside the home? How could they ever get everything accomplished that they need to at home and at another place of employment?" Jerusha asked, scandalized by the thought. Looking again at Joseph for permission, I took his nod to mean he was too curious to forbid me.

"Yes, more women work outside the home than stay home. We have so many devices that help make housework quite easy, and it's not so time-consuming now. It's possible to have a job and keep the house pretty clean also."

"But what happens to the children?" Emma asked.

"They take them to places called day-care centers."

"Which means someone else is raising their children, while they work," Mother Smith replied, not liking the thought at all.

"Did you do that, Jerree?" Emma asked, trying hard not to sound too judgmental, but I knew she was not approving of what she was hearing.

"No." I smiled proudly. "Tom wouldn't hear of it. He said he could provide for us without his wife having to leave the children to work. As a matter of fact, I was feeling very sorry for myself just before I arrived, because my youngest son had gone off to college and my mother had died. I felt I had no more use in my world."

"Then it's a good thing you found your way here," Joseph said, patting my head. I smiled fondly at him and nodded.

"If women are out of the home, what has happened to the family?" Mother Smith asked, cradling little Maria in her arms.

"The family has all but disintegrated. Sometimes it seems that only the Saints actually try to keep the family intact, although there are many others in the world who believe in our cause. We all hope the Savior comes soon. The world is in a horrible state."

They all shook their heads in despair, contemplating the awful state of the future.

"There are great wonders in my day also. The Church as spread throughout the world, technology had been advanced beyond anyone's wildest dreams—"

"All right, Jerree. I think we've heard enough about the future for one night. Let's keep our sights on our time, shall we? There's enough for us to do in this century," Joseph interrupted, reminding me of the agreement I had made when I arrived.

"You're right of course," Emma said, standing and pulling me up with her. "Besides, I don't think I want to know too much more. I can hardly cope with the hardships we must face right here and now. Come, let's get supper started." Linking arms we went into the kitchen, laughing and enjoying our time.

I hate being hot! I know I've said it before but I hate it, and Ohio is hot in the summer. Being forced to dress like a pioneer was a burden I'm not sure I could have handled, except for the fact that both Emma and Jerusha were pregnant and more miserable than me, yet did not complain. I was grateful not to be pregnant, and I tried to bear the heat with as much grace as they did.

In the fall the elders began reporting their success and failures. Joseph could hardly contain his excitement and called this time a season of joy. News came from New York that his cousin George Albert Smith, age fifteen, was baptized on September 10.

"It's about time," Joseph said, relating the fact that Father Smith had preached to his brother John in 1830 and now, two years later, George accepted the truth and was baptized.

September 22nd was a busy day in 1832. John Smith—Hyrum and Jerusha's first son—was born, healthy and strong, looking like a Smith through and through. Jerusha was tired but well, rejoicing in her new son. She shed bittersweet tears, still missing her little Mary. Hyrum was gentle and solicitous, thankful that she came through the ordeal all right.

A conference was held on the 22nd where Joseph was given the revelation that has become known as Section 84. The lineage of the priesthood was given and the functions of both the Aaronic and

Melchizedek Priesthood also. Building a temple to the Lord was mentioned more than once. The whole world lies in sin and groans under darkness and the bondage of sin. The Saints had treated lightly the things they received and were under condemnation. President Benson had reaffirmed that in my day.

Joseph's eyes filled with tears when he reported that the Lord considered them His friends, which was a greater honor than being His servants. The signs of apostles and those that believe were enumerated, namely wonderful works, casting out the devil, healing the sick, causing the blind to see, the deaf to hear, the dumb to speak, etc. Newel K. Whitney was called to New York to preach. Joseph decided to go with him, which sent Emma into a tizzy.

"You can't go to New York! This baby is coming in a matter of weeks and the weather is starting to get bad. I don't want to go through the whole ordeal without you!" Joseph smiled solicitously kissing the hand he was holding.

"I promise I'll be back in time for this little tyke to be born. Don't fret, Emma. I'm sure this one will live."

"Well, I'm not! And facing it all alone is too horrible to contemplate—not after Joseph M., and Little Mary." Her voice caught as tears swelled in her dark eyes. I had been finishing the stew for supper and turned to both of them.

"I'll stay with you, Emma. I think Jerusha is getting tired of me always underfoot."

"Yes!" Joseph exclaimed. "That's a wonderful idea. Now that we're finally settled in this new apartment Newel had remodeled for us and you don't have to worry about moving, you can relax and prepare for the baby's arrival. Having Jerree here will make me feel better, too. Besides, I can choose and order all the things we'll need for our store while I'm in New York, which will save me an extra trip later."

That seemed to placate Emma a little bit. She was looking forward to getting the store up and running, hoping finally to have something of their own. Of course the Church was putting up the money for the goods and the store would actually be the Church's, but Joseph would have a job and hopefully bring in much-needed funds.

I moved into the newly-remodeled store apartment with Emma, happy to be of service to her in Joseph's absence. He seemed happy to have me there and left with Newel, confident that all would be well.

Autumn flew by. Soon winter was gripping Kirtland again. When I look back, I'm amazed how well I adapted to life in a different century. It seemed as if I had always lived in the 1800s. I knew how to make soup, which herbs to pick for their medicinal properties, and how to sew without my Bernina. I could chop wood and build a fire better than most scouts I knew and had mastered cooking on an open fire, in a bustle oven, and on a wood stove. I was prepared now for anything the last days threw at me.

During the weeks that Joseph was gone, I taught Emma a few things, too. She was terrified of facing childbirth so I decided a little Lamaze would help her. I taught her proper breathing, focusing, and so forth. I promised to be her coach and together we'd bring her baby into the world, with or without Joseph, which is exactly what we did, November 6, 1832.

CHAPTER SIXTEEN

The contractions started a couple days before, slowly at first, just twinges now and then. Emma tried to be brave, but Joseph was still not home and her nerves were frazzled. As the pains became more frequent and harder, her reserve shattered and she broke into tears.

"Shhh…don't fret, Emma. It's going to be all right. Just remember what I've taught you. Come on, let me rub your back. You concentrate on breathing." She rolled onto her side, doing her best to breathe properly while I massaged the small of her back.

"I'm so frightened, Jerree. I want a child so desperately—Joseph's child—but going through the pain again…I'm not sure I can do it."

"Yes, you can. Every woman I've ever known has felt that way. The pain will be over before you know it and then you'll have a beautiful baby to love."

"But what if this one dies too?"

"This one won't!" I said with conviction, knowing that Joseph Smith III was about to make his entrance into the world. Seeing the look in my eyes, she nodded and sighed, trusting my words.

Lucy Mack Smith and Jerusha came, knowing Emma would need as much support as possible. The weather turned ugly on the afternoon of the fifth, a blizzard howling across the country. Emma lost any hope that Joseph would make it back and lapsed into an uncharacteristic silence, refusing to talk to anyone.

Night fell and Emma began hard labor. Mother Smith and Jerusha thought I was crazy when I began breathing with Emma, reminding her to focus. Emma clung to me, huffing and puffing as well as any 20th-century woman. They prepared for the delivery, boiling water, ripping sheets into rags, sterilizing scissors and searching for twine.

"I want Joseph!" Emma panted as a contraction subsided. I smiled and kissed her forehead.

"He'll get here. Just concentrate on having this baby."

Early in the morning of November 6, 1832, Joseph Smith III was born, upstairs in the Newel K. Whitney store in Kirtland, while a winter storm wailed outside. He was a healthy, strong boy with a set of lungs that helped him wail angrily at being thrust into such a cold, cruel world. Sobbing happily, Emma held her son close, kissing his moist head, breathing a prayer of thanksgiving. Lucy, Jerusha, and I left her alone after everything was cleaned, happy that this baby would live.

Joseph made it back immediately after the birth of Joseph Smith III. He refused to let the weather keep him from his family. I was glad to see him, but not as happy as Emma was. Needless to say, their reunion was of the sweetest kind.

✳   ✳   ✳

The reality about living through history is that important dates aren't important until they are recorded in the history books. Day to day living helped me forget that momentous things were going to happen at any given time. Keeping house, helping Emma with the children, and writing for Joseph when needed helped me forget that I had accidentally fallen into this life. This was not my time but I had adapted to it. Yet, when Joseph walked in with Brigham Young, I was totally unprepared.

Joseph went to his parents' house to help chop wood for the winter, while Emma rested with young Joseph. Julia and I were playing in the parlor, which was fast becoming known as the revelation room. Seventeen revelations were received in this room, but for Julia and me it was a quiet, spacious room where we could be alone to build many wooden block castles.

I heard them stomping up the stairs, Joseph talking merrily. "Come in! Come in! I know there's someone here who'll want to meet you." He excitedly ushered three young men into the parlor. They looked cold, tired, and hungry. Spying me on the floor, surrounded by blocks and Julia on my lap, seemed to enchant the men. They smiled fondly at me.

"Oh good! Jerree, I want you to meet three new converts. They've traveled clear from Mendon...New York." He bent down and took Julia from me, extending a hand to help me up. His eyes were shining excitedly. He watched my face intently as he introduced the men to me.

"Brethren, this is my cousin, Jerree James. Jerree, let me introduce you to Brother Brigham Young, his brother Joseph Young, and their good friend Heber C. Kimball."

Gasping, I looked at Joseph, who was marking my reaction with pleasure. I had long since stopped gasping at every new person I met but the coming of these men—especially Brigham Young—marked the beginning of the end of my stay here. I turned to the men and stared at them, finally giving in to the urge to extend my hand toward Brigham Young. Smiling, but a little taken aback by my reaction, he took my hand and shook it warmly.

Brigham Young was a huge man, not as tall as Joseph, but stout and well-built. His reddish-brown hair was shoulder length, which surprised me. Joseph wore his quite short as I just assumed all prospective prophets would. Of course he didn't know he was going to be a prophet, but I did, and by Joseph's expression, so did he. Brigham's eyes were smoky blue, reminding me of a stormy sky. His hands were big, calloused and strong. As I shook his hand, I could feel that he was the spiritual giant I had always heard he was.

"Brother Brigham," I said breathlessly.

"Sister Jerree. A pleasure to meet another one of Brother Joseph's family." He directed my attention to the other men whom I greeted warmly but my attention was drawn back to Brigham. Though not as handsome as Joseph, he was definitely, by today's standards, ruggedly handsome. In 1832, he was thirty-one years old, just recently widowed with two small girls, Elizabeth and Vilate.

Heber's wife, Vilate, was caring for them while he was away. Joseph invited them to sit down and warm themselves by the fire, reminding me that I did have certain duties. Taking my cue, I offered them something to eat, which they gladly accepted. I hurried to prepare something so that I wouldn't miss too much. Joseph seemed to understand, waiting to ask them about their conversion until after they were all seated around the table, food piled around them. He got a kick out of the fact that I was in as much awe upon meeting Brigham as I had been when I met him. Brigham Young would be referred to as the Lion of the Lord. Joseph would never have a truer friend.

All too soon they were finished. Joseph directed them to the staircase to meet Emma. In a few moments they all came down the stairs, laughing jovially at a joke Joseph had told.

"Jerree, will you help Emma? I'm off to a meeting and I'm not sure when I'll be back," Joseph asked as he donned his coat. Brigham and the others said their good-byes and went out to the wagon, patiently waiting for him.

"You've heard of Brigham Young, I see," Joseph replied, breaking his own rule. I nodded, afraid to say more. "I knew it! I could tell by the look on your face. Brigham Young is a good man, one of the best. He'll lead this Church some day." He laughed at the shocked look on my face, squeezed my arm again and was gone, bounding down the steps, plowing through the snow toward the waiting wagon.

The three men from Mendon stayed in Kirtland five days, meeting with the brethren and exhibiting their spiritual gifts, one of which was the gift of tongues. Joseph had never witnessed this before and was quite fascinated. Brigham seemed to be very blessed with this particular gift. Joseph professed it was indeed a gift of the spirit. He said Brigham often spoke in the pure language of Adam. Many people were unsure. I was still in awe of Brigham's presence, having heard so much about him all my life. He was indeed a wonderful, loving, humble man, and I enjoyed being near him. Emma was not sure she liked the man. Joseph had told her Brigham would one day lead the Church, and in her mind Joseph III was Joseph's rightful successor. When Emma asked for my opinion on the matter, I stayed silent, already knowing the outcome of that debate. This perturbed Emma, for she had a fierce love of her son, wanting only the best for him. It was hard for me to believe that some day, the sweet infant, Joseph III would lead the Reorganized Church.

The state of his world concerned Joseph Smith, and he insisted on being aware of everything that was happening. He was very concerned when South Carolina held a convention in November, declaring themselves a free nation. President Andrew Jackson sent out a proclamation against their action, deploying a large enough military force to squelch secession. It was a total surprise to me that South Carolina started making a fuss thirty years before the Civil War started. But Joseph did much more than worry and express concern; he spent hours in prayer over such matters. On Christmas Day, 1832, he received what we now call the Prophecy on War.

"Verily, thus saith the Lord concerning the wars that will shortly come to pass, beginning at the rebellion of South Carolina, which will eventually terminate in the death and misery of many souls;

"And the time will come that war will be poured out upon all nations, beginning at this place.

"For behold, the southern states shall be divided against the northern states, and the southern states will call on other nations, even the nation of Great Britain, as it is called, and they shall also call upon other nations, in order to defend themselves against other nations; and then war shall be poured and disciplined out upon all nations.

"And it shall come to pass, after many days, slaves shall rise up against their masters, who shall be marshaled and disciplined for war.

"And it shall come to pass also that the remnants who are left of the land will marshal themselves, and shall become exceedingly angry, and shall vex the Gentiles with a sore vexation.

"And thus, with the sword and by bloodshed, the inhabitants of the earth shall mourn; and with famine, and plague, and earthquake, and the thunder of heaven, and the fierce and vivid lightening also, shall the inhabitants of the earth be made to feel the wrath, and indignation, and chastening hand of an Almighty God, until the consumption decreed hath made a full end of all nations;

"Then the cry of the Saints, and the blood of the Saints shall cease to come up into the ears of the Lord of Sabaoth, from the earth, to be avenged of their enemies.

"Wherefore, stand ye in holy places, and be not moved, until the day of the Lord come; for behold it cometh quickly, saith the Lord, Amen."

I had read that section many times in my life. I knew that many of the things Joseph prophesied had happened before my day, including the Civil War. Wars and rumors of war were an everyday thing in my world, but seeing Joseph's face as he dictated the prophecy, I knew it was absolutely true. I did wonder what the Lord meant when said the Day of the Lord would come quickly. As of August of 1990, that day had not yet come. I knew then his definition of "quickly" was far different than mine.

A sense of gloom settled over the house. Many of us were inconsolable, saddened by the tragedies that would shortly befall the world. I shed many tears remembering Vietnam, Korea, and World War II, to name a few. So many conflicts had happened and were happening in my time. They had become commonplace in the world I grew up in. I hardly paid attention to the news reports of strife and conflicts in other countries. My generation seemed oblivious to the suffering and anguish caused by war because we weren't personally involved. Watching the Prophet Joseph Smith's face as he received Section 87 changed forever the way I felt about war.

We were so distraught that Joseph begged the Lord for some word of peace and hope. On December 27, he received Section 88, which indeed gave us cause to rejoice. So many promises, so much information, so many commandments! Joseph was told to build a house unto the Lord—in Kirtland—a temple! The Church was small, the Church was poor, but a temple would be built and with it, great blessings awaited us, including my ticket home.

*   *   *

1833 began busily and stayed that way. More and more people gathered to Kirtland, all burning with the fire of conversion. Joseph continued the translation of the Bible, completing the New Testament February 3, 1833. He also started a school, which quickly became known as the School of the Prophets. It was held upstairs in the northeast corner of the Whitney store, directly over the kitchen. Some people have said that Joseph Smith was an unschooled man, but I beg to differ. Only one man in this dispensation could say they had been tutored by Adam, Noah, Abraham, Nephi, Moroni—and that man was the Prophet Joseph Smith.

Having been raised in the "heart of Zion," I had a definite image of priesthood brethren and their meetings. It was the shock of my life to go into the room after the men had been taught by Joseph and be required to wash the floors because of tobacco juice, which had missed the spittoon, or air the room out due to the stale smoke. These men, holders of the holy priesthood, some even high priests, smoked and chewed tobacco while they were discussing important things of the kingdom! I couldn't believe it.

The cigar and pipe smoke filtered into the kitchen, causing both Emma and me great discomfort. I worried about Julia and young Joseph, having heard much about secondhand smoke. I voiced my opinion to Emma, who heartily agreed with me. I was fast becoming offended at having to clean up after such slobbish men. Didn't they have respect for their high and holy callings? It shocked me to know that Brigham actually smoked! I could hardly deal with that bit of information.

Finally, in the middle of February, Emma stormed down the stairs and into the kitchen, where Joseph was bidding farewell to several of the brethren. I followed her, curious to hear what she would say. It occurred to me that a revelation that would revolutionize Mormondom was about to happen and I wanted to be there.

"Joseph, I am extremely tired of cleaning that room after each meeting. It's disgusting, don't you think, Jerree?" she asked, turning her flashing eyes on me. I nodded at Joseph helplessly.

"Oh yes, Emma. Terribly gross," I stammered, earning a snicker from Brigham Young. I shot him a "look," having long since gotten over my awe of him. His gray eyes smiled at me, trying hard not to let his lips follow suit. Joseph tried to keep a straight face also, knowing it would only incite Emma's anger if he didn't take her seriously.

"I'm grateful you don't have such vile habits, Joseph, but I hardly think it's right to expect me to clean so filthy a floor. Surely the use of tobacco could not be fitting for men of God. Please, Joseph, ask the Lord about it. I personally think it would be a good thing if a revelation could be had, declaring the use of a tobacco a sin, and commanding its suppression."

My eyes grew round with surprise. Emma was certainly a bold one. Joseph couldn't hold it any longer, seeing the look on my face, and that of Brigham's. He burst into peals of laughter, wrapping his arms about his wife, kissing her forehead. I dared to crack a smile behind my hand. Brigham turned toward the door to keep from laughing out loud. I loved having such a rapport with Brigham Young.

"While the Lord's commanding we'll have to ask him about tea and coffee and how they affect the ladies," Brigham said jovially. With that all the other men in the room hooted loudly and left, readily agreeing with him. Emma shook her head, wriggled free from the circle of Joseph's arms, and headed back upstairs, muttering something about light-minded men. When I looked back at Joseph, he winked unrepentantly, causing me to giggle like a young girl. It was wonderful to see that Joseph could be so light-hearted.

"Hurry, Jerree! We have too much to do to be acting silly," Emma called sternly. I hurried up the stairs, leaving a chuckling Joseph behind.

Though Joseph had teased Emma about her reaction to the men's "vile habits," he did begin to think about what she had said. Day after day the men met, eagerly learning the principles God revealed to Joseph, puffing on pipes, chewing tobacco, missing the spittoons, surrounded by clouds of smoke. Knowing Emma and I would have to clean the mess weighed on his mind.

Though Joseph did not smoke, nor did he chew, he had not given much thought to the habits of the men around him. Tobacco use was just part of life. Emma's complaint started him thinking about it in a different light. Did God approve of such things? Was tobacco use only offensive to women, due to their more sensitive natures?

In the days that followed, these questions plagued him. No matter how hard he tried, he couldn't get the subject off his mind. Close to the end of February, it was obvious that Joseph inquired of the Lord concerning the use of tobacco. When he received his answer, he called the School of the Prophets together, inviting Emma and me to join the meeting. We assembled together on February 27, 1833.

"Brethren, sisters, I've asked you here to reveal the will of the Lord to all of us. Thank you for coming. We will begin with prayer."

When all the business of the day had been addressed, Joseph stood, looking over the small congregation assembled in the room. Smiling, his gaze lingered on Emma and me, knowing we at least had an inkling of what was coming. Emma looked over at me. I smiled, looking back to Joseph.

"After much consideration and prayer the will of the Lord has been made known. As in the days of ancient Israel, the Lord is concerned with the health of His people. I would like to read His Word of Wisdom to us."

February 27, 1833

"A word of Wisdom, for the benefit of the council of high priests, assembled in Kirtland and the Church, and also the Saints in Zion—

"To be sent greeting; not by commandment or constraint, but by revelation and the word of wisdom, showing forth the order and will of God in the temporal salvation of all Saints in the last days—

"Given for a principle with promise, adapted to the capacity of the weak and the weakest of all Saints, who are or can be called Saints.

"Behold, verily, thus saith the Lord unto you; In consequence of evils and designs which do and will exist in the hearts of conspiring men in the last days, I have warned you, and forewarn you, by giving unto you this word of wisdom by revelation—

"That inasmuch as any man drinketh wine or strong drink among you, behold it is not good, neither meet in the sight of your Father, only in assembling yourselves together to offer up your sacraments before him.

"And behold, this should be wine, yea pure wine of the grape of the vine, of your own make.

"And again, strong drinks are not for the belly, but for the washing of your bodies.

"And again, tobacco is not for the body, neither for the belly, and is not good for man, but is an herb for bruises and all sick cattle, to be used with judgment and skill.

"And again, hot drinks are not for the body or the belly.

"And again, verily I say unto you, all wholesome herbs God hath ordained for the constitution, nature and use of man—

"Every herb in the season thereof, and every fruit in the season thereof, all these to be used with prudence and thanksgiving.

"Yea, flesh also of beasts and of the fowls of the air, I the Lord, have ordained for the use of man with thanksgiving; nevertheless, they are to be used sparingly;

"And it is pleasing unto me that they should not be used, only in times of winter, or of cold, or famine. All grain is ordained for the use of man and of beasts, to be the staff of life, not only for man but for the beasts of the field and the fowls of heaven, and all wild animals that run or creep on the earth;

"And these hath God made for the use of man only in times of famine and excess of hunger.

"All grain is good for the food of man, as also the fruit of the vine; that which yieldeth fruit, whether in the ground or above the ground—

"Nevertheless, wheat for man, and corn for the ox, and oats for the horse, and rye for the fowls and for swine and for all beasts of the field, and barley for all useful animals and for mild drinks, as also other grain.

"And all Saints who remember to keep and do these sayings, walking in obedience to the commandments, shall receive health in their navel and marrow to their bones;

"And shall find wisdom and great treasures of knowledge, even hidden treasures;

"And shall run and not be weary, and shall walk and not faint.

"And I the Lord, give unto them a promise, that the destroying angel shall pass by them, as the children of Israel, and not slay them. Amen."

The room was silent save Joseph's voice, resonating with conviction as he read the Word of Wisdom for the first time. I watched the faces of the men register first agreement, then questions and finally astonishment. I was the only person in the room, besides Joseph, who was not totally shocked. The single question of whether tobacco should be used blossomed into an entire code of health that would set the members of the Church apart clear into the next century.

Questions were fired at Joseph as soon as he finished. Amidst the uproar, Emma and I excused ourselves, Joseph winking at us as we left.

Though the Word of Wisdom was not given as a commandment at that time, many people took it as such. Brigham, when he heard the revelation, readily gave up his use of tobacco, never again to pick up the habit. I was happy to see the priesthood gather together to direct the affairs of the kingdom without clouds of smoke, and Emma was happy not to have to clean the floor. She didn't even mind having to give up tea.

"If Brigham can give up smoking, then I'll give up tea and be happy to do it," she quipped when Joseph teased her about it. I laughed and put my arm around her waist.

"I'm just glad I didn't have any of those habits to give up."

"It's nice to see obedience," Joseph said, winking and placing a kiss on Emma's cheek. With mock anger she swatted at him, resuming her cooking. I joined in laughing, happy to be with these people.

CHAPTER SEVENTEEN

What can I write about this period that hasn't already been written? 1833 was busy, with ever-increasing numbers of Saints moving to Kirtland. A temple was being planned and a growing church needed more organization.

On March 8, 1833 the first Presidency was organized, with Joseph as president, Sidney Rigdon as first counselor, and Frederick G. Williams as second counselor. Ten days later they were ordained as Presidents of the High Priesthood, having equal authority with Joseph. The Church was beginning to look like the one I had grown up with. I knew that the Twelve would soon be called and then the hierarchy would be complete. I learned more about the function of the leadership of the Church in those few years in Joseph's house than I did in a lifetime of membership. Joseph made everything simple. It all made perfect sense when he taught.

George Albert Smith arrived in Kirtland on May 25th with his parents. John Smith, his father, was Joseph's uncle. The entire family was overjoyed to have them close at last. George A., as he was called, was a boy of fifteen, large like the Smiths, mild-mannered and jovial. He looked more like Hyrum than Joseph. He was immediately put to work in the stone quarry, being one of the first to haul rock for the temple.

God had called Joseph as a prophet, not just for the Saints, but for the entire world. Along with the excitement about the temple, the conditions of the world weighed heavily on Joseph's mind. He taught me that prophets have great love and concern for all the people on the earth, not just those they are associated with. So many people were suffering, and Joseph felt as if the entire population of the earth were his responsibility. He worried about the cholera epidemic rampant in big cities the world over. Clean water seemed to be more valuable than gold. He worried about the plague that broke out in India, taking thousands from the planet. He felt their plight as if it were his own. I found him several times in fervent prayer, weeping for the world and begging for relief.

How many prophets had done the same? Adam, Enoch, Noah, Abraham, Moses, Jeremiah, Isaiah, Christ himself, had all lamented the state of the world. When the love of God fills a man's soul, he longs to extend it to all men. Joseph Smith was such a man.

The most memorable event of 1833 was the laying of the cornerstones for the Kirtland Temple. It occurred to me that the building they were starting would stand in my own day. I knew the Savior would soon come to the temple, along with several prophets, to restore important priesthood keys to mankind.

July 23 was hot and humid, but I seemed to have finally acclimatized myself to it. I held baby John in my arms; at ten months he wasn't much of a baby anymore. He wiggled and squirmed, wanting to be with his father who was participating in the ceremony. Jerusha laughed and offered to take him. I shook my head, determined to be victorious over this small Smith. Emma leaned close, chuckling.

"I can see the family resemblance now, Jerree. You're as stubborn as any Smith I've ever met." I laughed and held on tighter to my little charge.

Most of the people in Kirtland had never witnessed the laying of a cornerstone for a temple. It had been done in Independence, Missouri, in 1831, but only a handful of men had been in attendance. Even I, who had been a member all my life, had never been to a cornerstone ceremony, and I would be the only one in my generation to witness the Prophet Joseph Smith presiding at one!

Twenty-three men helped, along with Joseph. He said that it must be done "after the order of the Holy Priesthood." I knew most of them. Jerusha pointed out the ones I hadn't met and told me their names. Nothing can describe my feelings as I stood with the Smith women and children, witnessing a momentous occasion in the history of the world. No group of people had tried to raise a temple to God since Herod the Great or the Nephites. I was truly humbled to be present.

In my naivete and ignorance, I assumed building this temple would be as easy as it was in my day. I would read about the plans for a new temple in *The Church News* and a few years later read about its dedication. I soon learned that the opposition to this temple would be unprecedented, due to the fact that this was the first temple. The powers of darkness didn't take kindly to the building of the house that would ultimately aid us in thwarting them.

The first anti-Mormon book written in this dispensation was by a man by the name of Doctor Philastus Hurlburt. He was a scoundrel and a liar. I had the misfortune to be in his presence a few times when he came to visit Joseph. He was arrogant, too sure of himself, and way too slick for me. He made a great pretense at piety, yet at the same time looked at me as if he could ravish me in two seconds. Why was it that evil men had to use sexual innuendo as part of their personality? Did it make them feel important or powerful? I was not impressed with him and after enduring Eli Johnson's abuse, I was not about to stand by and take Hurlburt's.

One of my duties as a member of Joseph's household was to make visitors feel at home and to provide any refreshment they might need. This was usually a joy for me, but in his case I hated doing it. I told Joseph so once, and he was shocked.

"Why would you feel so uncharitable toward a new convert?" Joseph asked.

"He gives me the creeps! He looks at me...in an inappropriate way. When I hand him something he always finds a way to touch me. I just don't like him."

"We must not be too quick to judge, Jerree. I think you just need to relax," he said patting my hand, smiling patiently. The only criticism I ever had about Joseph Smith was that he was far too trusting. He saw the good in everyone, trusting even those who didn't deserve his trust. So many took advantage of Joseph's childlike love and hurt him greatly because of it.

Hurlburt was called on a mission. While he was in the mission field, he proved to be immoral and deceitful. He was promptly excommunicated. That was, of course, not surprising to me. Bitterly angry, he began to vilify Joseph and the church. His book, *Mormonism Unveiled* was the worst collection of trash I'd ever read. It even outdid Simonds Ryder and Ezra Booth's articles. Hurlburt started a rumor about a manuscript written twenty years before by a man named Solomon Spaulding, which he claimed Sidney Rigdon stole and gave to Joseph Smith. He claimed that Rigdon and the prophet created the Book of Mormon from the manuscript.

"How could anyone believe that?" I questioned angrily. "Sidney didn't even show up until after the Book of Mormon was published!"

"Some people don't care to know the facts if they can hear something that will discredit me. I guess I should have listened to you when you said he was bad news," Joseph said, sighing tiredly. I reached across the table and took his hand.

"I happen to think you are wonderful." He smiled and squeezed my hand tightly.

"You are family. It just proves, once again, that Moroni was right when he said my name would be had for good and evil. I can't spend my entire life worrying about the lies being told about me. I have too many other things to worry about."

Philastus Hurlburt didn't stop there, though. He openly threatened Joseph, swearing he would wash his hands in Joseph's blood. Even Joseph thought that a serious enough threat to bring charges against him. Hurlburt was convicted, jailed for six months, and fined three hundred dollars. No one took much stock in his rantings after that.

Hurlburt wasn't the only one breathing threats against the Church and Joseph, however. Local enemies vowed the temple would never be built and that somehow they would find a way to kidnap Joseph. Emma lived in a constant state of panic, which caused Joseph to hire bodyguards; they were needed for the rest of his life.

Guards were posted on the temple site day and night. Sometimes there were three guards to every one laborer. George A. Smith insisted on guarding the Prophet. He spent the entire winter standing watch over Joseph, spending the first half of each night on his watch. Often Joseph would go somewhere other than his own home, hoping to keep Emma and the rest of the family safe.

"I'm so glad you're here," Joseph said one night, as he gathered a few things to take with him into hiding. I smiled, trying to keep the tears of frustration from showing.

"Why, Joseph? Why can't they just leave you in peace?" I asked. "Emma's sick with worry and your mother...I don't think she's slept all winter. I know George A. hasn't. He's going to fall dead in his tracks if he doesn't get a good night's sleep soon," I cried, taking his arm, needing to feel his strength. He patted my hand, trying to smile.

"It's going to be all right. The Lord has promised that Kirtland will be the stronghold of the Church for five years. We still have more time. This temple will be built and dedicated to the Lord...that I know." I nodded and pulled back so I could see his face. His steady gaze gave me comfort and I sighed.

"I know it too—the Kirtland temple stands in my day, though it's not owned by the Church." Joseph's gasp reminded me that I was saying too much.

"I'm sorry! I shouldn't have said that."

"No, probably not, but I've wondered...knowing we must leave Kirtland." He sighed. As he went back to his packing, he said, "Have no fear, all will be well. Please watch over and comfort Emma for me."

I promised I would and watched him leave, escorted by George A. and Heber Kimball.

One of the best things that happened in 1833 was that Brigham Young came to live in Kirtland. He had been on a mission to Canada and brought with him twenty or thirty converts. Joseph told him to go get his family and move to Kirtland to help build a stronghold for the Saints. He willingly complied and by the fall was situated with the Saints. I was glad, for I adored Brigham Young as much as I loved Joseph. I became quite close to his daughters, also.

Though opposition raged, more and more people gathered to Kirtland, including a woman by the name of Mary Ann Angell. She was a handsome woman in her thirties, committed to the faith she had embraced. I liked her right away, and we soon became good friends. Single and pretty, Mary Ann caught the eye of many a man in town. She often laughed at the obvious attempts to set her up with one or another of the brethren.

"I'm not in a hurry," she confessed to me. "I'm looking for a certain type of man. When I find him, I'll make my intentions known." Mary Ann Angell would have done well in my day.

It felt good to have made a friend of one of the people in Kirtland that was not a Smith and didn't know who I was. To Mary Ann Angell

I was just another convert, part of the Smith family only by marriage. If she only knew! One Sunday we were sitting together before church, when Brigham Young came in. He was an impressive man, well built—like a football player—with flashing eyes that could be one moment calm and blue as a summer's day, then turn instantly gray and stormy when he was provoked.

His reddish-brown hair was shoulder length. Though I was not partial to long hair on a man, I did have to admit it looked good on Brigham Young. Had I been young and single, my heart would have done a few somersaults at his appearance. As it was, I was thrilled just to be in the presence of the man I knew would one day be such a celebrated leader. Mary Ann noticed him too, leaning close to me to whisper in my ear.

"Who is he? I haven't seen him before," she said breathlessly watching as Joseph greeted him warmly.

"That's Brigham Young—Brother Brigham. He's just moved here from New York with his family."

"Oh," Mary Ann replied flatly. Never being one to overlook a chance to make a match, I took her hand, squeezing it fondly.

"He's a widower. His wife, Miriam, died a couple of years ago. He brought his girls, Elizabeth and Vilate, to Kirtland." Her smile told me volumes. I was sure Mary Ann had just laid eyes on that "certain type of man."

I had a hard time paying attention to the meeting, spending the entire time planning how to get my two friends together. They would make such a good match. Brigham was larger than life, outspoken and straight-forward. No one wondered where he stood. He was proud, industrious, and hard working, putting his all into everything he did. Mary Ann was confident, opinionated, and quite liberated for her day. She didn't rely on a man to shape her destiny or opinions. Her fierce love of the gospel matched Brigham's. They would make the perfect couple, and I was going to see to it that they met.

After the meeting was over, I made a beeline for Brigham, taking Mary Ann's hand and dragging her behind me. Brigham smiled when he saw me, scooping me up into a bear hug, chuckling fondly.

"Sister Jerree! It's so good to see you're still here! Have you helped Sister Emma convince Joseph to ask for any other revelations? You are looking well." When he put me down and stepped back, I giggled like a schoolgirl. Being Brigham's friend was one of the greatest joys of my life.

"Brother Brigham, Joseph tells me you're here in Kirtland to stay."

"Yes, I am. The girls are happy to know I'll be close to them and close to Joseph. I can't let him build a temple without me. Who have you brought with you?" He asked, looking appreciatively at Mary Ann.

"Oh…this is my good friend, Mary Ann Angell. She's just moved here from Providence, Rhode Island. She was baptized by someone I think you know—Brother John P. Green." Brigham's bushy eyebrows raised with interest at the mention of his brother-in-law.

"Really? He's my own brother-in-law! He is married to my sister Rhoda. How wonderful. Sister Mary Ann, I hope you will allow me to call and have you give me a full report on my family." He took her hand, holding it tenderly, looking down at the captivated woman. She was totally speechless, her cheeks red, her eyes staring at him in wonder.

Out of the corner of my eye I caught Joseph shaking his head at me, smiling broadly at my attempt at matchmaking. I shrugged my shoulders coyly, earning for myself a hearty laugh from the Prophet. Brigham and Mary Ann were totally oblivious of anything but themselves.

J E R U S H A

CHAPTER EIGHTEEN

Brigham Young was a powerful speaker. Joseph asked him to address the Saints that Sunday night to report on his mission to Canada. I, of course, sat with Mary Ann, who hardly noticed me after Brigham stood to speak. Though his speaking abilities differed from Joseph's, he certainly had an undeniable magnetism born of the Spirit. Turning to look at Mary Ann, I smiled to see how smitten she was with him. I was so glad. For two years, Brigham Young had been alone, preaching the gospel, trusting friends and family to care for his girls. His own mother died when he was fourteen and he felt the loss of his wife even more poignantly because of it. He deserved another chance at happiness.

Mary Ann had never been married. She told me that she feared, because of her high expectations for the right man, she might have missed her chance for marriage. Watching her interact with Brigham Young, I knew she need not fear. Sure enough, Brigham began calling regularly, and they began their formal courtship.

Tensions in Missouri continued to mount. The causes and effects of the Missouri period have been well documented. Being in Kirtland, living day to day with the Smith family, I confess that Missouri seemed as far away as it had to me in Idaho in the twentieth century. The cares of everyday life often left me insensitive to the plight of the Saints in Missouri, but I knew Joseph was concerned, for he talked and prayed about them often. There was as much to worry about in Kirtland, with threats being breathed toward Joseph, a temple to build, and no money to do it. I soon found out that the Lord had a plan to ensure my concern for the sufferings of the Saints in Zion.

Early in the year of 1834 I received a visit from Mary Ann Angell. She was ecstatic, her eyes sparkling, and her face beautiful with joy.

"He asked me! He actually asked me to marry him!" she blurted as I opened the door. She hurried in, the fire inviting her to come closer to partake of its warmth. I laughed and threw my arms around her.

"Brigham finally got up enough nerve to propose! Good for him. I'm so happy for you, Mary Ann!"

"Me too! I was just about ready to ask *him.* He needs a wife and a mother for those two precious girls; I'm ready and willing to fill the vacancy. We've set a date for the 18th of February. I would really love for you to stand beside me as my matron of honor." Tears filled my eyes as I looked at the happy face of Mary Ann Angell.

"Oh Mary Ann! I don't deserve such an honor." She took my hand, squeezing tightly, her eyes seriously boring into mine.

"Why, of course you do. You're the one who introduced us."

I smiled and squeezed her hand, shaking my head.

"I have a feeling you two would have met with or without me. I'm honored, really I am. Thank you, Mary Ann."

"Now don't go cryin' on me. Do you think you could get away and come to the store with me? I need to be choosing some material for a dress."

"I think I can. Let me go talk to Emma."

Brigham Young and Mary Ann Angell were married February 18, 1834. The day before, the first High Council was established in this dispensation. It was a busy time for everyone, but Brigham was determined to have a ceremony in spite of the activities. Because of the overwhelming poverty in Kirtland, white material was not to be found, but Mary Ann was just as pleased with dark blue. She was especially happy because her parents arrived shortly before the wedding, along with her brother Truman and his family. They were all pleased with Mary Ann's choice of husbands, especially Truman, who was an expert craftsman himself. He knew he and Brigham would work well together since the temple would take every available man.

Standing beside Mary Ann as Newel K. Whitney married her to Brigham, I was filled with an overpowering sense of sadness. I had now been in Kirtland for almost three years without my husband and children. Most days I was too busy to really worry about them. I had

132

been promised all would be well and that the Lord was watching over them, but looking at these two people so much in love, I ached to see Tom's face, to feel his arms around me. He would have loved this experience in Kirtland. He often commented how he'd been born in the wrong era. To rub shoulders with people like Joseph and Brigham was a dream he had wanted, and yet, here I was, fulfilling that dream.

With Brigham in Kirtland intent on building the temple, I knew my time here was quickly coming to an end. I was grateful for that and yet, it had been a wonderful experience. I would miss all my new friends, but I needed to go home to the man who loved me and to our children.

After the ceremony, I helped with the dinner Emma and I had prepared. I was glad to be in the kitchen where I didn't have to put on a happy face. I was so glad for Brigham and Mary Ann, but I was also homesick and I didn't want to spoil their joy. Joseph sought me out, ever aware of my moods, entering the kitchen with a large piece of cake in his hands that he was enjoying immensely. When he finished eating, he looked at me seriously, sensing my melancholy.

"The cake was delicious, Jerree. Mary Ann says you made it. You've truly become one of us. I remember when you first arrived and you couldn't even boil water over an open fire. You've learned a lot in the short time you've been with us."

I chuckled and handed him a dishcloth.

"Wipe your face; you have frosting all over it."

He took the towel and swiped it over his face haphazardly, laying it on the counter in a heap, like every other man I knew. He looked at me intently, his sapphire eyes boring into my soul.

"You miss them, don't you?" he asked, refusing to let me look away, the power of his gaze holding mine.

I sighed and picked up the discarded towel, twisting it in my hands.

"Terribly. Sometimes I can't remember if this life I have now is real and the memories of the past are dreams, or if this is all a dream and I'll wake up in my own bed at any moment. Everyone here means so much to me...I can't imagine loving anyone more than you...but I miss my family." He covered the distance between us in two strides and took my hands in his, stilling them from their nervous twisting of the towel.

"Of course you do. I'd think something was wrong with you if you didn't. But there are still a few things you need to learn, Jerree, before the Lord releases you from this journey. Some won't be easy—your very faith will be tried. Are you willing to learn the lessons God has for you?"

My heart leaped at the prospect of doing something more that would teach me the things I'd come here to learn.

"Oh yes! Whatever I'm asked!" I breathed.

Joseph smiled and took my hands in his massive ones, looking fondly down at me. How I adored this man. He was a friend, son, uncle, prophet.

"Are you so eager to go through tribulation, dear niece? Lessons learned from the Lord often include such. Don't fret; all is well—here and in your own time. I should go see to the guests." He placed a kiss on my forehead, smiled again and turned, reached for a tall glass of milk and gulped it greedily.

"Delicious cake," he said. He took another piece and left as quickly as he had come. Sighing, I gathered the dirty dishes and began washing, wondering what lessons the Lord had in store for me.

*   *   *

"Zion must be redeemed," Joseph said, looking at the congregation with love and determination. "I have journeyed much over the past few weeks, visiting branches of the church, asking for help from the brethren. If Zion is not delivered, the time is near when all of this church, where ever they may be found, will be persecuted and destroyed. It is our duty to go to Zion and assist them in reclaiming their inheritance. I plan to go; all who are willing are called to go and all who can help with monies are called to contribute. We will not escape the Lord's wrath if we forsake Zion."

Despite Joseph's stirring words, there seemed to be a division among the saints in Kirtland. Some stated there was no extra money to fund a military effort for Zion. Some thought all the manpower should be used to build the temple, which, they pointed out, was also commanded of them by the Lord. I heard some say Joseph was just plain bloodthirsty. I couldn't believe these people. Didn't they listen to what Joseph was saying? The Lord was requiring this of them, through the mouth of the Prophet, and all they could do was complain and find fault with him. All of this saddened Joseph who was only being obedient to the word of the Lord.

The plight of the Saints in Missouri had been a heavy burden on his heart. He wanted to be with them and yet the Lord had commanded him to build a temple in Kirtland, making it a stronghold, so that power could be received from on high. The Saints in Missouri complained, saying Joseph didn't care about them. Kirtland Saints weren't much better in their complaints against the Prophet. Joseph Smith shed many tears over the attitude of this flock. Because I lived in his home, I was aware of his pain. One rare afternoon at the end of April, he came home early, sequestering himself in his office, proclaiming that he wished to be left alone. After a while, curiosity overcame me; I poured a tall glass of milk and went to the office door, knocking softly.

"Come in, Jerree," came the weary voice of the Prophet. I swear he had X-ray vision. I really wanted to ask him how he knew it was me, but I knew he'd just smile and shake his head.

"I thought you might need a drink," I said lamely. He stood behind his desk, looking out the window. He smiled at me, nodding his head. I walked across the room and offered him the glass. He gulped the entire contents, and gave it back to me. I handed him a cloth to wipe the milk mustache from his upper lip. Sometimes he reminded me so much of my own son Joseph.

"All you women are the same—using food to pry the very thoughts from a man. I see that at least that won't change in a hundred years. So you wonder what is wrong with me, don't you? I'm tired!

"I long for the rest promised to those who are faithful—don't look at me that way. Don't you think every prophet that ever lived felt as I do? All the ones I know longed for death—Adam, Noah, Abraham, and Moroni. Sometimes I wonder why the Lord doesn't weary of this world Himself!"

The window by which he stood faced east, causing his face to be in shadow, the sun beginning its descent. The entire room began to darken. I wondered if I should light the lamps. He seemed so distraught, but I couldn't help smiling as I thought about what he had said. He probably really did know all the prophets he had just named. I'd bet there wasn't another man on the whole earth, since John the Baptist, who had been tutored by more angels than this man before me. At twenty-eight, he was one of the most learned men of his day, though he had had little formal education. He also insisted that those around him learn as much as they could and had kept the School of the Prophets going. He was determined that all who wanted to learn what he had been taught from on high should have the chance. He saw my smile and sighed, turning back to the window.

"You can't please everyone, Joseph. If you're right with God, that's all you can hope for," I said, putting the glass down and placing a hand on his arm. He smiled down at me, patting my hand.

"So true, my dear, so true. But I do hate being called a coward or a liar, or a fallen prophet."

His handsome face was etched in misery, the darkening shadows heightening the effect.

"Goes with the job, uncle," I said.

He chuckled, left the window, and sat down at his desk. I went to the mantel, found a taper and lit it, then lit the lamps around the room. When the room was bathed in the soft light of the lamps, I too sat down. He stared at me for so long that I wondered if he was even seeing me. I thought about getting up and leaving when he surprised me with his next words.

"The people of your day have become negligent in their duty to those of us who are fighting so hard to set up this kingdom. Wealth and greed have overcome their hearts. There is a purpose for you coming here, Jerusha."

My heart pounded in my chest so hard that I could hardly breathe. Many times I had been present when the prophetic mantle had fallen on Joseph Smith Jr., but now he was directing his words solely to me. He was bathed in an unearthly light. Though the sun was setting and lamps were lit, the room seemed brighter than it should have.

"Do you wish to know the Lord's will for you, Jerusha Walker James?"

"Oh, yes," I breathed weakly, a lump forming in my throat. The Lord was actually talking to me through a living prophet! That meant that He was mindful of me even in this time. Joseph smiled, seeming to understand my feelings.

"In a few days we leave for Zion—to accomplish her redemption. You are called to journey with us—to test your faith, to open your eyes, and to help you convince those of your day that they must seek first the kingdom of God and put aside the avarice of the world. For what profiteth a man if he gain the whole world and lose his own soul?"

"But...I'm a woman."

"Yes, the Lord is aware of that. There will be other women going also. We will need the help of our sisters, even in an army. Will you accept this call from the Lord, Sister Jerusha?" Joseph very seldom used my given name, yet he was using it now, while his face shone and the Spirit directed his words. The Lord must use my given name also, probably not impressed with the nickname I gave myself. I knew Joseph was serious, but I couldn't help but smile.

"Of course I will—on one condition." Joseph's eyebrows arched in surprise, his full lips trying to suppress a smile. He must have thought I was quite bold to put a condition on the Lord's call.

"Which is?" he asked curiously.

"I hate wearing a dress all the time. The women in my day wear pants—which makes hard work so much easier. If I'm going to march with Zion's Camp, I want to be comfortable." Joseph's laughter filled the entire room. He nodded and stood, stretching his hand out to me. I placed mine in his, laughing too.

"By all means, wear whatever you will, but don't complain to me when you're the subject of gossip and scorn."

"Better that than walk to Zion in a dress. I'll pack a dress for Sabbath worship," I said, picking up the glass I had used to approach the Prophet. I left with my heart soaring. Joseph was going to Missouri, and this time I'd be going with him instead of staying behind! Knowing the Lord requested it made the thought all the more exciting. Had I known the history of the Zion's Camp march, I doubt I would have been as excited. My ignorance was a good thing. Otherwise, I doubt I would have gone.

✻   ✻   ✻

The schoolhouse was filled to overflowing. It felt like a sauna with all the eager bodies waiting to hear what the prophet would say concerning the march of Israel's army. Several of the leaders took the stand, expounding on the virtues of redeeming Zion. Joseph sat, listening intently, nodding and smiling. At that moment, he would have made an excellent politician, never giving a clue what he was thinking by his facial expressions. It seemed forever before he stood and swept the room with his sapphire gaze. Everyone fell silent, knowing his words were the ones that we all wanted to hear. George A. leaned against me and whispered:

"It's about time. I don't think I could have stood one more discourse about our duties for Zion's redemption." I chuckled and squeezed his arm. He was fast becoming one of my favorite Smiths. It felt good to be around a teenager, and George Albert Smith was a typical teenager, his sense of humor sharp and to the point. He was never malicious but could pull off a whopping practical joke. I was happy to know he would be in the same company with me.

"Brothers and sisters, we've heard quite a bit about Zion's redemption and well we should. The Lord has commanded us to go, and we will be obedient. But brethren, I want to say to you before the Lord, that you know no more concerning the destinies of this kingdom than a babe upon its mother's lap." There was a collective gasp and hum of excited conversation. Joseph smiled and sought my gaze. My heart fluttered; though I wasn't sure what he would say, I knew it would be big.

"You don't comprehend it. It is only a little handful of priesthood leaders you see here tonight, but this church will fill North and South America—it will fill the world; it will fill the Rocky Mountains. There will be tens of thousands of Latter-day Saints who will be gathered in the Rocky Mountains and there they will open the door for the establishing of the gospel among the Lamanites. This mission is sanctioned by God. We must all keep the commandments. I promise that if we are united in faith, God will deliver us from our enemies. But, should there be murmuring against the Lord or his servants, the Lord will visit us in wrath and vex us in his sore displeasure. May we all be obedient and faithful is my prayer, in Jesus' name. Amen."

The Lord and his Prophet weren't going to put up with the murmuring that had been happening. It was time for action and there was no question about it. Looking at Joseph's face, I knew he had looked into the future and seen my day. He knew the future, without my testimony of it. Joseph Smith Jr. had been given the knowledge about a time that seemed almost a distant memory to me. I nodded, smiling broadly at him. He returned the smile, nodded, and turned to ask Brigham Young to offer the closing prayer.

CHAPTER NINETEEN

Excitement crackled in the air. My heart beat wildly as I finished packing the last of the provisions. A crowd had already begun to gather though it was still early. More than one person took a second look at me and most gasped when they realized I was in pants instead of a dress. I ignored them, knowing I would be glad I chose to dress this way. Though he was busy, Joseph took several opportunities to catch my eye and chuckle. I wrinkled my nose and went about my work.

"I do so envy you," Mary Ann Young said, giggling at the sight of me in homespun pants, a white shirt, and boots, which were a tad too big. I wiped my hands on the seat of my pants and laughingly walked over to her. She stood on the board sidewalk outside Whitney's store, holding a basket in her hands.

"Why do you envy me?"

"Because you are going where the excitement is, while the rest of us must stay behind."

"I don't have a baby coming like you do or one just born like Jerusha or little ones like Emma. The men need a cook and laundress, and so I go." She nodded and searched my face intently.

"Where is your family, Jerree? Brigham says you showed up one day out of nowhere without family or anything. There hasn't been a letter or visit from anywhere. Why is that?"

I smiled and squeezed her arm, filled with too much excitement to be offended by her question.

"It's a very long story, Mary Ann. It's really quite remarkable, but I don't have time to tell it. When I get back I'll tell you the whole story. Can you wait that long?"

"I suppose I don't have much of a choice. Can you do me a favor while you're gone?"

"Of course, you just name it."

"Will you keep an eye on Brigham? I know he was on his own for several years, but I've gotten quite used to caring for him and I'm afraid I'm going to miss him. It does make me feel better knowing you're going. I've made this basket of goodies—will you see to it that he gets some of them? If he knows I've made them, he'll give them all away without any for himself." Nodding, I took the basket, then folded her in my arms.

"I promise he'll get his fill. You take care of yourself and the baby." I laid my hand on her swollen belly. She sniffed loudly, nodding, then hurried off to find her husband. I sighed and went to the wagon to find a spot for Mary Ann's basket. All around me people were saying good-bye, laughing and crying. At that moment I missed my family so much.

What would Tom say if he knew I was about to march with Zion's Camp to redeem Zion? My own Joseph would insist on going. David would grumble, and Cory would be furious that I was going without him. Sarah would be envious of me but happy that she had stayed behind. I could see all their faces in my mind's eye. And yet, for all my homesickness, I would not have given up the past three years for anything. Everything I thought was important in the 1990s was of little use to me here except my love for my family and the birth of my testimony. 1990s worries would probably remain of little importance when I finally returned. Zion and her redemption were the only things that really mattered—in the 19th or 20th century.

By end of Zion's Camp March, I was one of twelve women. Several families joined along the way, planning to settle in Missouri, and that included women and children. Knowing other women would be there made me feel less conspicuous, though I was the only woman in pants. There were many comments about it, but I refused to complain about them, having promised Joseph I wouldn't. When someone mentioned my chosen outfit to Joseph, he just smiled and told them that I had a right to wear what I wished, as long as I was modest. Of course some people did not think trousers on a woman were modest.

On May 1st, a small group of men traveled ahead with four baggage wagons filled with provisions for the homeless in Missouri.

They were to go to New Portage and wait until the rest of us got there. I wasn't sure where that was but I knew I'd soon learn. Hyrum took a group north to Michigan to recruit more members. He left the same day we did. Lyman Wight accompanied him. Hyrum knew he must go, but he worried for Jerusha, who had just given birth to his son Hyrum Jr. on April 27.

"I don't even have the comfort of knowing you will be with her," Hyrum said before he left. I hugged him tightly, feeling an overwhelming sense of love for this man who was my progenitor.

"She'll be all right. Mother Smith and Lucy will take good care of her."

"I know; but she's not as strong as she used to be. It's hard being away from her so often."

I nodded, knowing how much he loved his family and, at the same time, how much he loved the gospel.

"She knows it's hard for you to leave, Hyrum. But she'd kick you out of the house if she thought you might shirk your duty to the Church to be with her." Hyrum's blue eyes filled with happy tears as he bent to kiss my cheek.

"You're right of course. Your parents were truly moved by the Spirit to name you Jerusha. You are indeed a blessing to our family. Thank you, Jerusha James."

As he walked away, I felt like sitting on the sidewalk and sobbing. To know that my great-great-grandfather, Hyrum Smith, approved of me was so wonderful that gladness swelled within me, spilling out of my eyes. For the first time, I felt proud of the name my parents had chosen for me. Jerusha Barden Smith was indeed a valiant, special, important woman, and I felt honored to have been named after her.

I was oblivious of all the people hurrying about me or the sounds of horses and oxen, or the smell of dust and animals. All that mattered was that the Smith family thought I was a good addition to their numbers. It had never mattered to me before. I had actually become tired of hearing my mother remind me who my ancestors were. But now, on May 5, 1834, the Smith's approbation meant the world to me.

"No time for tears, Sister Jerree. It's time to take our leave of Kirtland." Joseph Smith smiled down at me, stretching forth his hand. Sniffling, I took it and stood, following the Prophet to the head of Zion's Camp.

The company looked impressive, with all the men lined up as uniformly as could be expected for non-military men. Joseph was arrayed in his best suit, with a sword and a pair of pistols at his sides. He mounted his horse and proudly surveyed those who followed him. He loved this type of ceremony, with all its pomp and circumstance.

A banner, made from a white sheet had the word "Peace" written on it and was held by people I did not know. A considerable crowd lined both sides of the road, cheering us on as we marched out of Kirtland toward Chardon Road where we would turn south for New Portage. Finally, after several weeks of preparation, Zion's Camp was on its way to redeem Zion!

May 5, 1834

"Having gathered and prepared clothing and other necessities to carry to our brethren and sisters, who had been robbed and plundered of nearly all their effects and having provided for ourselves horses, wagons, and firearms, and all sorts of munitions of war of the most portable kind for self-defense—as our enemies are thick on every hand—I started with the remainder of the company from Kirtland to Missouri. This day we went as far as the town of Streetsbourough, twenty-seven miles from Kirtland. We stayed in Mr. Ford's barn...."

Joseph sighed and stood to stretch. I had been asked to scribe for him because he felt there needed to be a day-to-day account of the proceedings of Zion's Camp, and he hated to write. He claimed it pained his head and felt sure there were always people around him better equipped to handle the job. I don't think he ever knew how great he really was.

Mr. Ford's barn was large, but fifty plus people filled it to over-flowing. Some people opted to follow Brigham to Israel Barlow's place, three quarters of a mile away, which helped with the space. Because I was writing for Joseph, I was spared cooking for the night. Joseph rubbed his face and looked about him. Everywhere he looked, people were preparing to sleep. I knew he was feeling a bit over-whelmed because of the task he was undertaking.

"I'm weary, Sister Jerree. We'll continue this later. Go get something to eat."

142

"Would you like me to bring you a plate back?" I asked, wanting to put my arms around him but restraining myself. He smiled and took my hand in his, squeezing warmly.

"No, I'm too tired to eat."

"You need to eat to keep up your strength," I argued. Looking into my determined eyes, he knew he should not refuse.

"All right. If you insist."

"Good! Sit down; I'll be right back."

I knew he really didn't want to be mother-henned, but I refused to let him neglect his health. I fixed him a plate and set it on the makeshift table he was sitting behind. Without another word, I left him to his solitary meal. Joseph Smith hated to be away from his family. He adored Emma and constantly worried about her. He had confided in me that he feared she wasn't as strong as she could be, mentally and physically, due to the loss of the babies they had had. The birth of Joseph III had helped, but Emma still felt unworthy to be his wife. He had never wanted anyone but Emma, though he could not convince her she was far better than he deserved. The weight of leaving her so often, plus leading a military endeavor, cast him into despair. I wished I could make his burdens lighter.

We spent all the next day walking. The weather was not too bad—though we all could have done without the humidity. My feet were swollen and blistered after our twenty-seven mile march the day before. The boots that, two days ago, were too big, seemed to be shrinking with every mile we walked. My only consolation was that everyone else's feet were in just as sad of shape as mine. Spirits were high, though, for the most part. Everyone felt as if we were essential in the redemption of our displaced brethren in Missouri. Joseph said there was more to this trip than fighting a war—but no one understood what he meant.

New Portage was fifty miles southwest of Kirtland. We arrived at dusk, greeted by those who had gone before us. Thankfully, they already had the evening meal ready for us. I was almost too tired to eat, but this time Joseph made sure I got a plate.

"One good turn deserves another," he said, smiling wearily at me.

I was assigned to the tent with the children, being the only woman in the company without a husband. The children were as tired as I was, and they spoke very little. There was no fighting about going to bed or needing to have three drinks of water. These children were exhausted. They did tell me their names before drifting off to sleep.

Diana Holbrook and her two cousins, Sarah and Charlotte, Sara Pulsipher, John, and Eunice Chidester, were all lying on their bedrolls, exhausted and dirty. One little girl was already asleep and the others were too tired to tell me her name before they drifted to sleep. I knew I'd learn it before the trip was over.

All the wagons we brought were loaded with supplies, which meant we all walked—including Joseph. He did have a horse, but he refused to ride when so many of us walked. Old Major, his American bulldog trudged along, staying quite close to Joseph. He was very protective and had a cantankerous nature. I thought he was a funny–looking dog. They made quite a couple, the handsome prophet and his ugly bulldog.

The trumpet was sounded at 4:00 A.M., calling everyone for morning prayers. Joseph insisted on total participation in the morning devotional; having spent three years in his home, I was accustomed to them.

Some people did not agree with him, for instance, Sylvester Smith. He was young, attractive, and humility was not part of his nature. He often acted as if he were much better than those around him, especially those in leadership positions. He was the loudest grumbler in the mornings.

"As the army of the Lord, Brother Sylvester, it is only right and proper that we begin our day offering our oblations to Him whom we serve," Joseph patiently explained to him one morning. I, myself, was tired of hearing him complain.

"I understand that, Brother Joseph, but it isn't even light yet."

"Quite true, but much needs to be done before daybreak. Everyone needs to be fed and we must break camp. I want to be ready to march when the sun rises."

"I think that's sound reason, Brother Joseph," Brigham Young interjected, not taking kindly to Sylvester's complaining, either. Sylvester muttered something under his breath and went to take down his tent. Brigham shook his head and Joseph clapped him on the back.

"Don't fret, Brother Brigham. Some people must have more lessons before they learn obedience. I'm just grateful to have friends like you to support me in whatever the Lord commands."

"That I will always do," Brigham testified.

Joseph smiled. "I know, Brother Brigham. I know."

Joseph organized the camp at New Portage. He was considered commander-in-chief. F.G. Williams was appointed paymaster and went about gathering all the monies in the camp to be disbursed as needed. Zerubbable Snow was chosen as commissary general which put him in charge of the food and cooking assignments. George A. Smith was asked to be quartermaster, helping Brother Snow with food. He also became an arms-bearer. More assignments would be made when we met up with Hyrum.

One hundred and thirty men were counted as part of Zion's Camp in New Portage. Twenty wagons loaded with supplies accompanied us. Joseph spent the day organizing, teaching, and preparing us for our journey as the Lord's army. He divided us into companies of ten to twelve and admonished us to select our own captain. I was in Joseph's company as one of the two cooks. There were also two firemen, two wagoners and horsemen, and a commissary. Joseph wanted us to resemble, as much as possible, a proper military outfit. He did his best to see to it that we were.

Slowly, ever so slowly, we marched, day after day, braving the elements. Ever so often, we were joined by more volunteers, which were gladly received. Some were German. It was a refreshing change to have saints among us who spoke with a German accent. If the weather was warm, we fought dust, flies, and scarcity of water. If it rained, we battled mosquitoes, trudging through knee-deep mud. I truly missed a paved road and a mini-van.

We hadn't been out more than nine days before contention broke out in the camp. Not surprisingly, it centered around Sylvester Smith. He constantly complained about the shortage of bread and questioned Joseph's authority. His attitude grated on others, causing ill feelings. Joseph warned the camp about contention and pride, but I was sure Sylvester Smith turned a deaf ear to his counsel. I was beginning to dislike him immensely.

Sometime along the way, we met up with Hyrum's group. Joseph and Hyrum were happy to see each other; Joseph told me later it was nice to have someone in the camp he knew was totally loyal.

"Of course there's always you and Brigham and Heber, but Sylvester Smith is certainly a trial to my patience," he said, smiling wearily.

"That's the understatement of the century," I quipped. Hyrum laughed and put an arm about my shoulders.

"I'm glad to see you haven't lost your sense of humor, Sister Jerree."

"You've arrived on a good day, Brother Hyrum." Hyrum shook his head and squeezed my shoulder fondly. It was good to have Hyrum close by again.

Our company was getting larger, and though there was strength in numbers, it also put a strain on our food supplies. Rations were made smaller, which of course caused some complaints. Guards were placed about the camp due to the fact we were constantly followed.

On the night of May 15th, Joseph found Moses Martin asleep at his post. Joseph took his sword and left him asleep. The next morning, Joseph convened a military court martial, though I doubt there was ever one held with such love and tenderness as Moses Martin's was. No anger or hostility was present. Brother Moses was truly repentant and begged for mercy.

"I was so tired. I tried to keep my eyes open, but I couldn't. It won't happen again, I swear, Brother Joseph," Moses Martin pled. Joseph smiled compassionately, nodding his head.

"I believe you, Brother Martin. Hyrum, please return Brother Martin's sword. As commander-in-chief of this army, I recommend an acquittal. All those in favor raise your right arm to the square." All the leaders of the companies had been called to assist Joseph in judging Moses. The vote was unanimous. Moses broke into tears as Joseph embraced him. I was thankful to have been able to witness Joseph's compassionate leadership. He was truly a great man.

"Now let me say a few words about the importance of guarding our camp. As we grow in numbers, our enemies become more and more nervous. They are continually plotting to find ways to stop us. The Lord expects us to protect ourselves while we march toward Zion. We are all tired but must do our utmost to fulfill our duties. Let us remember our cause and earnestly strive to accomplish the task to which we've been called."

"With such a soft leader, I doubt we'll ever do anything except waste time," Sylvester Smith muttered to someone standing next to him. I turned around and gave him an angry look.

"Joseph Smith is the strongest man I have ever known. It takes more strength to forgive than to punish."

Sylvester's eyebrows shot up; his cynical eyes roved from my face to my feet, his disdain for me quite apparent. "This from a woman who aspires to be a man." Snickers were heard from those close to him. I hadn't realized Brigham had come up behind me until his hand touched my shoulder.

"That's quite enough, Brother Sylvester. I'm sure you have more important things to do than insult fellow camp members. Sister Jerree, Brother Joseph is asking for you."

Sylvester huffed off, mumbling his dislike for Brigham under his breath. Brigham chuckled and took my arm, leading me toward Joseph's tent.

"You are a extraordinary woman, Jerree James. Are the pants worth the ridicule?"

"Oh yes! I'd hate to walk a thousand miles in a dress."

"Come to think of it, so would I—though I must confess I don't think I'd want Mary Ann dressed like a man." I looked up into Brigham's gray eyes and chuckled. I think dear Brother Brigham was slightly chauvinistic. Linking my arm through his, I gave him my most demure smile, reminding him that yes, I was a woman.

"Not to worry, I doubt she ever would. I don't know another woman who would."

"No truer words have been spoken, Sister Jerree …but then we realize YOU are very different from all the other women we know, aren't you?" I looked at him in surprise and wondered how much he knew of me … really. I laughed nervously and nodded.

"Quite right, Brother Brigham. I'm definitely different than anyone I've met in Kirtland …but of course I'm from farther east."

"Oh yes …farther east." He emphasized the word "east" and laughed merrily, enjoying his little game. Before I could say more, he opened the flap of Joseph's tent and announced my presence, thus leaving me to wonder about my dear Brother Brigham.

On the same day as Moses Martin's court martial, we passed through a stand of trees. There was an overwhelming sense of sadness through the entire grove. Just when I thought it was my imagination, Joseph stopped and turned to Hyrum who was walking beside him.

"Do you feel it, Hyrum?"

"What?"

"The sadness—the oppression?"

"Yes—but I thought it was just me."

"Oh no. I can feel it; you feel it too, don't you Jerree?" I nodded. "There has been much bloodshed close by. Whenever a man of God passes through a place where many have been killed, he will feel a deep sense of melancholy and will sink in spirit."

His blue eyes looked about him, seeming to see things none of the rest of us could. A look of sad compassion etched lines on his forehead. He sighed and walked on, all of us following him. About forty rods (660 feet) further we came out of the trees and onto a farm. A large mound of dirt stood to the left of us, tall enough to be a hill. To our surprise, many remains of human bones were lying on the surface.

"This must have been a burial ground," I breathed. Joseph climbed on top of the mound and stared out over the land. His face was serious and forlorn, his vision seeing through the veil of time to another era. When he came down, tears stained his face. Most of the men had lost interest and went back to getting the camp set up.

"Joseph? Are you all right?" I asked, touching his arm. He nodded, smiling down at me fondly.

"Such scenes of war—such ferociousness, such hate. Can't people learn from the past and not repeat the cycle? You must warn your people —convince them that hatred is the father of such misery. I mourn for those who died here and for those who will die in your time."

I squeezed the arm I was holding, trying to make him feel better. He smiled down at me and touched my face. It was a sweet gesture of a loving uncle to his niece and I took it as such. Standing on my tip-toes I placed a kiss on his cheek, which was still moist from his tears. We had been standing close to the trees, looking up at the mound. All around us people were busy, oblivious of us.

"Joseph!" Sylvester Smith barked, eyes flashing as he witnessed something he was not taking as innocent. I moved away from Joseph, who looked at Sylvester steadily, refusing to feel guilty under his scrutiny.

"Hyrum is looking for you," he said, his eyes going to me. It wasn't hard to know what he was thinking.

"Thank you. Come, Sister Jerree." Joseph took my arm, steering me clear of Sylvester. I could feel his eyes boring into my back as we walked away.

"I can't stand that man!" I hissed.

"That's not very charitable," Joseph replied, wryly.

"He's contentious, he's rude and he has a filthy mind. I don't know why he's even here. How can the Spirit attend us with men like that around?" Joseph stopped and looked at me seriously. I thought I could see disappointment is his eyes.

"Do you understand the purpose of this journey?" he asked. Hyrum had come up beside us, a hammer in his hand.

"To redeem Zion," I replied, puzzled at his question.

"True. And where is Zion?"

"Independence," I said.

Joseph smiled and looked at his brother. Hyrum was watching us curiously. "Brother Hyrum. Where is Zion?"

"Here, Joseph." He placed a massive hand over his heart. Joseph nodded and turned back to me.

"Zion is the pure in heart. Zion is where ever the Saints gather. WE are Zion and as we go, we too will be proved. Some may not pass the test, but we will, won't we?" He looked at both Hyrum and me. We nodded.

"Good. Now help George A. with supper, please Jerree? I must counsel with Hyrum. It looks like he's having problems with hammering." Hyrum chuckled and led Joseph off to another part of the camp. I walked toward the campfire where George A. was busy beginning the evening meal. I felt that Joseph was more disappointed in me than he was in Sylvester Smith. He expected certain things from me, and he would not let me forget it.

Once again I wondered how one could be so loving and patient with someone so horrible. I remembered how I felt about Eli and knew that I had much to learn. Would I ever learn that one important lesson? Would the Lord keep me in the past until I did? Was this the purpose of my going on this journey? It was probably a good thing I had no clue about how many hard lessons I would yet learn while marching with the prophet in Zion's Camp.

CHAPTER TWENTY

Saturday May 17th

It was Saturday night and everyone was looking forward to a day of rest. We had walked forty miles since Friday. Many feet were blistered and bloody. After two weeks, our feet were still tender. I helped care for many, my own feet wrapped in rags. I wanted to go back to my tent and sleep, but many more people needed attention.

I eventually found myself in Sylvester Smith's tent, unwillingly administering first aid to him. I avoided eye contact and tried to hurry. Two other men lay on their bedrolls, awaiting my assistance. As I tied the last bandage on Sylvester's foot, he bent over and took my left hand, staring down at my wedding rings. The diamond flashed in the light of the lantern beside me.

"That's a beautiful ring. Where did you get it?"

"From my husband," I replied, trying to pull my hand from his. He held on tightly, ignoring the irritated looks from the others.

"Just where is your husband?"

"Back east."

"Where?"

"Release my hand, Mr. Smith," I said, my heart pounding furiously. I couldn't believe he would attempt to do anything with witnesses around.

"Why should I? You say you're married, and yet you see nothing wrong with kissing the Prophet. I'm a Smith—one should be as good as another." I gasped and met his gaze, hating him for his insinuations.

"Joseph is my—cousin," I stammered and finally freed my hand.

Sylvester laughed snidely.

"By marriage. Aren't you related to Hyrum's wife?"

"Yes. And I have the highest regard for Joseph and Emma."

"I've noticed that." The look in his eyes angered me to the point that Joseph's little speech about Zion and the pure in heart seemed irrelevant. Before I could stop myself, I slapped his face, earning for myself a round of snickers from the other men.

I hurried out of the tent, disgusted with his filthy mind and his insinuations about Joseph and me. Before I could get very far, Sylvester grabbed my arm and swung me around, anger filling his face. I wondered how I had ever thought he was handsome. He had no beauty in him—at least not at that moment.

"Don't you ever do that again! You're dressed like a man, and I'll be tempted to hit you back."

"Keep your hands off me, and I will be happy to ignore you," I hissed.

"Only want the prophet, huh?" he growled. If I had had a free hand I would have slapped him again. As it was, George A. came to my rescue, taking Sylvester by the collar and pulling him backward. Sylvester swung around throwing a punch, which George A. deftly dodged.

"You've made a big mistake, boy," Sylvester yelled. A crowd gathered, eager to witness a fight. George A., though a boy, was much larger than Sylvester and only chuckled at the threat. Growling like an animal, Sylvester lunged and found himself in a perfect half-nelson. Everyone cheered, seeing Sylvester Smith receiving his comeuppance at the hands of a boy.

"Release him!" Joseph's voice boomed above the din. There was instant silence, though George A. held onto the angry man.

"Let him go, George A.," Joseph said, walking to the two men locked in battle. George A. obeyed his cousin, stepping back and allowing Sylvester to face Joseph alone. He was breathing hard and poised, ready to defend himself again.

"Why is there a fight in the middle of this camp?" Joseph asked, looking from Sylvester to George A. to me. I refused to look at anyone.

"Sylvester was offensive to Sister Jerree," George A. said, casting a fond look my way. I smiled at him but still avoided Joseph's gaze.

"Is that true?" Joseph asked.

"She slapped me!" Sylvester replied, reminding me of a child who had been caught doing something wrong. Joseph turned to me. I had no choice but to look up at him, though I refused to act guilty of any wrongdoing.

"Why did she slap you?" Joseph asked, trying to hide a smile from the crowd. His eyes spoke volumes though, and I knew that he was not as angry with me as he could have been.

"How should I know?" came the rebellious reply from Sylvester. There was a murmured outburst. One of the men from his tent stepped up and stared angrily at him.

"He was being rude! Quite offensive, really."

"Yes! He was accusing you and Sister Jerree of...of...impropriety," another man testified. Joseph's blue eyes flashed with anger as he turned to Sylvester, whose attitude was cold and defiant. Joseph's gaze swept the entire crowd, his massive chest rising and falling as he breathed angrily. I could tell he was trying to control his indignation at such an accusation. All were silent, everyone shocked that such a thing could happen.

"Is there another man here who wishes to make such an accusation? "he asked, looking at each person in the crowd. They all shook their heads adamantly. Joseph turned back to Sylvester.

"On what basis do you state your claim?" he asked, his eyes boring into Sylvester's.

"She claims to be married but no one has ever seen her husband. She conveniently resides in your home and is now a part of this foolhardy scheme of yours. And I...saw her kiss you yesterday." There was a collective gasp, and I wondered if the people were shocked that he would actually talk to Joseph this way or if they believed what he was saying. Joseph smiled and looked at him.

"Quite true. I was sorrowing over the state of wickedness in the world, and Sister Jerree was comforting me. She is a member of my family. I hold her in the same regard as my dear mother or sisters. I am, after all, a married man."

"Since when has that ever stopped a man before?" Joseph took a step toward his accuser but was pushed out of the way by Brigham Young who took Sylvester by the front of his shirt.

"Say another word and I'll flatten that nose of yours. I will hear nothing so foul against the Prophet or Sister Jerree again! I'll deck the first person who looks like they might spread such filth."

Joseph placed a hand on Brigham's shoulder. Brigham looked at his friend and released Sylvester.

"Thank you, Brother Brigham. I can only hope I will have many such friends as yourself. I am deeply saddened by the spirit of contention manifest in this camp. We are the Lord's army and as such we are bound to act with more brotherly kindness. If we cannot show a more Godly spirit, we will meet with misfortune, difficulties, and hindrances before we leave this place."

"This from a womanizing hypocrite of a prophet," Sylvester yelled. Brigham made a move toward him to make good his promise, but Joseph stopped him with a look.

"Brother Sylvester! You will cease these accusations this instant or I will whip you myself! They are pernicious lies, and you know it! I command you to go to your tent and be confined until morning!" Though he did not yell, even Sylvester knew he was serious and dared not press his luck. Brigham and George A. took hold of his arms and marched him to his tent. Joseph looked around sadly.

"I am not perfect. I have my faults, but I did not do that of which I have been accused. If anyone else believes those lies, I will be happy to mete out that which I promised Brother Sylvester." With that he turned and walked away, his head held high, though his eyes were filled with agony. Joseph hated to be called a liar and to have those whom were supposed to be his friends accuse him of things they knew he would not do. Hyrum escorted me to my tent, which I shared with the children.

"I'm sorry, Hyrum."

"For what?"

"For causing such a commotion. I'm so impulsive sometimes, and I did kiss Joseph."

"Yes, I know. But was it in the way that Sylvester claimed?"

"Of course not!" I replied, wondering what Hyrum was thinking.

"That's right; therefore you are not at fault. Sylvester is; he has a filthy mind and a rebellious spirit. Don't fret. Go in and get some sleep. It's been a hard day."

"That it has," I said as I headed for my tent.

*　　*　　*

154

Because it was Sunday, I donned a dress and stepped out of the tent while all the children were still asleep. My feet were aching and I was grateful I didn't have to walk very much that day. George A. was already up, adding wood to the fire.

"Mornin', Sister Jerree," he said, smiling fondly at me.

"Good morning, George. I never got a chance to thank you for your defense of me yesterday. Thank you."

"No thanks necessary. Sylvester was being horrible to you—and to Joseph. No man should speak to a lady as he did."

"I haven't dressed much like a lady lately," I replied, handing him a spoon to stir the mush.

"But you are, Sister Jerree. A true lady, in my book."

"Thank you, George. I'm so glad you are my friend." I squeezed his shoulder and left him there to tend to breakfast while I went in search of a bush to use as my bathroom door. Before I reached camp again, a shout went up which brought men running from all directions. Hurrying, I found a crowd gathered around the horses. Many were lying on the ground, moaning. Some horses limped about, obviously in great pain.

"What happened?" I asked. Hyrum shook his head despondently.

"They've foundered—all of them."

"How? There's no way they could have gotten too much to eat. No one has enough, not even the horses," I argued.

Joseph looked up at me from where he knelt by his horse. His eyes were filled with sadness, unfathomable as the ocean.

"It seems God is not pleased with us. I told you if we could not manifest a more Godly spirit we would meet with misfortune. We must now humble ourselves and beg for mercy. We have twenty wagons. We cannot pull them ourselves. This testifies that God rules over all things, that His eye is upon us. If we are contrite and humble, these horses will be restored to health." A shiver ran down my spine. I could hardly breathe; the Spirit filled me with such force that I dropped to my knees before I even realized it. Everyone else followed suit, praying mightily, feeling convicted in our sins. Sylvester was the only one who refused to kneel. I wondered just what it would take to humble him.

I didn't have long to wait until I learned just what would humble Sylvester Smith. By noon, all the horses were as good as

155

ever—all but one. Sylvester knelt beside his horse, tears streaming down his face. Joseph touched his shoulder. He refused to look at him.

"I'm so sorry, Joseph...so very sorry."

"As am I. I hope now we can try to be better brothers. Please forgive me for being angry."

Sylvester nodded and stroked his horse's head once more. Joseph helped him to his feet and quietly asked someone to take care of the horse. I watched in silence as Joseph helped the grieving man to his tent where he embraced him, turned him toward the tent's opening, and watched him as he went inside. It never ceased to amaze me how loving and forgiving Joseph Smith could be. He genuinely loved everyone, no matter how awful they had been to him. I knew I was witnessing the same type of love the Savior must have had for those around Him. I felt ashamed at my anger and vowed I'd try to follow the Prophet's example. How much I had to learn from my uncle. How weak I truly was. Sighing, I went to help George A. prepare lunch.

> "Pioneer children sang as they walked
> and walked and walked and walked.
> Pioneer children sang as they walked
> and walked and walked."

That Primary song echoed in my mind as I trudged, day after day, across Indiana. The heat became unbearable. Water became scarce, oft times having wigglers in it so that we'd have to strain it. Some of the men would even strain it with their teeth. I thought it was a miracle no one got sick from it.

Everyone seemed to be more concerned with getting sick from the local milk than from the water. Joseph promised that if we had faith we wouldn't contract any illness from the milk. I had faith but boiled the water and scalded the milk just the same.

Many of the men worried over the rumors they heard about residents of Indianapolis threatening not to allow us to pass through the city. Rumor had it that the governor was heard to say that he planned to have us dispersed. Joseph promised this would not happen.

"How can we be sure?" complained Sylvester. I looked at him in disbelief. It was amazing that he would forget God's power so soon. Joseph sighed.

"I say, in the name of the Lord, if we exhibit faith in God we will pass through Indianapolis unmolested," Joseph replied.

Nothing else was said to dispute Joseph. When we came close to the city, we separated into smaller groups and took different routes through it. I walked with George A., Wilford Woodruff, Sarah and Charlotte Holbrook, and Orson Hyde. We went right down the center of town without being noticed at all. That evening we gathered and had a good laugh. It felt good to laugh and joke with the members of the camp. We hadn't done much of that since we began our trek toward Zion. Of course, some people could not see the miracle in the event, and I won't bother to mention names.

✢   ✢   ✢

Prairie. I thought I knew what a prairie was; I had watched *Little House on the Prairie* and every western ever made with John Wayne. But I found out I didn't have a clue what a prairie was until we came upon it. Miles and miles of open, flat land, covered with waist-high grass. Never before had I seen such an empty, uninhabited place. There were no roads, no houses, and no livestock—just flat, grassy land as far as the eye could see.

A few deer were sighted in the distance. Being tired of corn mush, several men ran after them, misjudging the distance by several miles. We had no deer that night. Water was almost nonexistent and what little there was, even the animals refused to drink. In the heat, we slowly, thirstily, plodded over miles of prairie.

Finally, we came to a small creek. After watering the animals, we crossed the creek and soon found ourselves on a homestead. I wondered why anyone would want to live so far from civilization.

Mr. Wayne, the owner of the homestead, was a jovial man, as thirsty for news as we were for the water in his well. He was happy to share, and we were happy to fill him in on all we knew about the news of the day. It felt good to come across someone who was not antagonistic toward us.

We continued on until we reached the Embarrass River. We crossed over and set up camp a mile west, on a small branch of the river. It felt so good to wade through the water. The heat had been oppressive. Dust covered my clothes and was caked on my face and in my hair.

I don't mind saying I immersed myself in the water several times, clothes and all. Many of the men followed my example. George A. even started a water fight with some of the children. Joseph stood on the riverbank laughing, glad to see some joviality in the group.

After our respite we began to put up the tents. While we were busy, three rattlesnakes were found. Some of the men thought it would be great to shoot them. Joseph hurried to the group, commanding them in a booming voice to stop. All activity in the camp ceased.

"Let them alone! Don't hurt them! How will the serpent ever lose his venom, while the servants of God possess the same disposition and continue to make war upon it? Men must become harmless, before brute creation, and when men lose their vicious dispositions and cease to destroy the animal race, the lion and the lamb can dwell together and the sucking child can play with the serpent in safety."

Chills raced up my spine. I loved seeing Joseph in his prophetic mode. His face, already handsome, shone with a light that was not earthly, making him all the more beautiful in my eyes. How I loved him. It was apparent that most of the men were moved by his speech. Sticks were found and the snakes were carried across the river.

"Let us not kill a snake, bird, or any other animal on this journey unless we are obtaining food," Joseph counseled.

That evening, Parley P. Pratt and Amasa Lyman returned to camp. Parley's job was to recruit men for the march. They had been in Eugene, Indiana. About twelve men came with them from the Eugene Branch. Parley, ever the storyteller, had quite a tale to tell.

"It was the strangest thing," Parley said, enjoying the rapt attention of the audience gathered around the campfire that night.

"I hadn't slept much for a few days and I couldn't keep my eyes open. I stopped about noon and let the horse loose from the carriage to graze. I laid back to rest and was soon so sound asleep I could have probably slept the whole day and night."

"Right there in the middle of nowhere?" I asked. He nodded, taking another big bite of the beans on his plate.

"I had only slept a few moments when a voice, more piercing than I had ever heard, fell on my ear and thrilled through every part of my system. It said: 'Parley! It is time to be up and on your journey.' I jumped up so suddenly that I didn't know where I was or what I was even doing."

We all laughed at Parley's animated features. He loved telling a good story. During my time in 19th–century Ohio, he had been one of the most outstanding storytellers I ever heard. Joseph smiled, nodding thoughtfully. Noticing he was not laughing like we were, we quieted and waited for the Prophet to speak.

"It seems you were awakened by an angel of the Lord. I would venture to say that it was the very angel that goes before this camp. He found you asleep and woke you," Joseph said matter-of-factly, as if discussing angels was an ordinary occurrence. Of course, with Joseph Smith Jr., it was.

"An angel?" George A. asked in awe.

"Yes, this whole camp is guarded by angels. I have seen them many times—haven't you?" He directed his question to George A. but we all knew the question was for everyone. George stared at his cousin for a moment and then smiled.

"No," he answered honestly. "But I have felt them."

Joseph smiled and touched his face lovingly. "Of course you have."

Parley then entertained us with more of his stories. It felt good to think of something other than the trials we had had to endure thus far. I was very comforted to know angels were attending us. I had a secret desire to see one. If nothing else was learned on my march with Zion's Camp, it was to be careful what you wish for—you may just get it.

✻   ✻   ✻

"Men and their games," I thought, as I watched the entire camp participating in a mock battle. I think Joseph was having the most fun, though they all seemed to enjoy themselves. They reminded me of my boys playing soldiers in the back yard at home. I felt a stab of homesickness so acute I wondered how I could get through the rest of my journey through the past.

The men of Zion's Camp were surprisingly adept at military maneuvers, and there were times it looked too real. Heber C.

Kimball was the only causality; he cut his hand on someone's sword. Joseph cautioned them not to 'play' so rough.

Looking back, I think that Joseph wanted the men to expend some of their pent-up frustrations. These men had come so far thinking they'd have to see battle, and so far they'd only battled thirst and bugs and the elements. The real battles had been fought for them by the Lord. This, of course, did not sit well with some of the men.

CHAPTER TWENTY-ONE

Sunday June 1, 1834

This Sunday would be known in Church history as a "puzzling religious service." That is an understatement. As we drew nearer to Missouri, threats came more often and we took care to hide our true identity. Joseph insisted we call him Squire Cook. I couldn't help but smile every time someone called him that.

Even at this early time, Missourians did not like Joseph and there was always someone after his head. I was surprised by this. I thought Missourians started hating him much later than 1834. I began to fear for his life more than ever.

Because it was Sunday, we decided to hold worship services. There were many "Gentiles" in our midst that day. It amazed me that so many people would be curious about our little group. Someone said they counted up to a hundred. To throw them off, the services were as phony as a three-dollar bill. John Carter gave a classic Baptist sermon. Some of the Gentiles were confused. They had been so sure we were Mormons. Then Parley Pratt, who had once been a Campbellite preacher, spouted Campbellite doctrine. He seemed to be having so much fun, I asked him later why he was going on so.

"Fooling our enemies does give me a strange sense of satisfaction," he confessed. I smiled, handing him a tin plate of food. I truly liked Parley Pratt and his wonderful sense of humor.

We camped near a river, which I learned was the Illinois. (That seemed logical to me, since we were trekking through Illinois!) My heart was heavy as we traveled, knowing that in this state Joseph and Hyrum would lose their lives. Of course that was ten years down the road, but it didn't ease the pain of knowing it would happen. Rumors had filtered to us that we would never cross the Illinois River.

Undaunted, we began ferrying over on Monday, June 2nd. The ferryman was a cross, filthy man. He smelled of sweat and tobacco; his clothes probably hadn't been washed in a month. He ferried us across the river, then tried to cheat us by saying he had counted 500 men going over on his ferry. We could have only wished for that many men. Ignoring his smell, Joseph wrapped an arm around the man's shoulder and flashed him a brilliant smile. I wondered how he could stand so close to such a foul-smelling person.

"Now sir, I know I've only got 150 men under my command. I'm sure you're tired after getting us all across the river. Still, we'll pay for 150 men—no more."

The man looked into the Prophet's blue eyes and nodded, seemingly unable to withstand Joseph's charm. Joseph smiled, gave the man another squeeze, then turned to Fredrick G. Williams.

"Fredrick, pay this good man. Time's a wastin'."

As we pressed on, we came upon more high mounds of dirt, much like the ones we'd seen earlier. Several men, including Joseph, climbed to the top of the highest one. There was a wonderful view of the river, the trees lining it, and the prairie. Three altars made of stone were still partially standing. Human bones were strewn about the surface of the ground.

Joseph called for a shovel. After digging about a foot down, he discovered most of a skeleton, an arrowhead between its ribs. Burr Riggs asked if he could have the arrowhead, and Joseph gladly gave it to him after he had examined it.

Joseph stood by the grave for quite a long time, as if he were seeing something the rest of us couldn't. Many of the men speculated about the identity of the ancient man lying in the grave, but Joseph took the question to the Lord, who answered him in vision. Joseph gathered us and put our speculation to rest.

"The skeleton that was found belonged to a white Lamanite named Zelph. He was a great warrior and chieftain who fell in the last great battle between the Lamanites and the Nephites. The arrowhead found in his ribs was Lamanitish. The Lamanite curse had been taken from Zelph—in part—and he was a righteous man. He was thick-set and large, a great warrior and chieftain under the great Prophet Onandagus, who was known from the eastern sea to the Rocky Mountains."

Zelph's remains were again buried, minus the arrowhead. I stood for quite awhile by the freshly-covered grave, allowing my imagination to take me to a time long since gone where Lamanites and Nephites warred, and rumors of war abounded. This was solid proof that they did, in fact, exist. No one doubted Joseph's words, for while he told us Zelph's story, his face shone with the Spirit's light. We all rejoiced in the knowledge that we were led by a true and living prophet. We were humbled to realize that God would tell us about someone that had lived so long ago.

"Rest in peace, Zelph. Your life and mission will not go unknown," I whispered, bending to place a bouquet of wild flowers on the fresh earth covering the chieftain.

At noon on June 3, Joseph climbed up on a wagon to address the entire company. I'm sure the Lord had had more things to talk about with the prophet other than Zelph. Joseph began by expressing his love for all of us and pleading for more humility and faithfulness.

"We are on the Lord's errand, and we must strive to behave as He wants us to. The Lord has revealed to me that a scourge will come upon this camp in consequence of the fractious and unruly spirit among us, and we will die like sheep with the rot—but if we repent and humble ourselves, the scourge, in great measure, will be turned away. But—as the Lord lives—the members of this camp will suffer for giving way to their unruly temper."

Waves of shock shot through me as I listened to him prophesy. I knew that look, I knew that tone of voice; Joseph Smith, the Prophet, was not speaking idle words. He was warning all of us to be less contentious. I was as guilty as some of the others, especially when it came to my feelings toward Sylvester Smith. It took me a long time to go to sleep that night. Joseph's words kept ringing in my ears. I felt condemned in my sins. I did not doubt that a scourge would visit this camp, I just wished I knew what it would be…at least I did at that moment. I later found that ignorance can, at times, truly be bliss.

I tried to justify my feelings for Sylvester Smith with the fact that he was an ungrateful, hateful man, but I knew that wouldn't hold water in the end. My responsibility as a member of Zion's Camp was to show forth a greater love and tolerance for everyone—even him. Isn't that what Joseph did? Was he not following the Savior's example? Could I do less? I wondered if anger was ever justified by the Lord. I had a feeling the type displayed in our camp was not.

Some men complained saying they were tired of the march and Joseph's pitiful prophecies. Of course, Sylvester Smith was the loudest complainer. There were times I wanted to stuff a sock in his mouth just to shut him up. Couldn't he see he was treading on thin ice, taking some of the camp with him? Again I wondered how much tolerance God would show me in regard to my lack of charity.

Some of the men had done some work for a Colonel Ross. He paid them enough money to buy honey and a dozen hams. Though they weren't the freshest hams, the thought of having meat seemed wondrous after so many days without any. Unfortunately, I was in Joseph's company, and we sacrificed the meat to the others, eating corn meal mush and honey. Joseph never wanted it to seem that his company got preferential treatment, and there wasn't enough meat to go around. Sighing, I sat down beside George A. and began to eat my mush. I doubted I'd ever eat corn meal mush again once I finished with this trip.

Before we finished our meal, two hams were tossed in front of the tent we were in. "We don't eat stinking meat," someone growled as they stomped off. I gasped and looked at Joseph. He turned to Zebedee Coltrin and replied,

"Brother Coltrin, would you be so kind as to see what has been delivered to our door?" His sapphire eyes flashed with anger, though his voice was clear and steady. One thing Joseph could not stand was ingratitude. Zebedee nodded and went to the door of the tent, peering out.

"Looks like two hams, Joseph." He bent and lifted one, inspecting it intently. "The outside looks rough but I'll wager they're not bad clear through," he said hopefully. Everyone looked eagerly at Joseph. My mouth watered at the thought of ham as dessert.

"Then let's cut off the bad parts and have a proper feast. George and Jerree, could you help?"

"Gladly!" we replied in unison.

I lay in my bedroll full and content for the first time in days. It seemed it had only been moments since I had climbed into bed when a guard brought a man to Joseph's tent, announcing Luke S. Johnson's return to camp. He had gone to talk to several influential men. We were so close to Missouri that the Missourians were getting nervous. They didn't want us there and were trying to stop us. Luke had been given letters and told that 400 men waited on the Missouri side of the river, ready to "use up" the camp.

Joseph felt uneasy after Luke's report and refused to rest, preferring to keep sentry himself, patrolling the entire camp several times. Just before midnight, gunshots were heard, first in the east, then in the west—like some sort of signal. Joseph woke everyone, ordering us to be alert and ready to defend ourselves at a moment's notice. I spent many frightful hours, standing close to Brigham and Hyrum, wondering just what the Missourians would do. Nothing else happened, but we spent a long night up and ready, just in case.

June 4th found us ferrying across the Mississippi River toward Missouri. The river was a mile across with an island in the middle. We set up camp on this island, which I later learned was called Snye Island. Some men wanted to hunt in the trees but Joseph advised them against it. They disregarded his advice and came back to camp with quite a few eggs.

"My mouth is waterin' for a fresh omelet," Sylvester said, holding several eggs in his hands. I must admit, an omelet sounded heavenly.

"I wouldn't eat those if I were you," Joseph said, coming to stand beside me, inspecting the eggs. I groaned inwardly; so much for an omelet. "Those are snake eggs. You'll be sick if you eat them."

"They're turtle eggs. Several turtles were seen close to where these were found," Sylvester argued. I looked at Joseph hopefully. He smiled but shook his head.

"Nevertheless, they are snake eggs and not fit to be eaten." That was good enough for me. A prophet had spoken and I wasn't about to disregard his counsel. Sylvester snorted, stomping off, muttering something about blind faith and sheep. Joseph sighed and took my arm, heading toward Brigham and Hyrum. Of course the eggs were eaten, against the advice of Joseph, and soon all those who disregarded his words were terribly sick. Joseph said nothing, but refused to administer to the disobedient, letting them suffer the consequences of their own actions. He also let those who were sick look after themselves. I was grateful I had obeyed Joseph's words; I slept quite well that night.

It took two days to get across the Mississippi. We camped on the Missouri side in a grove of oak trees. Hostility prevailed in the camp, brought on by disobedience and sickness. Joseph became depressed; those who had become sick were blaming him. They muttered and whined against him. He hated being talked about and anger among the brethren grieved him. When everyone finally made it to the Missouri side and camp was set up, Joseph "rose up" and began to address us. Old Major, Joseph's bulldog, stood protectively at his heels, growling ferociously. He seemed to sense the hostility of some of the men toward his beloved master and didn't appreciate it.

I thought Old Major looked a lot like a pit bull and wondered just what would happen if someone really came at Joseph. I doubt they'd get too far with that dog around. His mere presence in camp incensed some people, especially Sylvester. Old Major disliked Sylvester the most—and who could blame him? Some of we humans could hardly stand to be around him, either.

"I am deeply saddened by the hostile spirit manifest in this camp. The Lord is displeased, also. As the army of Israel we should show brotherly kindness and love at all times. Instead we fight and quarrel and threaten one another. Let me explain. If any man insults me or abuses me, I will stand in my own defense at the expense of my life, and if a dog growls at me, I will let him know that I am the master."

Before Joseph began speaking, Sylvester had been checking the horses. He returned as Joseph was talking about the dog. Thinking Joseph was singling him out, his face turned beet red. He pointed a shaky finger at Old Major, who growled ominously.

"If that dog bites me, I'll kill him!" he yelled, earning for himself another deep-throated growl from the dog at Joseph's heels. Joseph swung around, his massive chest rising and falling in righteous anger. I think he was at the end of his rope with Sylvester Smith. Joseph seldom got angry—really angry—and it was something to behold. It reminded me of the story of the Savior's cleansing the temple.

"If you kill this dog, I'll whip you," Joseph breathed, his voice very soft but effective. My heart was beating hard against my chest. Everyone could feel the tension between the two men.

"If you lay one hand on me..." Sylvester began. Before he could finish, Joseph was in front of him, his gaze silencing the man.

"This is exactly the type of spirit that drives away our God and His protection. I'm ashamed to say that I was a part of this wicked and un-Christian conduct. The very thought offends the eyes of truth and justice." His voice was barely above a whisper but we all heard his words. With a sigh and a look of genuine pain he turned and walked toward his tent, Old Major at his heels. A look of intense hatred played across Sylvester's face, and my blood ran chill.

"The Lord has revealed to me that a scourge will come upon this camp in consequence of the fractious and unruly spirit among us and we will die like sheep with the rot."

I had no idea what the "rot" was but Joseph's words echoed in my mind, and I felt sure his prophecy would come to pass.

While we marched toward Zion, the Saints there were trying to seek redress from the government. Letters were sent back and forth to Daniel Dunklin, governor of Missouri. He was sympathetic to the plight of the Mormons, even stating:

"A more clear and indisputable right does not exist, than that of the Mormon people, who were expelled from their homes in Jackson County, to return and live on their lands."

Dunklin then tried to convince them to give up the lands refusing, to take sides with either party. This indecision gave the mob courage to continue to harass the Saints. Rumors ran rampant about a huge army coming to help the Mormons. Had the Saints in the East heeded the call to send men and money, we could have had a great army, but as it was there were probably only 200 men. This fact weighed heavily on Joseph, who had hoped for so many more.

Some of the politicians of the 19th century were just as greasy as politicians in my day. Promises were made to help reinstate the Saints to their lands and in the end were not kept. Dunklin ordered General Lucas to return the firearms the militia had taken in November. Lucas resigned. I heard he was a real Mormon-hater.

On Saturday, June 7th, we arrived at the place called Salt River. We camped near a spring in the woods. A branch of the Church had been established nearby. We spent five days here, washing clothes, inspecting firearms, organizing the camp, and drilling the men in military maneuvers. We all needed the rest. Orson Hyde and Parley Pratt were sent to Jefferson City to talk to Governor Dunklin, to see if he was going to help the Saints. He, of course, did the great political sidestep.

Now that we were in Missouri, we were constantly followed by the mob and harassed. We traveled on, hoping to get to Jackson County in one piece. Orson and Parley returned on June 15th, reporting that the governor did indeed refuse to help reinstate the Saints on their lands. This news cast a depressive pall over the entire camp.

"We were in perils and threatened all the while, we were much troubled to get provisions, and had to live principally on corn meal and were glad to get that," Joseph wrote.

I was not glad. I hate corn meal mush—johnnycakes—or anything like it. But I did eat it to keep up my strength for walking day after day. I would have given my diamond ring for a T-bone steak.

We traveled onward, crossing a river called the Chariton, camping on the west side. Edward Partridge came into camp, having come from Clay County.

"Edward! It's so wonderful to see you! You look so good! How's your family?" Joseph asked, drawing his friend into a bear hug.

"We're all fine, no thanks to the mob. They refuse to stop harassing us. It has done one good thing, though. I don't think we've ever been so close—as a people, I mean. I'm proud to say we are united as a church.

"That warms my heart. I wish I could say the same for this camp. Come, we need to gather the brethren to hear your report," Joseph replied, linking arms with Edward and leading him to the heart of the camp

We crossed the Grande River on the 16th. The ferryman was another dishonest soul who tried to cheat us. Joseph again talked the price down. It was hot, no air was stirring, and thunderclouds were boiling overhead. We all hoped it would rain because we hadn't had decent water in days. When it finally did rain, we caught water in hats and even drank from the tracks of the horses. I really wished for a Brita water filter as I took a drink from George A.'s hat.

Martin Harris, often a proud and boastful man, did a stupid thing by playing with a snake he found, teasing it with his bare feet. Naturally the snake got tired of the ill treatment and bit Martin on the left foot. Martin was horrified, begging someone to get Joseph. When Joseph heard the story, he invited me to join him in seeing to Martin. He then took his time, stopping to visit several people before he reached Martin's tent. Martin was flushed and terrified by the time Joseph lifted the flap and entered.

"Oh, Joseph! Please bless me! I know I'm going to die if you don't!"

Joseph knelt beside him, looking him over sternly. Martin quickly realized that he was angry. He grabbed Joseph's hand and began to weep.

"I'm so sorry—I was just—"

"I know what you were doing, Martin. You were puffed up in the pride of your heart and tempted the Lord and the snake. How preposterous of you to provoke that snake to bite you. How can you expect to have any claim on God's promises if you tempt Him?"

"I know—I'm sorry—please forgive me!" Martin gasped hysterically, squeezing Joseph's hand until his knuckles were white. Joseph pried his hand from the frightened man and motioned for one of the other men to come and help him administer to Martin. When the blessing was over, Martin lay quietly on his bedroll, breathing more easily. Tears fell from his eyes as he stared up at the Prophet.

"Thank you," he whispered.

"Don't thank me—thank the Lord—and don't do anything so foolish again," Joseph said tenderly. Martin nodded and drifted to sleep.

CHAPTER TWENTY-TWO

Tuesday June 17, 1834

We crossed another river by ferry and were informed that a mob was gathering to attack us in the night.

"I don't think we should stay here tonight," Joseph said, looking about him in concern. Ahead of us lay the prairie, at least twenty-three miles of it.

"But there are no trees or water out there!" Sylvester growled angrily, pointing out toward the prairie. "We don't have much food or water! I can't believe you would even suggest going on."

A group of men gathered around the two men, some dumbfounded that Sylvester would dare oppose the Prophet. Joseph turned to Hyrum, whose eyebrows were cocked in surprise.

"I think we should gather some food and water and continue for eight or ten miles. What do you think, Hyrum?"

"I know, in the name of the Lord, that it is the best if we go on," Hyrum answered, sending chills down my spine at his quiet response. Joseph nodded and slowly turned, looking at each person standing around them.

"All right. You're the oldest and I know you speak the truth. Start gathering wood and filling everything you can with water. We leave within the hour."

Excited conversation began as Joseph walked away. I followed him, accompanied by Hyrum, Brigham, and George A. I was busy gathering wood when Lyman Wight stomped past me and rudely let himself into Joseph's tent.

"What are you doing, Joseph? Are you trying to get us all killed? We should stay close to the river!" Lyman didn't even try to keep his voice down.

"The Spirit says otherwise, Lyman," I heard Joseph reply calmly.

"You mean Hyrum says otherwise!" Lyman countered.

"Brother Lyman, I am telling you that the Spirit has whispered that it is not safe to stay here, and we will heed that warning!"

"I am the general of this army and I say NO!" Lyman's voice rose in pitch until he fairly squeaked out the word "no". I wished I could have been in the tent to see Joseph's face. I was sure his eyebrows arched, his jaw clenched, and his blue eyes flashed.

"I'm the commander–in–chief, general, and the Lord's anointed. We will move on." There was no questioning the authority in Joseph's voice. I doubted that even Sylvester would have had anything to say at that moment. Lyman stomped off, so angry he didn't notice my smile. Joseph did, though, and winked. I stifled a giggle and went about my work, loving the way Joseph could see the humor in almost any situation. He was definitely my hero, forceful but compassionate, kind but even willing to offend for the Lord's sake.

As we began to march onto the prairie, Sylvester pompously stood in the middle of the road, trying to convince the men to stop.

"Are you going to follow your general or some other man?" he asked as we passed. About twenty men stopped, aligning themselves with Lyman and Sylvester. Joseph forged ahead, refusing to acknowledge the mutinous behavior of two of his men. I wanted to sucker-punch Sylvester but followed the Prophet's example and just ignored them.

We made a camp about eight miles from the river—without Wight's men. It was hot and water was scarce. I wondered if I would ever again get enough water to drink. Two powder kegs had been filled with water but the water was gross. The water standing in puddles was full of wigglers. It looked as though we could spend another night without water. I was glad the animals had been watered at the river. I wondered how the other camp was doing.

Wight's camp showed up about eleven P.M., apparently not willing to stay by themselves for the entire night. Joseph gathered them together and reproved them.

"This is the army of Israel and though we are divided into companies we are led by Christ, who is our head. When His Spirit whispers, it behooves each of us to obey. General Wight—never disobey me again!"

"I won't Joseph—I promise it. I'll stand by you forever," Lyman answered contritely. Joseph smiled and extended a hand, which Lyman gladly took. Everyone seemed pleased—everyone but you know who.

George A. arrived at my tent early the next morning, winded and concerned. "Sister Jerree!" he wheezed, "Could you please come quick! Joseph is sick!"

"Oh no! I'll be there in a moment, George," I cried, pulling on my boots and scraping off more scabs than I should have. Rushing from the tent, I followed George to Joseph's tent. Joseph lay inside, listless and pale. I placed a hand on his forehead. He was burning up.

"Joseph, what can I do for you?" I asked, brushing a lock of hair from his eyes.

"Water—I need water," he croaked through cracked lips. Tears filled my eyes.

"There's not much," I whispered.

"I know," he replied, trying to smile. He took my hand and gave it an affectionate squeeze. As sick as he was, he was still trying to comfort others.

"Have you had a blessing?" I asked.

"Not yet; George went to get some of the brethren."

"When did you eat last?"

"I don't know," he moaned.

"Just rest. I'll be right back," I said. Outside everyone was beginning to break camp. I found Jesse, a cousin of George A. and Joseph. I asked him to find some water.

"There's none that's any good," he said. Jesse was young, maybe even younger than George A. He was sweet, unassuming, and ready to help whenever he was needed. I liked him as much as any of the Smiths. I smiled and put a hand on his shoulder.

"I know; just get me some. I want you to take it and boil it, strain it and bring it to me as soon as you can. Joseph is very sick. He needs some water."

"Sure thing, Sister Jerree," he replied.

I squeezed his shoulder and hurried away, looking for
Zerubabel Snow, who was in charge of the food for the camp. I asked
him what was available.

"All we have is cornmeal," he replied sadly.

"There's no meat at all?"

"No, Sister Jerree," he said apologetically.

"All right, then we need to send someone hunting. Brother
Joseph is very sick, and he needs something more nourishing than
cornmeal."

"Hunting? I doubt there's any big game around here."

"Probably not, but there's bound to be rabbits or ground
squirrels or snakes! Just get me some meat," I ordered, in no mood
for excuses.

"Well, Hyrum Stratton found two snakes just this morning,"
Brother Snow said, his eyes lighting up, "but they were carried out
of camp."

I groaned. Joseph was adamant about treating snakes with
respect and he had insisted each man in camp be obedient to this
edict. No one wanted to go through what Martin Harris had gone
through. I looked at Zerubabel and smiled.

"Well then, go find them. I'm sure Brother Joseph won't mind if
we used our serpent friends to help him get better." I walked away,
Zerubabel Snow shaking his head and running a hand through his
hair. When I reached Joseph's tent, Jesse stood with a bucket
teaming with wigglers. I looked at it and sighed.

"Don't forget to boil and strain it," I said as I lifted the flap to the
tent and entered. Lyman Wight, Hyrum, and Brigham stood around
Joseph's bedroll, listening to their leader.

"We need to keep moving. We are not safe here...until we reach the
Saints in Clay County. Lyman, take command and get this army marching."

Brushing past the men and going to Joseph's side, I touched his
forehead and found that he was still burning with fever. "You are
burning up, Joseph. You can't march today. Are you sure you want
Lyman..." Joseph silenced me with a glance, his physical misery
apparent in his face.

"Heber has offered to let me ride in his wagon. Don't worry,
Sister Jerree. I trust General Wight. He repented of his folly and I
know he'll be obedient. Now brethren, get going."

174

The tent emptied in a moment, leaving me to minister to Joseph in peace. He smiled up at me, his fondness for me showing in his blue eyes.

"You are a true friend, Jerree. I'm grateful for your support. But you must try to find a bit more tolerance for those with less valor than yourself."

"Oh, Joseph, I have no valor. But what Lyman did was inexcusable! He should never have listened to Sylvester."

"True, but it is not for us to judge. Better to leave that to God. There's so much more to worry about."

"You're right, like getting you better." Jesse came into the tent holding a mug of steaming water. I cooled it and offered it to Joseph. He drank it greedily, ignoring the stream that trickled down his chin. Jesse left me to my ministrations, saying that he'd be close if I needed him. I nodded, turning my attention back to Joseph.

"Where....?"

"Don't worry about that. Just know that sometimes my 20th-century knowledge is advantageous." Joseph nodded and sighed contentedly. Brother Snow arrived with freshly cooked meat, refusing to meet Joseph's eyes. I smiled warmly at him, gratefully taking the plate from him.

"Thank you, Brother Snow."

"Don't thank me yet. Let's see how Brother Joseph appreciates it."

"He will," I assured him, and smiled as he left the tent. Joseph ate the meat with relish, commenting on the scarcity of meat and my ability to get things that were unavailable.

"You're not the only one who can perform miracles," I teased. He laughed weakly.

"Maybe you should have been general," Joseph quipped, taking another bite of his food.

"I'd be a lot more loyal than some. In 1990, I actually could be a general, but I doubt the men of this century would take too kindly to listening to me. I'm content to be of service to you—and Zion."

"If every person in this camp felt as you do there'd be no contention. I think, dear Jerree, that you are beginning to understand the great reason for your presence here."

I took his plate from him and stood. "Get some rest. I'll check on you a little later."

He nodded and lay back, grateful to be fed. I worried about him all day as we marched toward Clay County. I hated to be away from him but I had other duties, so I did not see him again until the evening. Heber had driven slowly so that he wouldn't jostle Joseph too much. When the wagon train stopped for the evening meal, Joseph insisted on getting up to inspect the camp. His brow was knit together with worry.

"We're not safe here. The mobs in several counties are gathering together to come against us. I can't feel right about staying here."

Deep in thought, he moved toward the thick hazel brush. I hurried to him, taking his arm in my hand.

"Joseph, you need to go back to bed. You still have a fever," I pleaded, touching his forehead. He covered my hand with his, smiling fondly down at me.

"Thank you for your concern, Sister Jerree, but I need to commune with my Father more than I need to rest." I watched him enter the brush and knew all would be well; there was a prophet in our midst.

We ended up staying the night there, receiving peace of mind from Joseph who had been assured by the Spirit that we'd be safe through the night. Early the next morning, we hurried onward, marching quite quickly for nine miles.

We were warned by a black woman, working in a garden, that a company of men was waiting to kill us as we passed through Richmond. I was shocked to find out that Missouri was a slave state and that the woman was a slave. Having been raised in another century by parents who taught me that prejudice was wrong, I was horrified to actually see the reality of slavery. Tears stung my eyes as Hyrum explained these things to me.

"Don't you have slaves in 1990?" he asked, seeing my distress.

"No. Joseph's prophecy on war has been fulfilled. Though some countries still have slaves, the blacks in America are free."

"I'm glad," he said.

We stopped for breakfast close to a farm. Sometimes Christian behavior is found in the least likely places. Missouri, in 1834, was not a tolerant place for Mormons, so kindness from a citizen was a welcome surprise. Milk was offered to the entire camp by the owner of the farm. Brother Snow had found some bacon to purchase. We had quite a feast with cornmeal pancakes, bacon, and fresh milk.

Joseph thanked him profusely, offering to pay for the milk. He flatly refused saying, "He is a mean man that will sell milk; I could have let you have more, if I had known you were coming. You have many enemies about here, and you may meet with some trouble. It's a damned shame that every man can't come up and enjoy his religion and everything else without being molested."

"My sentiments, exactly," Joseph countered, extending a hand to the man. They shook hands, Joseph leaving a blessing on him, and we were off again.

Some people would say we were plagued with bad luck, but I think things happened the way they did to show who was in charge. Joseph wanted to leave this part of Missouri so he urged us on. We hadn't gone very far when several wagons broke down.

Because it would take longer than a few hours to fix them, Joseph surveyed the area and chose a spot to make camp. He was still weak, but his fever was gone and he insisted on taking command again. He walked to the top of a bluff, which overlooked the Big Fishing and Little Fishing Rivers. An abandoned church stood on the bluff. I thought it seemed strange to have a building there, but before the night was finished, I was grateful for it.

JERUSHA

CHAPTER TWENTY-THREE

"Sister Jerree! Come quick! Brother Joseph says you're to go with the other women and children!" Jesse Smith hurried to me, his chest heaving and nostrils flaring with fear. I was busy making corn dodgers. My hands were caked with corn meal, my hair plastered to my head from sweat. In the middle of June, Missouri was sweltering. There wasn't much of a breeze or a cloud in the sky, though I would have welcomed a bit of rain just then.

"What's wrong?" I asked, fear shooting through my body at the look on his face. I put my arm around his waist, trying to give him a bit of comfort.

"Missourians! Five of them! They're riding toward us! Joseph wants all the women and children to take shelter in the old church." My heart leaped to my throat. Wiping my hands on my apron, I took Jesse's hand and ran with him toward the church building. The rest of the women and children of the camp were already there, huddled together in a corner. I hurried to Mary Chidester whose children, John and Eunice, were clinging to her, whimpering. Jesse stayed as close to as he dared without looking cowardly.

"It'll be all right; Brother Joseph is in charge. He won't let anything happen to us," I soothed. Mary nodded, swallowing hard. "Jesse, sit down here next to Sister Mary. I need to find George A."

Several of our men entered the building to guard us. Guns in hand, they stood by the windows, watching intently.

"Has anyone seen George A.?" I asked.

"He's with Joseph," someone replied. I nodded and started toward the door. One of the men stepped in front of it, refusing to let me pass.

"I've got to find George," I said, my voice trembling with fear. The guard shook his head, his eyes filled with compassion.

"Sorry, Sister Jerree. Joseph said no one is to go outside, especially the women. He'll take care of the boy. Just go over there and stay out of the way."

Sighing, I made my way back to the Chidesters. Jesse smiled up at me, taking my hand, and helping me to the floor.

It seemed like hours, waiting, inside that Baptist church, wondering about our fate. It was extremely hot; sweat flowed from every brow. We knew five Missourians were not much of a threat…but where there were five there were bound to be more. Finally, Joseph entered the church, George A. trailing close behind. I sighed in relief. Joseph smiled at us reassuringly, though I could tell he was still quite concerned.

"Sisters, brethren, our guests came to inform us that we will be receiving quite a welcome party. Several counties have joined together to try and discourage us from crossing the river and reaching the Saints." Several people gasped in fear. Joseph raised a hand, silencing them in one action.

"Have no fear. We are the Lord's army and He is mindful of us. I want the women and children to stay close to this building. These brethren will stay to protect you…."

At that precise moment a clap of thunder interrupted Joseph's speech. We all rushed to the windows and were shocked to see dark storm clouds roiling in the distance, moving toward us at an alarming speed. I sought Joseph's eyes. He watched the clouds with rapt fascination, looked down at me, smiled and winked. The fear in my heart lifted. I smiled back at him, knowing that this was no ordinary storm. Joseph patted my face, went around to all the women and children, and gave them words of comfort. He then asked George to follow him. They left the church. I followed after them, ignoring the protests of the others. I hurried to the edge of the bluff, looking toward the confluence of the Fishing Rivers.

Several Missourians had ferried to our side of the river. The ferry was on its way back, where several hundred men waited to ford the river. With a pounding heart, I looked to the northwest in disbelief. Minutes before, there had been no clouds in the sky, but now it was covered with dark, menacing, mountainous clouds. Wind, rain, and hail began to pelt the ground, accompanied by lightning and loud blasts of thunder. Before we knew it, tents were being blown down and bedding and clothes scattered, getting soaked. Joseph turned around, his eyes registering surprise at seeing me outside.

"Get back to the church building!" Joseph commanded, taking my arm and turning toward the church. "George, go with her and see to it that she stays!"

"Yes, sir." George took my hand and tried to get me to follow him.

"Joseph! Where are you going?" I yelled.

"No questions, Jerree! I expect you to obey me!" Joseph replied and took off toward some of the other men, shouting orders, helping keep track of the animals. George and I ran to the church. I looked back only when I got to the door. This definitely was no ordinary storm—and I knew now how the Lord was going to fight our battles. As I entered the safety of the church, I sent a thankful prayer heavenward.

Before long, the church was filled with wet, anxious people. Those who couldn't get inside found shelter under wagons. Joseph finally came in, shaking water off his clothes and hat.

His eyes were shining with excitement, his handsome face smiling. "Boys, there is some meaning to this," he said. "God is in this storm."

He could hardly hold back his excitement. I imagined Moses must have looked similar to this as the Red Sea parted to save the children of Israel from Pharaoh's army. There was no fear in the Prophet, only anticipation of what the Lord would do for his little army.

The storm lasted for hours. Wind and rain pelted the little church we were in. The children squealed as thunder rumbled and lightning flashed. Even George A. and Jesse sought me out, sitting close—saying they wanted to make sure I was all right. I smiled at them, knowing how frightening a storm could be for children. In spite of Joseph's excitement, fear prevailed, until I could stand it no longer. Jumping up, I looked around, took a breath and began to sing the first song that came to mind.

"A mighty fortress is our God
"A tower of strength ne'er failing."

Joseph turned. He had been standing by a window, watching the storm with Hyrum and Lyman. Smiling broadly, he joined me.

"A helper mighty is our God
O'er ills of life prevailing."

Soon everyone was singing, the fear dissipating as the Spirit descended within our midst. I felt warmed by its sweetness, and tears flowed down my cheeks. Jesse stood, taking my hand, singing lustily. George joined us, taking my other hand.

"He overcometh all,
He saveth from the fall.
His might and power are great.
He all things did create.
And He shall stand reign forevermore."

Friday June 20th, 1834

Lightning lit the sky through the night, and thunder made the earth shake, but the calm of the morning was almost as deafening as the night's storm. Zion's Camp rose, marveling at the mighty battle God had fought for us. Very little hail had fallen in our camp; though we were drenched and weary, we were all safe and unharmed. That was more than we could say for the Missourians.

For nearly a mile all around us, crops had been destroyed, limbs torn from trees, the trees themselves grotesquely twisted from the force of the wind. The river was full and rising—Joseph said at least thirty feet.

There wasn't a Missourian in sight. We heard later that one man died, hit by lightning; another lost his hand trying to hold onto his frightened horse. The Missourians said if that was the way God fought for the Mormons, they might as well go about their business.

Standing on the bluff, I was amazed at the destruction surrounding us. Heavenly Father didn't mess around when he decided to fight for His people. All this devastation was biblical in nature. My heart went out to those people who were the targets of such tremendous indignation. Is this how Moses felt in the wake of the Red Sea incident? How did Joseph feel? I didn't have long to wait to find out.

Joseph gathered the entire camp and we bowed before God, giving thanks for His mercy. The injured Missourians were prayed for, as were their families. Tears streamed down my face, knowing that the Prophet Joseph Smith felt no malice toward those who were trying to harm us. How grateful I was to have been a witness to his love for God's children, no matter who they were.

After the prayer, all the men were ordered to gather for a weapon's inspection. I began to prepare breakfast, the other women following suit. Each man was to shoot his rifle to ensure the gun was dry. Most shots were good, proving that the men could care for their firearms even in a deluge.

Everyone was still in a state of shock as they looked about. Even Sylvester was subdued. There was no way to doubt the power of God. It was evidenced in all we saw. Joseph came to me, standing close to the fire, watching my preparations as if he'd never seen cooking before. I finally stood, looking at him questioningly.

"What is it, Joseph?"

"You are a brave woman," he said quietly. I smiled, patting him on the arm, and turned back to my work.

"I am related to a prophet, you know," I said flippantly. He chuckled, shaking his head.

"You have an inner strength that is more than blood. Thank you for what you did last night."

"I sang a song. Nothing more."

"And that was just a little rainstorm we were going through."

"All right...thank you. It means more than I can say to know that you think I'm brave."

"It means a lot to me that you trust me and my words. I'm glad you came...and I don't mean just on this march." He reached down, touching my cheek, a look of pure love shining in his sapphire eyes. A lump formed in my throat. I wanted nothing more than to fling my arms around him and sob into his chest, but I knew there'd be trouble if I did, never mind that I was old enough to be his mother and was feeling the tenderness of a mother toward a great and honorable son. I settled for nodding and placing a small kiss on the palm of his hand. Then, so as to keep people from talking, I turned back to my cooking, tears pricking my eyes.

Joseph Smith, a prophet, my great-uncle, approved of me. He was one of the greatest, most wonderful men that walked this earth and he approved of me. What more could I ever ask for? Only to have the Savior look at me one day as His prophet had.

We traveled five miles that day. No one was willing to stay too close to the Fishing Rivers. No sense tempting the Missourians to get their dander up. A few men were sent ahead to try to procure food for the camp. We set up camp early that afternoon so everyone could rest. Zion's camp was suffering from "post-traumatic stress syndrome."

Saturday found us entertaining a Colonel Sconce and two political leaders from Ray County. They had come to find out what our intentions were, seeing "there is an Almighty power that protects this people."

Joseph laughed heartily, extending his hand, gripping the colonel's shaking one. He seemed uneasy to be in our camp. Joseph called for a stool to be brought.

"Bring these gentlemen some water, too," he requested. The three men looked at me in surprise as I served their drinks. I had forgotten that a woman in pants was such a novelty in 1834. Joseph chuckled, putting an arm around my shoulders.

"This is a cousin of mine. Colonel Sconce, may I introduce you to Sister Jerree James. She's invaluable to me on this march." I extended my hand and demurely greeted the colonel. He stuttered a greeting, his face beet red. I smiled sweetly and went about my work. Joseph was having a great time watching their discomfort.

"I started from Richmond, in Ray County, with a company of armed men, determined to destroy you. The storm kept us back," Colonel Sconce said, still trembling, obviously terrified of the Lord's army. Joseph nodded, rising, looking at the three men before him.

"Gentlemen, I will not deny that God has fought our battles for us, for I know He has. We have not come here as enemies of Missouri, but to bring relief to our fellow saints. They have been driven from their homes, robbed of their belongings, and left homeless to fend for themselves—all this for the sake of our religion. We want only to help our brethren and to furnish necessary goods, which they now lack. Yes, we wish them reinstated on their lands, which they purchased legally, but we intend no harm to any one."

"Why are you armed then?" one of the men asked, his eyes darting back and forth to the armed men standing around Joseph.

"What man or group of men goes into the heart of his enemies' country without means to protect themselves? We are aware of the animosity some Missourians have for us, and I would be a poor leader if I allowed my men to come unprotected. There are many stories that have been circulated that are false. We are a peace-loving people, wanting only to live on our lands, worshipping according to our God-given right, molesting no one. Those people who were spreading the lies do so to procure our destruction."

Had I not been there, I would never have believed the change that came over the three men. Of course I felt the Spirit as Joseph talked, as did all his followers, but it soon became evident that the Missourians had felt it too. With tears in their eyes, they stood and extended their hands to Joseph, smiling broadly.

"Well, Mr. Smith, I believe you. I promise to use all my influence to defuse the excitement, which seems to be everywhere about you and your little army. My heart is grieved to know my people have caused yours so much pain," Colonel Sconce said, his eyes filled with unshed tears. Joseph nodded, gripping the colonel's hand heartily.

"Thank you. That is more than we dared hoped for. Thank you all."

June 24, 1834

CHOLERA! The word struck fear into the hearts of every 19th–century human being. I had heard of cholera but had no idea what it was until it struck Zion's Camp.

Two years before, in 1832, cholera swept the globe in epidemic proportions. Thousands died an agonizing death, suffering from horrible stomach cramps, diarrhea, and dehydration.

Having spent the past two years in Joseph's house, I had seen him pray for the people suffering the effects of the disease. We had many discussions about it, but in the Western Reserve of Ohio, on the brink of civilization, people's pain, even as close as New York City, seemed a world away.

The disease was a mystery. No one was really sure how it started. Some assumed because it began in India, affecting heathen, dirty and ignorant people, Americans wouldn't be as affected. They were obviously more pious, prosperous, and enlightened. I chuckled at that point of view. Americans weren't any better than anyone else, a view Joseph agreed with. I was sure cholera flourished so well, even in America, because, as a whole, these people lived in filthier conditions than most Americans in my time. Good, clean water was so rare I wondered how anyone in this century made it to adulthood.

The rivers carried carcasses of dead animals, sometimes dead people, human waste and garbage. There was no sanitation system, and the government didn't seem strong enough to enforce one if it had been in place. People poured urine in the streets from their chamber pots. This was a grotesque practice I refused to perpetuate. I had always had a vision of how pristine, clean, and pure water and land must have been in the "old days." I was never more wrong in my life.

While Joseph was talking to the Missourians, Ezra Thayre and Joseph Hancock became ill. Had the Missourians known cholera was in camp, they never would have ventured near us. A while after they were gone, Joseph came to me, asking me to join him in the tent of the sick.

Both men lay on their bedrolls, writhing in agony from severe stomach cramps. The stench from vomit and diarrhea was enough to make me turn around and walk out of the tent. Surprised, Joseph followed me, taking my arm, turning me around to search my face.

"Jerree? Are you all right? Don't tell me you've never encountered cholera before."

"I haven't. Cholera is all but unknown in my day," I replied, taking deep cleansing breaths to rid myself of the horrid smell of cholera.

"Really? How was that achieved? Can we do it now? You must help us."

"We've learned ways to purify water...and frankly things are much cleaner...it would take too long to explain. I don't know what I can do to combat this disease, but I'll do all I can. And Joseph, no matter how strange the things I want done may seem, they must be done exactly as I say."

"Of course! Anything," he breathed, grateful for my knowledge and willingness to share it. I felt like I knew nothing.

"First, anyone attending the sick should wear a mask--something over their mouths and noses--a kerchief or something. Hands should be washed often, in hot water. Do we still have soap? Good. I want as much water as possible to be boiled; have someone doing it constantly. No one should drink any water that hasn't been boiled."

"People need to start keeping themselves, the camp, everything cleaner. Anyone who owns gloves, those of us handling bedding, or clothing, or anything the sick touch, should wear them, especially when attending the sick. Then they must be burned. I want those two men washed, all of their clothes and bedding destroyed, and the tent aired out. I can't work in such stench. Select only a few people to help me with the sick. Make sure they are as healthy as they can be. The rest of the camp needs to stay away." I took a breath, looking up at Joseph, who was smiling, a merry twinkle in his eyes.

"So, you'll help us?" he asked teasingly. I laughed nervously, brushing a stray lock of hair from my face, realizing I had all but taken over the nursing responsibilities.

"Yes. But remember my instructions need to be followed explicitly."

"Of course, Sister Jerree." He bowed with a flourish, and turned hurriedly to find help for me. Suddenly, I was filled with overwhelming fear. I knew nothing about cholera... or how to control it. All I had was my common sense and years of caring for my children. Would I end up catching it while I was busy helping others? For a moment I thought about refusing to help, but a calm feeling of peace settled over me, giving me assurance that whatever happened would be the Lord's will. Taking a deep breath, praying silently for strength, I went to my tent to find a kerchief and gloves. Walking back toward the tent that would become the hospital, I couldn't help think that we were now going to feel the Lord's wrath. We were in the midst of the scourge He promised us. I prayed we would be able to overcome this. For once I had no desire to know what the future held. Helping the sick was all I needed to concentrate on.

"I can't see how any such strange practices are gonna help," John S. Carter complained, when I explained what I expected from those who were helping me. Joseph had rounded up about ten people, including Jesse and George A. He had the other women in camp busy boiling water on the fires. The men in my small group of hospital workers seemed frightened and worried. I looked at Joseph for support against this contentious man. He smiled, his eyes twinkling, but said nothing, knowing I could hold my own.

"I've had some practice in taking care of sick people, Brother Carter, and this is the best way I have found to prevent a full-blown epidemic. I insist that you wear this bandanna and your gloves if you plan to help me," I said, knowing I was lying about my experience. No need to tell these people. I did keep up on current news reports and articles about medicine, so I was more knowledgeable than the rest of these 19th–century people. Joseph hid his laughter behind his massive hands, though I knew he was having a great time watching me try to lead these skeptical people.

"I say we bless these men. The priesthood is the only medicine that is sure to work," Brother Carter countered, refusing to take the bandanna. I shoved it into his hand. He snorted, dropped the bandanna on the ground, and turned to leave. Joseph grasped his arm.

"I agree, Brother Carter, the priesthood is our best weapon against this disease, but we also need to be wise enough not to spread the infection. Therefore we will take as many precautions as we can. That includes you." The man whipped around, looking at me with angry eyes, noticing my determined face and pant-covered legs.

"You may tell me what to do when you look and act more like a lady, Sister James," he said snidely and stomped off. Joseph shook his head, knowing I was ready to go after him. I questioned him with my eyes. He just shrugged and passed out freshly-laundered bandannas to each person helping me, commanding them to wear them, being strictly obedient to me. No one else defied him or me.

"It does no good to go against God's decrees, brethren. Not even the priesthood will keep the plague from us. We were promised a scourge and we have one. Do all you can to help those who are sick without contracting the disease yourself. I have every confidence in Sister James. Do as she asks."

Joseph then followed Brother Carter. Sighing, I organized my little group and we all set to work, forgetting about John S. Carter... for the moment.

I have never seen a disease spread so quickly as cholera did. First two were sick, then five. I wondered if it moved this fast naturally or if God was helping it along. I have had children sick from vomiting and diarrhea, but never had I tried to help grown men wracked with horrible cramps try to stay clean and not spread the disease anywhere else.

John S. Carter was struck with cholera after trying to rebuke the sickness by the power of the priesthood. He was in great agony, the cholera attacking him quite violently. He moaned, grasping my hand, begging me to help him. Joseph helped carry him into my makeshift hospital and shook his head, his blue eyes swimming with tears. I tried to smile down at Brother Carter, knowing that when God declared a punishment on a people, trying to change it was futile— often deadly.

Mercifully, Brother Carter did not last long, dying comparatively fast, even for cholera victims. My eyes clouded with tears as his body was wrapped and carried out by two of my workers. No casket was built. John S. Carter's body was laid solemnly in a shallow grave a half-mile from camp and hurriedly covered, hoping to keep the infection from spreading. I knew then that Heavenly Father meant business and we all had better humble ourselves or we'd have the same fate as John S. Carter.

CHAPTER TWENTY-FOUR

My whole existence became caring for the sick. I have no idea what anyone else did, outside of my hospital tent. I'm amazed that so much was being done, which I learned only after later reading Church history.

Joseph steadily tried to work things out with the government. This seemed futile to most people, but Joseph said later that he needed to give the government officials the chance so that they would later see God's judgments as just. He left camp quite often to comfort the homeless Saints and organize the Church better in Zion. I didn't know it at the time; I was so focused as the chief-of-staff of my little hospital.

In spite of our efforts, more people died and more became sick. Soon several tents were designated as the hospital. More people were called to help. I had to repeat my instructions many times, but no one questioned my methods. I think some were even relieved. It made sense to them to keep their faces and hands covered.

The entire countryside was filled with fear as word spread about cholera among the Mormons. I wondered how many Gentiles would be afflicted, though I didn't have time to worry about them. The sick in Zion's Camp were my priority. I organized a schedule, giving each person four hours off to wash, eat, and rest. They were then awakened to work four hours. I hoped this would keep people from becoming too exhausted. I even had to resort to wearing a dress so that one of the women could wash my other clothes.

Finally Joseph could not handle the cries of pain and death any longer. Calling Hyrum to his side, they commenced to bless the sick.

They began in the tent I was laboring in. I wondered why they were there until I saw Joseph take out a vial of oil. Gasping, I rose, afraid for the Prophet and his brother. He placed his hands on the sick man's head, but before he could speak, he was seized with violent cramps. Hyrum also fell, grasping his stomach.

"George! Go get Brigham and Lyman!" I cried, rushing to the fallen brothers. George A. fled the tent to do as I asked. Jesse was beside me before I even realized it. I knelt by Joseph's side, weeping wearily.

"Oh Joseph! Why? You said yourself it wasn't any good to go against God's decree. Why did you?" I wept.

"I...I couldn't....stand it! I hoped....maybe...now...He would revoke...the decree..."

"What should I do?"

"Nothing to do," he gasped. "Hyrum?" He turned his head so his tear-filled eyes could focus on his brother. I'm so sorry." Hyrum only shook his head, trying to smile.

Jesse helped me get them onto bedrolls. I used all my energy to make them comfortable. Brigham knelt beside the brothers, asking what he should do. Joseph clutched his hand, seeing something in Brigham that no one else could. He smiled wanly, nodding weakly.

"If my work were done here, you'd have to put me in the ground without a coffin," he joked. Brigham's eyes darted to me. I was weeping.

"You can't leave us, Joseph. No one is ready to lose you," Brigham said with more insight than he was aware of.

"Keep the Saints calm," Joseph rasped and was seized again with violent cramps.

Because people were dying so quickly, we were forced to wrap the bodies in blankets and bury them without coffins. George A. and Jesse got the unpleasant job of burying the dead. They made a travois, secured it behind a horse, and dragged the bodies the half-mile to the new graveyard.

While attending to one such burial, Jesse Smith was attacked with cholera. George picked him up and carried him to me. With angry tears, I nursed him, wondering why an innocent boy would be cursed. Some of the men in this camp deserved to suffer, having grumbled and fought against Joseph most of the way, but not dear, sweet, obedient Jesse. I prayed fervently for God to remove this curse. The brethren also began earnest prayer, covenanting to do all that was asked of them. During such a prayer meeting, an Elder Wilcox died. Miraculously, Joseph and Hyrum spent only one day sick.

"That was enough to convince me to be obedient. Also, it is wonderful to know that our dear mother would pray for us. I saw her in vision, kneeling in prayer as I was attacked by the disease. I believe that is the primary reason we were healed."

"I think the fact that you are the Lord's anointed had a little to do with it," I quipped.

"So true, Sister Jerree," he laughed. As soon as they were well enough, Hyrum and Joseph were off to western Clay County to meet with the Saints there. They were gone a week or more. I learned later that some of the Saints had contracted cholera also. Sidney Gilbert died, which caused me much sorrow. Jesse continued to be tormented by a disease I had learned to detest. George A. was ever vigilant, helping me care for Jesse. I was grateful for all those who helped me, such as Brigham, Joseph Young, and Heber C. Kimball who were always there.

Hiram Page came into camp saying he had been instructed to have Jesse and George taken to Joseph, who feared for them. By now, George was sick also, though not as violently as Jesse.

"No! You will not move them!" I said adamantly, surprising even Brigham. I had never questioned Joseph's word before and no one could believe I was doing it now.

"But Sister Jerree, Joseph has asked for them," Hiram said patiently. Everyone knew how many hours I had spent nursing the sick, so they were willing to try and reason with me. I was beyond reason.

"I don't care! You tell Joseph if he's so worried about these boys to get back here! I'm not allowing them out of my sight!" Brigham came to my side, taking my hand, looking down at me compassionately.

"If Joseph has asked for them, then it is our duty to obey," he said quietly, trying to calm me. I think I would have been convinced if Hiram Page hadn't opened his mouth.

"Dr. Williams said Jesse is over the cholera, now."

Ripping my hand from Brigham's, I whirled around to face Hiram.

"Dr. Williams has no idea what Jesse has been through! He's in town with Joseph! He hasn't seen him in days! I could care less what his professional opinion is. Jesse has suffered for seven straight days.

He needs to stay down until he's strong enough to walk, not be traipsing after his cousin who is too busy to come and see him!"

George stood up shakily. "I can make it," George said weakly.

I scowled at him for his mutiny. "You want to go?" I asked incredulously.

"If Joseph says I should, I do," he replied simply.

"I suppose if Joseph said to jump off a cliff you'd do that too, the lot of you. I may not be able to stop George, but I won't allow Jesse to be taken," I said defiantly, looking at the group of men surrounding me. None of them dared oppose me. I'm sure they figure they'd let Joseph deal with me. Well, I was ready to tell Joseph Smith a few things anyway.

George was able to get on a horse, but was attacked with cramps before they left the camp. He wouldn't listen to my pleadings, setting his Smith chin and forging on. He rode fifteen miles that day, getting to Joseph before dark.

I sat stoically by Jesse's bed as he became weaker. By now I'd seen enough death to recognize it when I was looking at it. Jesse had that look. I held his hand as he struggled for life, tears streaming down my face.

"Don't cry, Sister Jerree. I'm not afraid to die," he said weakly.

"But you're so young. You've hardly begun to live."

"I believe there's a greater mission for me elsewhere. Thank you for caring for me." He lapsed into a coma soon after our conversation. In the early hours of July 1st, Jesse N. Smith went on to his greater mission.

I insisted on accompanying the brethren to Jesse's grave. He too was wrapped in his blanket, placed on the travois, and hurriedly buried. Brigham dedicated the ground but no other service was held. I stood there long after everyone else left, weeping bitterly for the loss of such a good boy. It was harder for me to bury this boy than it had been to bury my mother. I felt as if I had lost one of my own children.

"Jerree," Brigham said softly, coming to escort me back to camp. He put his hand on my arm. Turning, I collapsed against him, burying my face in his huge chest. He allowed me cry until I was too exhausted to weep more. He led me back to my tent, insisting I go to bed and rest.

"How can I? We've just buried one boy and sent another one off to be close to Joseph! Joseph wasn't even here to say good-bye! He's Jesse's cousin, for heaven's sake! I can't believe an innocent boy was taken. Jesse didn't deserve to suffer so! How could God be so cruel?"

Brigham tried to calm me, but I wrenched myself free. I did not wish to be comforted, even by Brigham. I was angry with Joseph, angry with God, and angry with Brigham for trying to find excuses for either one of them. For the first time since I arrived in this century, I found fault with Joseph and allowed my grief to feed that fault-finding.

"Joseph can't be everywhere, Jerree. He's trying to help the Saints in Zion."

"Zion! Don't tell me about Zion! It won't be redeemed now or anytime in your lifetime or mine! I doubt it ever will!" I screeched. He took my arms and shook me, telling me later he was sure I had lost my mind. At that time, he did not know I was from the future.

"Let me go! Why don't you go over to Clay County to be with Joseph? Help him redeem Zion while people are dying all around you!" Suddenly my stomach was seized with the most horrible pain I'd ever felt. If Brigham hadn't been holding me, I'd have gone to the ground. He picked me up, carrying me to the hospital. Fear filled my heart. I had been speaking against the Prophet, the Church, and God. Would I die as John Carter had?

I found myself in an agonizing world of pain, wishing I could die. Cholera was the most horrible sickness I had ever experienced. I'm grateful that it had almost been wiped out in my century. Brigham tenderly cared for me. Sometime during the week I was sick, Joseph returned to camp. I was vaguely aware of his presence, though I wondered if I was dreaming. I was told later that he cared for me also.

My body was not prepared for such a violent disease, and I was positive I would die. I welcomed death, I embraced it, knowing I would be reunited with my mother.

"Jerusha." I opened my eyes, finding myself in a beautiful garden, the most beautiful flowers growing everywhere. I knew that voice, the one calling me. I looked around, spotting my mother sitting serenely on a bench in the midst of the garden. I ran to her, throwing my arms around her. I sobbed with joy.

"Finally! I've missed you so much, Mom!" My mother smiled tenderly, touching my face.

"You can't stay, Jerusha," she said.

"Why?"

"Your work isn't finished. There's so much more for you to do."

"I'm so tired. I can't go on. I want to stay with you."

"You only think you do. Your family needs you."

"I'm not even with my family," I cried. Mother's eyes twinkled, her hand warm against my cheek.

"Of course you are. The Smith family is as much your family as Tom and the children. Joseph needs you...Tom will need you too. You must go back and learn all you need to know...and you must never speak ill of Joseph again. He has done all he can to help mankind."

I felt ashamed that my mother knew of my tirade against Joseph. Tears welled up in my eyes. I laid my head in her lap. She combed her fingers through my hair as she often did when I was little.

"I'm sorry. I know I was wrong, but I was so tired...so upset about Jesse."

"Jesse has greater glory and power now than he would have ever achieved on earth. Don't mourn for him. He is happy. Go back and support Joseph. Trust him. He will never lead you astray." Kissing my forehead, she stood, smiled down at me and walked away, apparently unaffected by our separation.

"Mother! Mother!" I cried weakly, looking around, seeing nothing but darkness. Joseph hurried to my side, holding a lantern up to see my face. He smiled, wiping my brow with a cool hand.

"Welcome back, Sister Jerree. I wondered if you had given up," he said kindly. I stared at his face, wondering if I was dreaming again or if I was really with the Prophet Joseph Smith.

CHAPTER TWENTY-FIVE

July 8th found me lying in the back of a wagon that was heading toward Kirtland. Joseph, Hyrum, Fredrick G. Williams, William McLellen, and George A. traveled with me. Joseph insisted I rest and would not allow me to walk. I didn't argue, feeling weak and drained from my bout with cholera.

Despite my mother's advice, I did mourn for Jesse. He had become such an integral part of my life during the march to Zion that I wondered how I could live without him. His father was going to be devastated.

It took three and a half months to march to Zion. Taking a wagon got us back home in less than a month. We reached Kirtland August 1st and were greeted warmly by family members who had missed us sorely. Emma and Jerusha fawned over me, hearing how sick I'd been.

"Are you sure you're all right?" Emma asked. "You look so pale."

"I'm fine…just a little tired still."

"Then rest. We'll take care of you. Joseph tells me you nursed all those men during the scourge. It's time you were looked after," Emma said, handing me a hot cup of herbal tea.

"Thank you."

It didn't take long before Mary Ann was at my side, glad to see that I had survived the ordeal. She was now well advanced in her pregnancy, looking healthy and happy.

"Was it really so horrible?" she asked, envying my adventure.

"Not horrible—just hard. I hoped we would go to Zion and help the Saints regain their lands and homes. I never thought it would turn out the way it did."

"There was a reason for the march…though we may not find out what that is right away. I'm just so glad you are home."

"Me too," I sighed, knowing I wasn't truly home until I was back in the 20th century. I reached over and patted her swollen belly.

"You look so good. How do you feel?"

"I feel fine. I'll be happy to have this baby on the outside. He punches like a boxer."

I laughed, squeezing her hand. It felt good to be with her again.

Upon his return to Kirtland, Joseph had no time to spend with his family. He was thrust back into the thick of Kirtland affairs. Emma seemed quite hurt that he could not spend time with her after being gone over three months. But the work of the Church needed his attention, and he would not put it off.

Sylvester Smith, who had to my astonishment escaped the scourge, took great delight in telling everyone who would listen how horrible Joseph had been to him on the march. He accused Joseph of taking delight in publicly rebuking him, that Joseph prophesied falsely, threatened to whip Sylvester, and then threw a bugle at him. The allegation that angered me the most was when Sylvester claimed that Joseph had been improper with a married woman—namely me! Emma was livid, threatening to sue him for libel. Joseph tried to calm her, telling her he'd take care of it.

A high council meeting was held, which ended up lasting several days. Many people were called to testify. I wanted to but was never asked. I'd have given the high council an ear full. Of course, Joseph was aware of that and refused to let me have a say. In the end, Joseph was found innocent of every charge—the council satisfied that "President Smith had not acted in any respect contrary to righteousness before the Lord."

Sylvester was asked to publish an apology in the *Evening and Morning Star* so that "he could yet remain a member of the Church, otherwise he would be expelled from the same." He did publish an apology, although in my estimation his attitude was not as humble as it should have been. I stopped him in the street after the letter was published to try to make amends.

"Brother Sylvester, could I have a word with you?" I asked, getting his attention by touching his arm. He frowned when he realized it was me but stopped and extended his hand. I placed mine in his and looked up into his handsome face. It was too bad he was such a jerk; he could be charming if he wanted to be.

"Of course," he said curtly.

"I appreciated your letter. I know it is hard to realize we've done something wrong. It took great courage to admit it. I hope that you accept my apology for my attitude toward you. Joseph and his family are very important to me—as is the gospel."

His eyes shone with sarcasm. He smiled, tightening his grip on my hand. At once I knew it was a mistake to try to make peace with this man.

"I know Joseph is important to you. It remains to be seen just how important the gospel is."

I gasped and tried to wrench my hand from his. He chuckled menacingly. All at once Joseph was at my side, clasping a hand on Sylvester's shoulder. He instantly freed my hand. Joseph stood, staring at Sylvester, his blue eyes flashing with anger.

"Do you want to know how important the gospel is to Sister Jerree? I'd be happy to tell you, Brother Sylvester. She has come to us at great cost. She has had to give up a husband and four children to be with the Saints—the SAINTS, Brother Smith, not me. What have you ever given up for the gospel's sake?"

I stared at Joseph in wonder. I had never thought of my presence in Kirtland in such a light before. Joseph was making it sound like some noble sacrifice instead of a dumb accident. I looked back at Sylvester, who for once, looked utterly ashamed.

"I'm sorry...I...didn't know," he replied weakly.

"Of course you didn't know. Sister Jerree seldom discusses it. But let me set the record straight. Sister Jerree is an honorable, pure woman and a member of my family. I hold her in the same regard as my mother and sisters. To insult her, you insult me. I will cut you off myself if I hear you have said one more hurtful word against her." Joseph's voice never rose; he didn't speak angrily, but Sylvester knew he meant what he said. Joseph had allowed the high council to deal with Sylvester and his allegations but he refused to stay silent any longer. Sylvester nodded. Turning to me he said:

"Please accept my deepest apologies, Sister James. I was totally out of line."

"I accept, Brother Smith, and extend a hand of fellowship." Six months ago I might have had a hard time accepting his apology, but after having spent the summer marching toward a dream, watching a Prophet work to create a proper army of God, I could do nothing less than follow his example and feel compassion for this man who saw no vision. I extended my gloved hand, which he again took, this time bending over to place a kiss on it. He then straightened, bowed his head at Joseph and hurried away, leaving me to a puzzle over such a paradoxical man.

Joseph took my arm, leading me toward the Whitney store. So many questions flooded my mind I didn't know where to begin. I remained silent, relishing this time I had with the Prophet.

"Sylvester has great wells of goodness in him. If he can overcome the pride that rules his heart, he will be truly great," Joseph said, opening the store's door and escorting me in. I nodded, too overwhelmed to speak.

"Why didn't you tell me?" Mary Ann asked, looking at me with tears in her eyes. I was busy in the kitchen. She had come to visit. I had no idea what she was talking about.

"Tell you what?" I asked, wiping my hands on my apron.

"About the sacrifice you've made to be with the Saints." I stared at her in confusion until realization dawned as to what she was talking about. It seemed Sylvester Smith had wasted no time telling my sad story to half of Kirtland. I sighed, put the dough I was kneading back in the bowl, poked a hole in the middle and draped a towel over it. I sat in the chair next to Mary, wiping my hands before I took one of hers.

"The story Sylvester is telling is...well...not accurate."

"What do you mean?"

"This is hard; no one knows the real story—except the Smiths. Most people probably wouldn't believe it if they were told anyway."

"You can tell me. I'll believe you, Jerree. You know I think of you as a sister."

I smiled at her. I loved the fact that she was willing to listen to my story and take my word as the truth. I hoped she'd feel that way when she heard it. I hardly believed it, and I was living it.

"All right. But first you must promise to listen to the whole story before you say anything...please don't get up and leave." Her eyes grew round with curiosity and her hand grasped mine tightly.

"I promise," she vowed.

I breathed deeply and exhaled, praying that the story she was about to hear wouldn't change her feelings for me.

"I arrived in Kirtland in March of 1831. Joseph found me lying in the middle of the street. He thought I was Hyrum's wife, Jerusha, but he soon learned that I wasn't."

"You do look enough like her to be her sister," Mary Ann agreed.

"Yes, and we are related."

"She's your cousin, right?"

"No, Mary Ann, my name is Jerusha Mary Walker James. My father, David Walker, was a direct descendent of Hyrum and Jerusha Smith through their daughter Lovina."

"I don't understand. Lovina is only seven..."

"I know. I was born in the year 1940...in a place called Idaho..."

"Don't you mean 1780 something?" She asked, all the color draining out from her face. I shook my head.

"No, I mean 1940. I don't know exactly how, I don't even know the reason why, but somehow, through some miracle, I found a doorway from my time to yours. I stumbled into Kirtland in 1831. My family—my Mormon family—is still in Idaho in the 1990s. I have a daughter Sarah, who has two children, a son David, who also has two children, and sons named Joseph and Cory. One is on a mission and the other is off to college. My husband, Tom, is a high councilman in our stake. Both of us were raised in the gospel. My family has always been proud of our heritage—having prophets as our ancestors. My mother named me after my great-great-great-grandmother—Jerusha Barden Smith."

Mary Ann sat staring at me for what seemed like an eternity. I was afraid she'd get up and walk away, thinking I was crazy.

"You look just like her," she breathed.

"Yes...and my son Joseph looks a great deal like the Prophet Joseph."

"How can this be? I've never heard of such a thing...traveling through time...I just don't know," Mary Ann mumbled. Nodding, I squeezed her hand.

"I know just how you feel. Joseph says my being here is good thing. If you don't believe me, go talk to him. Emma, Jerusha, Hyrum, Mother and Father Smith, they all know."

"If you found your way here, why haven't you gone back? You've been here four years. Don't you want to go home?"

"More than anything. But I can't go back until the vehicle by which I was brought here is made."

"Oh! And what is that?"

"A chest of drawers with a beautiful mirror, made with scrap wood from the Kirtland Temple."

"Oh! And construction on the temple has just begun. Who makes the chest?"

"Brigham." Mary Ann's eyes widened, then filled with tears.

"Doesn't he know?"

"Not yet."

"How did your family get something made by Brigham?"

"It was given as a wedding present when…" I stopped, realizing I was about to reveal future events, and that was not permitted.

"When what?"

"I can't say. Joseph told me I was not to reveal what I know about the future. Everything that is past to me is future to you." Mary Ann nodded, a bit disappointed.

"So the Church does survive into the next century. I take it the millennium hasn't started in the 1990s?" I shook my head. "Where is this place…Idaho?"

"Right here…in America, just further west."

"Oh. Since you're from the future, did you know about me and that I would marry Brigham? Is that why you introduced us?"

"I'm sorry to say, I wasn't the best student when it came to learning about the history of the Church. I've learned so much more here than I ever learned in all my life in the future. Joseph says that's the main reason I was allowed to come here. My generation hasn't paid enough attention to the past or to those who suffered to give us what we have. I do know some about Brigham. Your descendants will flourish in my time." Mary Ann's eyes brightened. She pulled me into a tearful, tender embrace.

"Oh, Jerree…. your story is so strange, but the Spirit whispers that it is true! I promise I'll make sure that dresser gets built so that you can return to your family. I know I'm grateful you came here. How else would I have found Brigham?"

"Oh, I think the Lord would have found a way to get you two together."

"I think you're right," Mary Ann said laughing merrily. I joined her laugher, happy to have shared my secret with this woman who was one of my dearest friends.

CHAPTER TWENTY-SIX

The next eighteen months were busy but peaceful, for the most part. The Kirtland Saints put all their energy into building the temple. Though our enemies said it would never be built, it grew steadily, purported to be the largest religious building in America.

Every available person 'tithed' as much time as they could to the work of raising a house to the Lord. I sat for hours sewing, by hand, clothes for the workers, weaving rugs, and making the veils that would hang in the temple.

Joseph was intent on building up Zion. He ever diligently worked to improve and restore all that God wanted him to. In the spring of 1835, Joseph said it was time to restore to the Church the Quorum of the Twelve Apostles. He also organized the First Quorum of the Seventy.

When I learned the names of those called, I knew one purpose for the march of Zion's Camp. All but three of the Apostles had been on that march, and every Seventy had been. Zion's Camp had not been a failure after all. The march had tempered an army of witnesses for Christ—a much better cause than a killing machine, in my estimation. Even Sylvester Smith was called to the Seventy. He had humbled himself so much that he published a contrite letter saying he had falsely accused Joseph and that he was truly sorry. He even stopped by the house to beg my pardon. I embraced him gladly, happy to have finally made peace with a brother.

In 1835, the Doctrine and Covenants was published. One hundred revelations and twelve lectures on faith were compiled as the first edition. Joseph gave me one of the first copies to come off the press.

"Thank you, Joseph! I will treasure it always."

"Always? Don't tell me your generation has forgotten God's words to his prophet Joseph?" he teased.

"Oh no! We have the Doctrine and Covenants—it's just—this came from you," I replied, hugging the book to my breast.

"The one in your day came from me, too. It should be just as treasured," he replied, smiling, then left to find Emma.

I thought about what he said. It was true. The Doctrine and Covenants in my day also came from Joseph Smith—from the Lord to Joseph Smith—and should be just as treasured as the book I now held. Did we, in my day, treasure the word of the Lord through his prophet? Were we guilty of neglect and complacence? I vowed never to be so again.

In the summer of 1835, a man came into Kirtland bringing Egyptian mummies and papyrus scrolls. His name was Michael Chandler. He had heard that Joseph could translate ancient languages. Upon reaching Kirtland, he came straight to Joseph's house, requesting an audience with him.

Joseph greeted Mr. Chandler warmly but listened to his claims with not much interest—until he produced the papyrus scrolls. Joseph's sapphire eyes perused the scrolls, then looked at the peddler in amazement.

"Do you mind if I look at them over tonight? I would be so very careful. Come back in the morning, and I will let you know what they say."

"Very well. I feel I can trust you, Mr. Smith."

"That you can, sir."

When Mr. Chandler was gone, Joseph stood, rolled the scrolls lovingly, started toward his office, then turned.

"Jerree, please go get Oliver. I think he's at the temple site. I'm going to need him."

Nodding, I rushed to the door, looking back in time to see Joseph wiping tears from his eyes before he headed up the stairs.

I escorted Oliver to the office door, knocked, and followed him in, wanting to know what was going on. Sensing my interest, Joseph allowed me to stay as he excitedly talked to Oliver.

"These scrolls are from God, Oliver! They are the writings of Abraham—at least the one I've been reading. I've found some written by the Joseph who was sold into Egypt!"

"Joseph...son of Jacob?" Oliver asked incredulously.

"Yes! The very one. The Spirit whispers that these are important, and we are to obtain them. Are you willing to scribe for me, old friend?"

"Ready and eager, Joseph."

They spent the remainder of the night sequestered in the office. Early the next morning the entire family gathered, having heard about the scrolls and wanting to know what Joseph had learned from them. He and Oliver came down to breakfast, tired but ecstatic, looking very much like two school boys in their delight.

"Well, son, what did the man bring to you?" Father Smith asked, no longer able to keep silent.

"Oh Father! It's wondrous! We have in this very house the writing of Abraham—the father of Isaac!" Everyone gasped, unable to believe their ears.

"There's also some of the writing of Joseph of old!" Oliver blurted, hardly able to contain his excitement.

Father Smith smiled and looked with fondness on his prophet-son.

"This fulfills the words of your patriarchal blessing which I myself pronounced just this past December.... remember?" Joseph nodded, enthralled with his father's words.

"I bless thee with the blessings of thy forefathers, Abraham, Isaac, and Jacob; and even the blessing of thy father Joseph, the son of Jacob. Behold he looked after his posterity in the last days, when they...wept before the Lord. He sought diligently to know from whence the son should come who should bring forth the word of the Lord, by which they might be enlightened, and brought back to the true fold, and his eyes beheld thee, my son: his heart rejoiced and his soul was satisfied, and he said: 'As my blessings are to extend to the utmost bounds of the everlasting hills, as my father's blessing prevailed above, where the blessings of his progenitors and as my branches are to run over the wall, and my seed are to inherit the choice land whereon the Zion of God shall stand in the last days, from among my seed, scattered with the gentiles shall a choice seer arise, whose bowels shall be as fountain of truth, whose loins shall be girded with the girdle of righteousness, whose hands shall be lifted with acceptance before the God of Jacob to turn away his anger from his anointed, whose heart shall meditate great wisdom, whose intelligence shall circumscribe and comprehend the deep things of God, and whose mouth shall utter the law of the just: His feet shall stand upon the neck of his enemies, and he shall walk upon the ashes of those who seek his destruction; with wine and oil shall he be sustained and he shall feed upon the heritage of Jacob his father; the just shall desire his society, and the upright in heart shall be his companions: No weapon formed against him shall prosper, and though the wicked mar him, for a little season he shall be like one rising up in the heat of wine, he shall rear in his strength, and the Lord shall put to flight his persecutors: He shall be blessed like the fruitful olive, and his memory shall be sweet as the choice cluster of the first ripe grapes. Like a sheaf full ripe, gathered into the garner, so shall he stand before the Lord, having produced an hundred fold'."

It was wonderful to behold. Father Smith, the Patriarch of the Church and the head of the Smith family, sat, suffused in light, reciting a blessing he had given months ago as if he had just given it. Joseph rose, tears in his eyes, and knelt before his father, who took his face in his aged hands.

"How the Lord has blessed me, to have given me such a son," he whispered, and kissed Joseph's forehead. We all sat quietly, watching. My mind had been caught up in the imagery of his words, and I could see Joseph, glorious and triumphant, standing with the Lord in righteousness. I had been told all my life that he was great, I had lived in his home for the better part of five years and I knew him, but it wasn't until this moment that I realized WHO he really was. He was Joseph...son of Joseph...descendent of Joseph... son of Jacob... son of Isaac...son of Abraham. He had come from prophets to become a prophet...the Prophet of the Restoration. Joseph of old had seen him and rejoiced in him. Now I had seen him also and I too rejoiced in him, as one of his posterity who had been blessed by his life and mission.

I don't know if Michael Chandler was impressed when he was told the scrolls contained the writings of Abraham and Joseph, but in the end he sold the mummies and the scrolls for $2,400. Oliver and W.W. Phelps acted as scribes as Joseph translated the words of

Abraham. They later said it was one of the most thrilling experiences of their lives. Chandler told Joseph that he believed the translation of the scrolls was true. Joseph just smiled warmly and testified that it was.

The artifacts became a point of curiosity, and many people came to see them. The visitors were charged a quarter to help repay those who had given their money to purchase them. The mummies were interesting, but it was the words of Abraham and Joseph that were the real treasures received from Michael Chandler by the grace of God.

One of the most exciting things to happen that fall was the birth of Brigham and Mary Ann's first child, Joseph Angell Young. I felt privileged to be there to help Mary Ann. I must admit I had become quite a good mid-wife.

Both parents were so proud of their new baby. Brigham's two girls were ecstatic about having a baby brother. Elizabeth was ten and looking forward to caring for the small child. Five-year-old Vilate was happy not to be considered the baby any more.

I was happy that I was still in Kirtland when this baby was born. I knew my time here was almost completed. I had seen Mary Ann and Brigham meet, fall in love, and marry. It seemed only right that I should witness the birth of their first child.

Winter came again to Kirtland. I felt torn between wanting to stay and knowing I needed to return to my own time, to my own family. Of course there was never a dull moment living in the Prophet's house.

Sometime in December, a new convert arrived in town, full of zeal and determination, ready to contribute all she could to the cause. Petite and proper, the brunette, slender woman stood in the parlor, waiting to pay a visit to the Prophet. I opened the front door when she knocked.

"Hello. May I help you?"

"I hope so. I'm looking for the prophet, Joseph Smith Jr. Is he here?" she asked. She was definitely an educated woman, well dressed, with impeccable manners and speech.

"I'm afraid he's upstairs in a meeting at the moment. Come in and warm yourself by the fire. He's been up there for several hours, so I expect him down at any minute."

"Thank you. Are you his wife?"

I laughed, shaking my head. Leading her to the stove, I turned to add more wood to the fire.

"No! I'm a cousin. I don't think we've met." I looked at her carefully. She was a pretty woman, with classic features and a refined deportment.

"I'm sure we haven't, since I've barely arrived in Kirtland. My name is Eliza... Eliza Roxcy Snow." She extended her tiny hand, smiling brightly at me. My heart skipped a beat, and I wondered if she realized just how stunned I was. I gave her my hand, staring at her in awe.

"And you are...?" she asked.

"Oh! I'm Jerree James. Sister Snow, I'm so honored to meet you. I've been an admirer of yours for...a while now."

"Why thank you," she said in a puzzled voice.

"Please have a seat. I'll run upstairs and see if Joseph is ready to take a break. Don't go anywhere." She assured me she wouldn't as I rushed out of the room.

Eliza R. Snow! I couldn't believe Eliza R. Snow was actually in this house! She was one the greatest women of this century! She wrote poems and songs and married two prophets. She would become a plural wife to both Joseph and Brigham. This was certainly a day to remember!

Joseph answered my knock, smiling at my excited face.

"Sister Jerree. How nice of you to come and remind us we need to rest from our labors. What can I do for you?"

"There's...there's someone here to see you," I breathed. I'm sure he realized this was no ordinary visitor to me. His eyebrows arched, his blue eyes shining.

"Well, I guess I'd better go down and meet them. Brethren, I think we can call it a day. Go home and visit your families. I'm sure your wives will enjoy that." The men in the room laughed and gratefully prepared to leave. Joseph allowed me to take his arm and excitedly escort him down to the parlor. Eliza was sitting with her back to the door, warming her hands at the fire.

"Sister Snow, Brother Joseph," I announced and watched as Eliza turned to greet Joseph. I watched closely as Eliza smiled up at the Prophet. Joseph's eyes became quite round, his smile genuine if not a little shy. He shot a look my way. I just smiled, looking as innocent as I could with the knowledge I had about these two people.

"Hello, Brother Smith. I've just arrived from Mantua. I've come to gather with the Saints. I wanted to ask if you knew of any employment in Kirtland for a single woman, such as myself."

"Well, Sister Snow, I'm not sure...I'll have to talk to my wife... she knows about such things better than I do. How was your journey?"

"Cold...but exciting."

"I assume you've been baptized, then."

"Yes...in April."

"But didn't I come to your house about three years ago?" he asked, pointedly. Eliza blushed prettily, nodding her head.

"Yes...but I'm quite stubborn and it took me a while to make up my mind."

"Well, it does my heart good to see that you finally did. Do you have a place to stay?"

"Oh yes. Sidney and Phoebe Rigdon have invited me to stay with them for a while."

"Good," Joseph replied, finding it difficult to continue the conversation. Eliza, being astute, knew it was time to go. Extending her hand to Joseph, she smiled up at him again, said her good-byes and left, leaving me alone with the flustered prophet. I again fed the fire with fresh wood.

"You know who she is, don't you?" he asked, watching me as I tended the fire.

"Yes. She's well-known in my time," I answered.

"No...you KNOW who she is and the role she'll play... someday...."

"Yes Joseph, I do. But don't worry. I'll never say a word to anyone." Joseph smiled, his eyes swimming with tears.

"It's not you I worry about, Jerree. Emma will never accept her...and you know it."

I nodded, refusing to voice what I knew. Joseph sighed, excused himself, and went to seek solace from the One Source he could always count on.

Emma and Eliza R. Snow became fast friends. Emma was taken with her refinement and education. She insisted that Eliza teach the children. Eliza R. Snow was one of the most educated women in

Kirtland and Emma wanted the best education for her growing children. She insisted that Eliza move into their home, which gave me a roommate. I figured if I was to have a roommate, Eliza R. Snow would be the best choice.

We also became fast friends. I found myself helping her establish a school for young ladies. Most people called it The Prophet's Family School. Eliza was impressed by my education and I became one of the teachers for the school. It was a joy to work beside Eliza R. Snow, getting to know her, watching her interact with the children and the Saints.

Joseph was busy with the business of the Church, but at times I would catch him watching us, looking at Eliza with awe. Joseph wanted always to obey the Lord in His commandments but the law of plural marriage was the hardest commandment to even consider. He loved Emma; she was the choice of his youth. How could he possibly tell her that the Lord would soon command him to take other wives, especially one so obviously refined, educated, and pretty as the twenty-seven-year-old Eliza R. Snow? I worried about Joseph, knowing that in the end he would obey, and Emma would hate Eliza and cause Joseph grief. I think it made him feel better knowing I was aware of Eliza's role in his life and that I understood, though we never talked of it again.

1835 came to a close with the temple nearing completion. Crushed glassware and china, donated by the sisters and added to the exterior stucco, gave the walls a glistening effect in the sunlight. Many women had given their choicest pieces of china for this cause. It was a sacrifice willingly given, which would soon be miraculously accepted.

Not surprising to me, Brigham was put in charge of finishing the interior. As a carpenter and glazier, there was no one better. He took great joy in beautifying the inside of the Lord's house.

Eliza, one day talking to Emma, learned that the building committee was in need of a substantial amount of money to pay for the supplies for the temple. They were in dire straits and wondered where to get so much money from a people so financially needy. Eliza promptly picked up her cloak, asked me to accompany her, and went to the head of the building committee. She handed him a purse containing a sizeable amount of money.

"Sister Snow! I can't accept this money! How will you live?"

CHAPTER TWENTY-SIX

Eliza smiled, refusing to take back the purse.

"Sir, I have very few needs, which are being taken care of by teaching in the Prophet's school. I feel it is a privilege to be able to give this money for so worthy a cause."

"Well, I must tell you, Sister Snow, that we were fairly worried where we'd get the money to make our payment, and you have relieved our minds considerably. God bless you."

"He already has. Thank you."

"Thank *you*. We will make up a promissory note and give it to you soon."

"I require no such note," Eliza replied, taking my arm and escorting me out of the building. I looked at her in wonder, which she noticed, laughing merrily.

"Don't look so surprised, Jerree. I've been raised in comparative wealth. I would be an unprofitable servant if I did not repay the bounty that has always been mine. Don't you think?"

"Yes. It's just so wonderful to see such generosity. Most people would never part with so much cash."

"I hope you realize by now, Jerree, that I am not like most people."

"Oh, believe me, Eliza, I know that."

One day in early February, 1836, Mary Ann came to Joseph's house, her eyes full of excitement. When I let her in, she pulled me into her arms, laughing and crying.

"Get your cloak! I have something to show you," she breathed.

"I can't! I've got bread in the oven and I'm tending young Joseph and Julia.

"Is Joseph home?"

"Yes, but he's busy." She released me and hurried to search for the Prophet, bringing him into the kitchen after a few minutes.

"Tell her, Joseph," Mary Ann demanded, her eyes shining. He was smiling, though I could have sworn I saw sadness in his eyes.

"Go with Mary Ann. I'll tend the babies...and the bread. You need to do this." His voice caught, and his eyes filled with tears.

"What's going on?" I asked, fear gripping my heart.

"Nothing—go! This is a day you've been waiting for." Joseph's voice was strained as he took the cloak Mary Ann gave him and wrapped it around me. His hands stayed on my shoulders, squeezing them tightly. "Go," he whispered. I looked into his sapphire eyes. A look of such love filled them, that for a moment I could not breathe. Mary Ann took my arm and led me out the door, though I turned just before the door closed. Joseph had taken a seat at the table, his face buried in his hands.

Mary Ann would not allow me to be sad. She chattered all the way to her house. She told me about the progress of little Joseph, about his father's joy in him, and the girl's enchantment with their brother. I wanted only to go back and ask Joseph why he was so sad.

Soon we were in Mary Ann's kitchen, warming our hands by the fire. "He brought it home last night, proud as punch! It's beautiful and I knew you'd want to see it immediately," Mary Ann said, taking my cloak from me.

"See what?" I asked, realizing I hadn't been paying much attention to her words.

"Come...I'll show you." She smiled, took my hand, and led me to her bedroom, opening the door with a flourish. I gasped when I looked in, beholding the dresser that had been such a part of my life. It looked as I remembered, though it must have been refinished in my time, for now the wood was lighter in color. It had three long drawers in the middle and three shorter ones on each side. The oval mirror was attached. It looked brand new. Brigham had created this dresser exactly as it was in my room, and I had never described it to him.

A small box sat on top—a box I remembered well. Tears sprang to my eyes as I stood in the hall, staring at the vehicle that would carry me across the chasm of time—back home.

"Oh, Mary Ann! It's my dresser!" I whispered, walking to it and touching it lovingly.

"Actually it's mine—for now. Is it just like you remember?"

"Exactly...except...the wood is stained darker in my day—but everything else is the same."

"Then you can go home whenever you wish," Mary Ann said sadly. All at once I felt like Dorothy in "The Wizard of Oz," when she was told she could finally go home. If I remembered correctly, she had a hard time going back too. I sighed, turned to my friend, and smiled.

Home! Tom...the children...the grandchildren! All that I loved waited for me just beyond that mirror resting on the dresser. All I had to do was take the steps necessary to get there.

"How do I leave Joseph, Emma, Hyrum and Jerusha....and you? The temple is almost done. I so wanted to see it finished."

"Your family needs you," Mary Ann said, touching my arm. I nodded.

"I need to talk to Joseph," I cried, running out of the room and out of the house without my cloak. I was frozen and heartsick when I reached the house, tears freezing to my face. Joseph still sat at the table, looking at the loaves he had just taken from the oven. He stood, took my hands and led me to the parlor, invited me to sit by the fire, then rubbed my hands tenderly to warm them. Hyrum had come while I was gone and now stood beside me, a hand on my shoulder.

"Don't cry, Jerree. You should be rejoicing," Joseph said softly. Hyrum nodded in agreement. I looked from one to the other, thinking how much I loved them both.

"I am...but how can I leave? You are all so much a part of my life now. How do I live without seeing you...asking your advice...sharing in your lives? How do I live now?"

"The way you did before. We will never really leave you...you share our blood and our faith. You will never really leave us, either. But the time has come..."

"But must I leave before the temple is dedicated? I worked to build it too! I can't leave before I see it given to the Lord. I've looked forward to this day as much as the next person. Please don't make me leave until then...please."

Joseph looked into my pleading eyes, then at Hyrum, who smiled and nodded. Joseph smiled, touching my cheek.

"We would never force you to leave; I hope you know that. But it is God's will that you go home. I don't think He'll mind if you stay a few more weeks, though."

"We really can't dedicate the temple without our Sister Jerree. Please stay, dear, dear, Jerusha."

Hyrum joined Joseph and I on the davenport, taking my hand in his. I wanted to fling myself into his arms, feeling suddenly as if this grandparent of mine was older and wiser than I. In this moment of time, I was the elder, but he was my grandfather and I needed to feel his love. He seemed to understand and folded me gently against his chest. Joseph placed a hand on my back. I sobbed quietly against Hyrum for a while, both brothers there to comfort me.

"It's settled then," Hyrum said softly.

I knew I would be going home soon to my family, my husband, and my life before I fell into this time, but for some reason I could not find the joy I should have felt at such news.

Sunday March 27, 1836

I don't think anyone in Kirtland slept the night before the temple was to be dedicated. The excitement was tangible. The entire family rose early, knowing we would have to get in line soon to get a good seat. Joseph was long gone when I finally made it downstairs where the rest of the women had gathered to walk over together. Mother Smith, Emma, Lucy, Mary Ann, Eliza, Julia, and Lovina kept me company while we waited. Jerusha stayed at home, having just given birth to her fifth child, Jerusha, in January. The baby had been named in honor of me.

The sun rose, shining brightly in the crisp blue sky. Birds sang happily, a slight breeze blew, all testimonies of the fact that the whole world rejoiced over the first temple completed in centuries.

As I stood in line, my mind wandered through the past few years. How blessed I felt to have had this experience. How could I have gone my whole life without this burning in my bosom for the gospel? How could I have not seen that Joseph Smith was the man my mother said he was? I loved him; I loved the gospel with all my heart. I knew I'd never be the same, and I was thankful for it.

Finally, the temple doors were opened. Joseph personally led us to a row of seats in the front. I was speechless as I gazed around me. I hadn't had the time to come and see the finished product after helping with the veils. This temple was beautiful, with white gleaming walls and large Gothic-arched windows, allowing the light to shine into the room. The lower room was huge, with a vaulted ceiling; the north and south ceilings had been lowered with beautiful columns supporting them.

The room was filled with compartments of pews, backless and waist high, so that the congregation could choose which direction to face. In the center of both east and west walls were pulpits, which, I learned later, were for the priesthood brethren. They were four tiers high, measuring at the highest eight to ten feet above the congregation. The lowest had a built-in table so that the sacrament could be administered.

Benches sat on both sides of the pulpits for priesthood holders. I sat down by Eliza and Mary Ann and listened as she praised the workmanship of her husband. Brigham had truly outdone himself. This building was every bit a fitting place for the Lord to dwell.

The congregation faced west, where the Melchizedek Priesthood was assembling. We waited an hour, while the temple filled with happy, excited Saints, finally realizing the fulfillment of their dream. At 9:00 A.M. Sidney Rigdon stood. He had been chosen to conduct this session of the dedication. So many people had come that Joseph promised to repeat the services again for those who could not gain entrance. I marveled that this was the practice for a temple dedication even in my day. Thursday was set aside for the next dedicatory session. The school house to the west of the temple was full of those who couldn't fit in the temple. They were holding their own worship services. I appreciated the modern technology available in the 20th century. In my day, the people in the school would have been able to hear and see everything that was going on.

Sidney smiled, looking rather proud. His austere features softened with love as he gazed upon the congregation. He had a great gift as a speaker, and outdid himself that day.

"My dear brothers and sisters, my heart is filled with gladness on this wondrous day. I wish to begin by reading the 96th Psalm:

"O sing unto the Lord a new song: Sing unto the Lord, all the earth!" His voice cracked as a wave of sweetness washed over the entire room. Indeed the heavens were rejoicing as power was given to man, and a prophet walked among men. I looked up at Joseph, who sat smiling, tears glistening in his eyes. As his gaze took us in, his handsome face shone with the love he felt for all of us. I could not contain the tears that insisted on flowing. Sidney continued on with the psalm.

"O worship the Lord in the beauty of holiness! Fear him, all the earth."

The room was totally silent, save Sidney's rich voice filled with emotion as he read. When he finished the 96th Psalm, he turned to the 24th. I gasped as he began.

"Who shall ascend into the hill of the Lord? Or who shall stand in his holy place?"

"He that hath clean hands and a pure heart." Were my hands clean? Was my heart pure before the Lord? Should I even be in this house, knowing what great things would happen here?

215

"Lift up your heads, O ye gates; and be ye lift up, ye everlasting doors; and the King of glory shall come in."

"Who is this King of glory? The Lord of hosts, he is the King of glory!"

I was fairly weeping as the choir began to sing. Though I had never heard the hymn before, it was beautiful. I learned later that Parley P. Pratt had written it.

Sidney then offered the invocation. I hardly remember the words, but I will never forget the warmth of the spirit there. Brother Davis then stood and once again led the choir in song; this hymn had been written by W.W. Phelps. The choir members proudly held the new hymnals that Emma and Brother Phelps had worked so hard to finish.

Sidney then began a discourse on the 18th chapter of Matthew touching mostly on verse 20.

"Verily I say unto you, whatsoever ye bind on earth, shall be bound in heaven." He spoke for two and a half hours, though it seemed much shorter. He recounted the toils to build this house and the many tears shed in prayer for this temple.

"The foxes have holes, and the birds of the air have nests, but the Son of Man hath no where to lay His head. This building, this beautiful, magnificent building, constructed from our sweat, blood and tears, is worthy of the name 'The House of the Lord!' May He accept our sacrifice, I pray."

He said much more but I fail to remember it all. He then began the sustaining vote, acknowledging Joseph as Prophet, Seer and Revelator. Never before had I been as thrilled to raise my hand to the square in sustaining someone. Joseph Smith was indeed a prophet! When all the officers were sustained, Sidney bid us all stand in assent to these officers. We rose eagerly.

Next, we sang, "Now Let Us Rejoice." Though the hymn was new to those around me, I could sing the entire song without looking at the words. This had always been one of my favorite hymns. Becoming personally acquainted with W.W. Phelps now made it even more my favorite. Joseph then called for an intermission, which lasted twenty minutes. Very few people left their seats, not wanting to lose their places.

Another hymn was sung—"Adam-Ondi-Ahman." There were other things done at this time but my mind began to wander, feeling as if my heart would burst with love for these people. How could I leave such wonders? How could I go back to a world full of technology and noise and evil? I looked at Joseph, who was standing to read the names of all those who should be sustained from the various Priesthood quorums, down to the deacons. Joseph Smith was a beautiful man. His goodness shone in every feature of his face. I could see where he had gotten older while I had been in Kirtland. Little lines were etched on the corners of his eyes—from joy and from sorrow.

His voice was deep and resonate, with a slight whistle, the legacy he received from that horrible night in Hiram when he was tarred and feathered. His front tooth, broken and never completely repaired, caused a whistling sound as he spoke. The broken tooth did not detract from his appearance, however. No one cared about his teeth while he was speaking with the Spirit's power.

In his thirties, he was in the prime of his life. His body was strong. No one could best him in any sport he participated in. His hands were huge, well-worked, yet still tender enough to minister to the weakest of the Saints. He had a slight limp caused from the operation he went through as a child, though it was hardly noticeable unless he was quite tired. Having been in close proximity to him for the past five years, I could tell when he was exhausted, just by the way he walked. How thankful I was to know that the man standing at the pulpit was not only human, with faults and defects, but was a mighty prophet chosen by the Lord to do a great work in these last days. Yes, I adored Joseph Smith Jr.

Another hymn was sung. Joseph then rose to read the dedicatory prayer. This prayer had been given to Joseph by direct revelation. He read it just as it was given to him by the Lord.

"Thanks be to thy name, O Lord God of Israel, who keepest covenant and showest mercy unto thy servants who walk uprightly before thee, with all their hearts..."

Joseph spoke every word that appears in that dedicatory prayer in our Doctrine and Covenants. I will never be able to read it without his resonant voice ringing through my mind. On he read, recounting the sacrifices of the Saints, pleading for the wicked, praying for Jews and Gentiles, pleading for his family, the Saints and the Church.

"Oh hear, O hear, O hear us O Lord! And answer these petitions and accept the dedication of this house unto thee, the work of our hands, which we have built unto thy name…that we may mingle our voices with those bright shining seraphs around thy throne, with acclamations of praise, singing Hosanna to God and the Lamb!

"And let these thine anointed ones be clothed with salvation and thy saints shout aloud for joy. Amen and Amen."

His voice rang through the building long after the last amen. No one moved for a long time. We all just wanted to feel the spirit that pervaded the temple. Mary Ann looked at me with tears streaming down her face. We smiled at each other, taking hands, linking ourselves to each other in true sisterly love.

The choir stood and sang "The Spirit of God Like a Fire is Burning." That song has thrilled my heart more times than I can count but, there in the Kirtland Temple, listening to a small choir sing, I felt as though I had never really heard it before. Every fiber of my body seemed infused with the music, as if it were part of me and had been forever.

Joseph asked if we accepted the dedicatory prayer. We all agreed that we did and then he announced we would have the sacrament of the Lord's Supper.

Don Carlos officiated, blessing both the bread and the water. Several elders distributed it among the congregation. Never had I been in a meeting where it was so quiet during the sacrament. I sat, my head bowed, eyes closed, left hand firmly grasping Mary Ann's, thinking of all the things I had heard and seen this day. It took quite a long time to pass the sacrament to the thousand or so people squeezed into the building.

I was enjoying the sacred silence, when I heard a noise, like the rustling of skirts. Someone was walking right in front of me. Opening my eyes, I looked toward the sound. The most beautiful man I had ever seen passed by, looked at me and smiled. He seemed to know me and I could feel great wells of love coming from him to me. He walked on, looking at those around me with joy. I couldn't breathe. He was dressed in a long, white, flowing robe, so shiny I thought I would be blinded.

I looked at the pulpits and noticed several other people similarly dressed, all smiling, all walking through the congregation basically unnoticed. David Whitmer seemed to see them, as did Joseph. He looked at me, smiled, and nodded. Angels! Angels were in the midst of the Saints, worshipping beside us. Again my eyes filled with tears. I sighed contentedly.

When the sacrament was completed, Oliver stood and bore his testimony. F.G. Williams stood, testifying that he had seen an angel enter the window while Sidney was saying his first prayer and the angel took his seat between Father Smith and F.G. Williams. The angel stayed until the prayer was over.

Smiling down at me David Whitmer testified he had seen angels also. Hyrum stood and gave a few remarks. Sidney closed the meeting with a prayer. Joseph invited us to stand and taught us the Hosanna Shout. Taking a white handkerchief, we raised our hands to the heavens and shouted, "Hosanna! Hosanna! To God and the Lamb! Amen, Amen, and Amen!" This was repeated three times.

Brigham remained standing when the rest of us were again seated. His face shone with the same light that rested on Joseph, when the Spirit was upon him. Mary Ann gasped, taking my arm.

"Look at Brigham!" she whispered. I nodded, hardly breathing. All at once he began to speak, but the language he spoke was not one I had ever heard. A wave of shock flooded the whole room. All eyes were fixed on Brigham. A few moments later, David W. Patten rose and began to interpret Brigham's words. I was so intent on listening to Brigham, I barely noticed Brother Patten. When they were finished, Joseph stood, pronounced his blessings on us in English, and dismissed us. It was just after 4:00 p.m.

CHAPTER TWENTY-SEVEN

How do I describe the conflicting emotions that were mine as I prepared to return to my own time? I was caught between wanting to stay and witness more history and knowing I must return to my time and try to help a sleeping nation awake and prepare for the events that would shortly befall them.

I don't know how I bridged the span of time and ended up in Kirtland in the 1800s, but I do know it was not a mistake. I shudder to think what my life would have become without this glorious experience. My testimony was now fixed and immovable. I doubted there would ever be anything that could shake it. I knew God lived; I knew Joseph Smith was indeed a prophet, that he brought forth the Book of Mormon and restored the Church of Jesus Christ to the earth. I knew the C'hurch was true. Thank God for this experience. Thank God.

I stood in Brigham and Mary Ann's bedroom, holding the treasures I would take home with me. Joseph had given me a Book of Mormon and Doctrine and Covenants. Emma had given me a handkerchief.

"Think of me whenever you use it," she had whispered, embracing me. Jerusha had taken a lock of her hair and made a necklace for me. I wore it around my throat at this time. Hyrum had written a letter, placed it in the Book of Mormon, and told me to read it when I got home. He took my face in his hands and searched my eyes intently. I tried not to cry, but knowing I'd never see him again in this life added to the tears.

"I am so proud of you, Jerusha. You are a credit to your name and to this family. God bless you." He placed a kiss on my cheek and fled, unable to control his own emotions any longer. Father Smith gave me his reading glass. He, too, kissed me, holding both my hands in his aged ones.

"Good-bye, my dear. Go with God."

I regretted that I could not say good-bye to Eliza. She did not know that I was from another time. I knew I'd miss her terribly. I wrote her a small note and asked Emma to give it to her. She promised she would.

Now here I stood, having said all my good-byes. Only Joseph and Mary Ann stood beside me now. Emma was pregnant and not feeling well. Mother Smith preferred to say good-bye in her home. I had visited last night and hugged them both tightly. Who would have known that six years ago I would have hated leaving so much? Brigham had come by first thing in the morning, saying he had much work to do but wanted to bid me farewell.

"I knew there was something different about you, right from the start. I got the distinct impression that you knew me the first time we met," he said, shaking his head, chuckling.

"Well, I didn't know you...personally, but I had heard a lot about you. You'll be quite famous some day."

"Oh, right! Now I know you're pulling my leg."

"No, I'm not, but the Lord has said I can't tell what I know about the future."

"Then be obedient, Sister Jerree. I am grateful to have known you. Remember what you've learned."

"I will, Brother Brigham." Without much thought, I threw my arms around him and hugged him tightly. Brigham wrapped his arms around me, holding just as tight.

"Thank you," he whispered. Then he kissed my cheek and left.

Joseph stood beside me now, smiling sadly down at me. I clutched my treasures to me, staring at my uncle. He touched my face tenderly.

"Go with God, Jerusha. Remember all you've seen here. Warn your generation and prepare them for the Savior's return."

"I will. You take care of those babies...and Emma...and yourself." My voice caught. I wondered again how I could ever leave this great man. "I love you, Joseph—more than I ever thought I could. I'm so proud to be a member of your family.

"And I'm proud to know there are people like you carrying on the work."

Sobbing, I rushed into his arms, knowing I would never see him again. How did one exist without such goodness once it's been felt? He let me cry against his chest for a moment, then stepped back, and motioned for Mary Ann to come. She was crying also but smiling. She kissed my cheek, asked me never to forget her, and then hurried out of the room.

"The time has come. You must go to your family now. Remember, no one must know of this door between our times. You must teach your generation, but knowledge of this door could be disastrous. You have been given a great gift; don't take it for granted."

"I won't. The greatest gift I've been given was to meet you. Many great things are yet to come, Joseph. I wish I could be here to witness them—but I know I need to go home."

"Yes, you do." He bent, kissed my cheek and walked out of the room, looking back once more as he closed the door. For a moment I wanted to run after him, begging him to let me stay...but I knew this was God's will for me. Taking a deep breath, I approached the dresser.

Placing Father Smith's glasses on my nose, I stared at the mirror. In a moment, my image faded into streaks of water. Through the streaks, the reflection of the Young's bedroom melted away and I began to see my own bedroom. With a pounding heart, I stood as close as I could, held my breath and bent into the mirror....

"Jerree! Jerree! My goodness! Are you alright?" Tom's voice penetrated the fog that wrapped around me. My entire body ached from the jolt of falling onto my bedroom floor. All the things that had been on the dresser were strewn around me. Gasping, I tried to sit up, clutching to my chest the treasures I had received from the past. The room was pitch black. The digital alarm clock read 3:00 A.M. Tom was kneeling beside me, dazed, half asleep, wearing sweat pants and a garment top. Joyously he folded me into his arms, sobbing heartily.

"Dad! Dad! What's going on?" One of the boys was pounding on the door.

"Come in! Joseph, she's home! Your mother's home!" Tom yelled. The door burst open, flooding the room with light from the hall. Joseph flipped on the light switch, then hurried to my side, kneeling next to me.

"Mom! How did you get in? Where have you been? Good heavens, what's happened to you?"

Together my two men helped me stand, then led me to the bed. Still disoriented, I couldn't answer the barrage of questions they fired at me.

"Joseph, go call the other children and tell them she's home. Look at her. She's totally out of it."

"But...but, Dad!"

"Settle down," Tom soothed, putting a hand on our son's shoulder."We'll figure this all out with the whole family."

Joseph nodded, looking down at me once again with great concern. "Mom, I'm so glad you're home," he said, kissing my cheek softly before he left the room.

"Jerree...do you know where you are?" Tom asked, sitting beside me on the bed, wrapping his arms around my shoulders.

"Yes. This is our room. Oh, Tom! It looks so good—you look so good! There were times I wondered when I was ever going to see you again."

"Where have you been, Jerree? You look...you look like you've been through war. Your hair—it's almost totally gray—and your hands—I've never seen them so worn. Were you abducted? Were you hurt? Where have you been for the past eighteen months?"

"Eighteen months? I wasn't gone eighteen months. I've been gone six years!" I exclaimed, breaking loose from him to go to the dresser and peer into the mirror.

I couldn't believe it! I was amazed at the change in me. I had aged much more than Tom had. He didn't look much older than he did the last time I saw him. He had a few more worry lines around his eyes, but that was it. My hair was more white than auburn now. How could that be? How old was I? I thought I should be fifty-six, but I looked so much older.

"Sweetie, you were gone eighteen months—from August 1990 to now, February, 1992. Why would you think you were gone six years?"

"I don't know! I'm so confused, Tom, and tired. Please don't ask any more questions right now. All I want is a nice hot bath...and for you to hold me."

"All right. Let's get you into the bathroom. You're home now, and that's all that matters."

With trembling hands I removed the dress I had been wearing, wondering if it would survive a washing machine. Tears filled my eyes as I removed my garments. This one pair had stayed intact the entire time I was gone. They had protected me against an attack and weathered all the storms I went through in Kirtland. So many miracles, so many things I could not explain had happened in the past six years—or eighteen months, whichever it was.

How could I have lived six years in the past while only eighteen months had passed in my own time? What would make time move so differently? I had aged six years—at LEAST six years! I looked like a hag! Would Tom even want me now?

I took my bath. It was heavenly! I'd almost forgotten what a hot bath was like. I stayed in the tub until the water was cold. Tom gave me the privacy I needed, waiting downstairs for the rest of the family to arrive.

I had no time after I dressed. My entire family surrounded me, touching me, gawking at me, weeping at my return. It was so good to see them.

David, my oldest son, was there with his wife, Michelle, and their two children, Mikey and Tommy. Then there was my dear daughter Sarah, a mirror image of me, and therefore of Jerusha, her husband John, Sean, Julie and little Jerree, born while I was away. My son Joseph, so much like a prophet I now knew well, sat beside me, holding my hand, his blue eyes shining with tears. My youngest son, Cory, rested his head on my shoulder. It was great to have all my kids crowding around me. How I had missed them!

Tom told me he had come home to an empty house the Sunday after I fell through the mirror. No one knew where I had gone. It seemed as though I had vanished into thin air, which wasn't far from the truth. A nationwide search had been conducted, to no avail.

"I never gave up hope," Tom said, touching my face. "Still, I could hardly believe it when I saw you tonight. Jerree, where have you been?"

"I don't know how to explain. It's all so confusing...I remember falling and bumping my head...and feeling very lost—I didn't know where I was..."

"You brought strange things home with you, Jerree...a very old copy of the Book of Mormon and the Doctrine and Covenants. A letter was with them... from Hyrum Smith to your namesake, Jerusha. It must have been written after she died; it wasn't dated...and you were holding a handkerchief...and wearing a necklace made of hair, I think. You had glasses on...very old ones. Where did you get those things?"

I shook my head...unable to come up with appropriate answers. Joseph had told me I must not talk about my journey through time. My entire family became convinced that I must have wandered off, suffering from amnesia for all those months. If they only knew....

"Where's the letter?" I asked.

"In the Book of Mormon. Right here." Joseph picked up the book that just yesterday was new. Now it had the appearance of being quite old. The letter was yellowed and beginning to fall apart. Joseph carefully opened it and began reading:

"Dearest Jerusha,

I write this knowing I will never again see you in this life. Your leaving me grieves me deeply. I have grown to love you far more than I thought possible. Having you in our lives has been a miracle. I thank God every day for it. I pray I can live worthy to be reunited with you in a place where time has no control. Until then, know we all love you.

Hyrum."

I wept silently as my son read the letter. Hyrum had written so that no one would ever know he was writing to me. Tom took my hand, trying to comfort me.

"Mom?" Cory asked.

"I'm fine...really I am...just tired."

"We'll let you rest. Come on."

All the treasures I received from the Smith family are now lovingly placed in the box Brigham made out of the Kirtland Temple wood. The scriptures sit next to it, on the dresser, the letter to me from Hyrum marking section 76—that glorious vision I had the honor to listen to on that wondrous February day in 1832. I smile when I think of this letter. I know something Hyrum didn't know. I found another letter in that box—written to me in 1846 by Hyrum's second wife, Mary. I left the past in 1836 and didn't meet Mary

Fielding while I was there. Jerusha was still alive when I left, nursing a new baby. So how could Mary Fielding know me unless I was to make a second journey into the past? Hope fills my heart when I think of returning. I don't know when, or why, but somehow I know I will. Already I miss my Smith family terribly. Hugging Mary's letter to my chest, I peer into Brigham's timeless mirror and smile. For now, I thank God I'm again with my husband and family. My future in the past can wait. I'm content with my present.

JERUSHA

EPILOGUE

I've often reflected on my experiences in the 19th century. I'm still not sure why I was permitted to travel there. Joseph said it was to comfort them and prepare me for all that will surely come—and come soon. Whatever the reason, I know I'll never be the same. The testimony my mother prayed I would receive burns brightly in my heart and I KNOW Joseph Smith Jr. was indeed the Prophet of the Restoration. Seeing him as he dealt with people day by day, sitting at his feet as he taught, helped me understand why so many people sacrificed everything to follow him. Joseph radiated goodness; the light of God glowed in his eyes, illuminating his whole countenance. All in all, I'm filled with peace. Though I can't share my experiences with my family, I treasure them. Reading the library of Church history books my mom left to me helps me feel close to all the Saints I left behind. I have kept my promise to Joseph, trying to educate this generation about our wondrous ancestors and the great sacrifices they made in our behalf.

A year has passed since my adventure in the 1830s. I think my family has stopped being anxious every time I go to town by myself. Tom took an early retirement, invested some money and made a killing, enabling him to spend his days with me. Having me older hasn't cooled his love for me, which makes me happy. I'm enjoying our "second honeymoon," as he likes to call it.

I still have no idea how I lived six years in the past when only eighteen months passed in the present. I guess it's one of those mysteries I'll just have to live with. Another is how I could have traveled through time by falling through a mirror. How it happened I don't know—but it happened, and I'm glad.

Life is sweeter now. My outlook has definitely changed. All about me I see the blessings my ancestors worked so hard to give me. At times, I miss them so badly my heart aches. I know someday, when the time is right, I will return. Of this I have no doubt. Until then, I'll just have to be happy with reading the scriptures given to me by my great uncle—the Prophet Joseph Smith.